ONE EIGHTY

A Novel

by Milt Mays

PREFACE AND ACKNOWLEDGEMENTS

Those who go to war must sometimes, depending on their injuries, put themselves back together to function. We as doctors in the Navy and VA help, but the individual soldiers and sailors bear the brunt of it. As do those they leave and return to. It has been my pleasure and honor to serve those who have returned and found function. I salute you and hope those who read this book will do the same. It is more than difficult. And yet those brave men and women continue to do it for us 24/7, 365. Some even return with a sense of humor, like Var.

It takes a wealth of help and constructive criticism to finish a book like this. My wife begins the process with bouncing back my comments and being the first and last to read the book with patience and very keen observations. Thanks, Babe. My writing critique group (Jean, Jane, Carl, Beth) see me every two weeks. Their encouragement and positivity keep me going. Their critiques have been invaluable. I thought this book ready two years ago. But since then it's gone through several iterations, finally sent to my editor, Kim Catanzarite, who deftly set me right on several areas. Thanks, Kim. After more changes, it went to several beta readers (Sandra, Bob, Greg, Greg, Jennifer, Carl, Jane) and I thank them. Thanks to my daughter Jennifer for her read and comments and for her superb cover design.

I gained most of my knowledge of wars and combat

injuries from years of study at the Naval Academy and subsequent experience with my patients and their families. The internet has a profound amount of data that must be combed through to find pearls. One in particular relating to Var and Angela, was entitled, *7 Myths of Lost Love Reunions*, by Dr. Nancy Kalish. A great VA physical therapist, Evan, helped me better understand mirror therapy for phantom limb pain, and music therapy for war injuries. Other current books that gave me more insight and more reality about the wars in Iraq and Afghanistan, including the Battle of Fallujah were: Filkins, Dexter. *The Forever War.* Knopf, New York. 2008 where he gives credit for the lyrics I used from *Hells Bells* © 1981, J. Albert & Son PTY.Ltd. Copy right owner; and O'Donnell, Patrick K. *We Were One.* Audiobook. Blackstone Audio, Inc. 2007. I strongly recommend everyone read or listen to both books. They will open your eyes even more.

The Next Day
The first in the *Dan's War* Series

THE BEST KEPT SECRET AFTER 9/11.
Did Iraq have secret Weapons of
Mass Destruction?
Was there a biological attack on the US
that almost killed millions?

Alex Smith just wants to do his job—modify viruses in a secret US lab in Brazil—then go fishing. But something causes changes in Alex. Could he have been accidentally exposed?

After 9/11, Jabril El Fahd wants to finish the job—kill ALL the infidels with a modified virus. But when he is exposed, horrible, evil changes occur to him, and he loves it.

Can the new Alex stop the new Jabril from killing millions?

DEDICATION:

To the men and women who protect our freedom
around the globe.

One Eighty

CHAPTER 1

Var

One eighty saved my life, twice. It can save yours, too. It made me a bit wacky in the head, a bit off kilter. But it's an off-kilter world, so why not? Sometimes I connect a lot of dots in microseconds. Sometimes I overuse words. Sometimes my brain pauses and restarts. It's what losing a lot of heartbeats does to a person. But I still have to tell this story. Try to stay with me. I keep getting better, and I hope, with time, I'll be closer to normal.

What exactly is one eighty? Degrees indicating half a circle? Diametrically opposed, starting one way, ending another? Kinda like my new, revised thinking style. Or maybe on a compass it's the point directly south, give or take a few degrees of declination?

Could be a straight line connecting two points, going on forever in two exactly opposite directions.

How about an amount of, say, money? Approximately: just under two bucks. Exactly: eighteen dimes, thirty-six nickels. Relatively: depends on the year—1910, thirty-six loaves of bread—now, not even one loaf. Inflation. What a difference a hundred years makes.

So, if it's money, one eighty can be quite variable in value.

What if it's, say, um, seconds? A hundred and eighty seconds. Tick, tock. Wouldn't matter if it was in 2010 AD or 1910 BC, still can't make it go faster or slower. It goes. Once it's gone, it's gone. Bye-bye, so long. Farewell. Fsst. Fizzle. Can't bring it back.

It so happens, you can.

Three minutes: the most common length of a recorded song. At least for most of the music I love.

There are good songs and bad, love and hate, joyful and depressing—just about—well, probably for sure, any emotion known to man. Or woman. Yeah. That's for damn sure.

You can get lost in a three-minute song, but you can only run so far in three minutes. If you're really fast, you might make it three-quarters of a mile. Then you're spent, out of breath and feel like you're gonna croak. Been there, done that, can't do it anymore. I prefer a road bike.

But three minutes of a song … that can make your whole day. Enough of them might even change your whole life, maybe even the whole world.

John Lennon believed that it's possible to save the world with a song. Cool.

♪ ♫

I started out this morning with the full intention of enjoying every minute before I helped my client. Not a patient, a client. There is a difference, despite what HMOs and the VA says. I don't take money for my after-hours clients. I get paid enough from my VA pension and as a doctor. Besides, if I took money I'd need a license. A private eye license. I didn't really want that. Lisa has one and that's fine with me.

But, getting back to this morning, I had used a couple

of weeks of vacation from my practice and now was ready to help my client in court.

One eighty has taught me so many things. Enjoy every moment, even driving.

As the garage door went down and I backed my gray 4Runner out of the driveway, I selected "Sweet Home Alabama" by Lynyrd Skynyrd. Not being directly from Alabama, but having roots and relatives there, and having had an extended stay in a hospital as close to southern Alabama as you can get and still live in Florida, I've always identified with that song. Also, my therapist played it during my second hospital stay. She played a lot of old songs.

Anyway, before long I was Sweet-Home-Alabama-ing it so hard that I ...

Missed two lights.

I'm not sure if I ran them when they were red, or if I went through them legally when they were green. The part of my brain that drives while I sing must have done the right thing because there were no sirens. Or maybe the cops had been listening to music, too. Anyway, that's what happened to that. ... I think maybe it was more like a hundred and eighty-six seconds. Not exactly one eighty, but hey, it was pretty close.

I usually get lost in a song that I'm close to mentally or emotionally. Pretty sure that is why one eighty works. And occasionally a song will hit home that is ...

Just weird.

Like "30,000 lbs. of Bananas," by Harry Chapin. I've never been a truck driver. I like bananas, and I've driven on the Pennsylvania Turnpike, so maybe I do have a few emotional attachments to the song. But mostly it's just a catchy tune by an artist I love.

That's what was playing when I lost the next little bit down the road. I was really getting into the part when he's coming down the hill and he loses his brakes, and he's going to run right into this town with his huge rig full of bananas when ... I ... um ...

Missed my turn.

No big deal, really. I just turned at the next road. Sometimes things happen. When those hundred and eighty seconds get going you can't—except for the song—bring 'em back. But, you know, maybe I don't wanna bring them back. Maybe if I'd made that first turn I'd have run somebody over. You never know. Things happen good or bad that you cannot predict.

Is that fatalistic? Certainly not impressionistic. Maybe it's depressionalistic? Anyway, I'm optimalistic. My feeling is that I just got a chance to ...

You know, look around some more. I got to see that incredibly yellow tree.

It was ... like ...

Yellow.

I mean, I was listening to a song about bananas, and there was a yellow tree.

That's just too weird.

That brings me to another point. Some people spend a lot of time when they compile recordings, getting the songs in the perfect order. I mean, I had a roommate in college who made a lot of playlists, seriously, a *lot* of playlists. He had tons of different artists. And they had to be in the exact order—*his* exact order. I mean ... I guess ...

Ah, geez. What's wrong with just allowing the right brain to ... kinda ...

Enjoy the moment. To hell with the left.

Though, you know the latest about the left, right? The right brain and the left brain—everything is connected and works together. You can lose some speech areas in the left brain, for instance, and still learn to speak again. Pretty cool.

I happen to know this because of my near-death experiences. My brain has proven its ability to coordinate both sides. It even floats around in space and picks up the thoughts of others.

I didn't believe it at first, either.

Anyway, the point I was making is that there is a bit of artistry in making a good playlist. Especially with the new high-res digital stuff. Takes up a lot of memory, but the sound ... ooh-rah! Yep, I was a Marine. ... Well, that's not precisely true. I was a Navy doctor with the Marines for almost a year, before I got injured.

Getting back, I like my recordings to have a random order. Kinda like life. When I record, I look at what I have out and go with the flow. Sometimes I'll pull out some really old suckers. You know, $33^1/_3$ on plastic. Yeah, plastic. (They call it vinyl now. Who wants a piece of plastic?) That was back when you had something you could identify with, not just electrons floating around in some digital matrix using laser beams or ... whatever. No, you had metal, or like, diamond needles that converted plastic squiggles to sound. Talk about cool. Now it's all about smoke and mirrors, digital mumbo jumbo, magic crap that only physicists can understand.

In honor of oldies but goodies, I think it appropriate that I played "Yesterday" by the Beatles. Cool, huh? Now you try to sing along with that and you can do it, but it's tough, man, unless you have a really high voice, at least if you're a guy. Have you ever noticed how a lot of the great songs by guys are almost, like, soprano? Like Rod Stewart. What's with that? Anyway, I diverge. Could be from a little too much of ...

Well, you know. We don't want to get into that. Not just yet.

Anyway, "Yesterday" is playing when I pull up to the courthouse, and, of course, I have to sit and listen to the whole song. You can't cut something like that off in the middle. It's just not right. And Lennon is getting to the last line, "I be-lieve in yest—"

There's a knock on the window. How can you do that to me? I mean, *Come on!* I'm obviously sitting here, in rapture, listening to a wonderful song, a world-changing song, and you , like, knock on my window? It's not like I'm doing anything illegal: smoking a ... you know, or laying half naked with a babe or something. And I don't have, like, a gun sitting on my dashboard. So, *what the hell!*

I look around and ...

I have to turn the music off.

Sometimes that hundred and eighty seconds can help you. Sometimes the opposite.

Anyway, she's been helping me a long time and she's ...

Nice. You get what I mean when I say nice, right? So, yeah, I open the door. Immediately.

"Lisa, how are ya? Man, what a nice morning, huh?" Yes, it's a beautiful morning, but I said nice.

Lisa has reddish-brown hair, maybe you would call it auburn. It's not real long and it would look really cool in a spiky do, but she's not into that. Though, she does like rock and roll, and the old tunes I play. But she's worldlier than me: listens to NPR, constantly tells me about podcasts that taught her about physics or astronomy or our founding fathers, not to mention all the forensic stuff. She visits her paralyzed sister in a nursing home every day.

No, Lisa's way nicer than I am. She's got eyes that in the right light look yellow, but I think they're really greenish brown; you might even call them buckskin. When I first met her in Afghanistan, I thought she was wearing contacts. Like, they did a number on my brain. Maybe she's part cat or something. Weird. But it's okay. I like cats. With her, I've taken it a bit further than like. I think.

She's shouting. Not really happy this morning. Her eyes have dark circles under them.

"Var!"

Yeah that's my name, a nickname. Hang on.

"Var. You're running late. Come on. Hurry!"

Lisa has a serious Type-A streak. I'm glad because I need it.

She helps me with my, you know, accoutrements. Chair is in the back. I don't normally need it but keep it in case. Yesterday I fell off the last four feet of the climb with O.J. Cromwell and bent my leg prosthetic, so I can't walk right. We pull the chair out and I'm good to go. Battery's all charged. Yeah, that's why I have the solar panels on top of the 4Runner. It helps in case I get lost sometime during another one eighty and forget to plug the battery in at night. But last night I remembered. So it's all charged and ready, and I scoot on in beside her as she walks. I want to get behind her, wave her ahead a little, enjoy the …

Yeah. You get it. But I have control over my urges.

Sure.

"Go ahead, Lisa. I'll follow you."

She knows, I think. I start to fall behind.

Aw, crap.

I push the forward toggle with my good hand, the right one. The chair boogies up beside her before Dork-meister down there gets control of every thought. I'm glad I still have those urges, believe me, but it's hard being a guy sometimes.

"Bad night, huh?" I ask.

"Yeah. She's getting worse. Ever since the stroke. ..." Her voice falls off. "I don't want to talk about it."

Lisa doesn't say that for fun. That's her way. I'm used to it, and I respect it. Doesn't talk about her problems. I know to shut up.

Besides, I need to get my head in the game. It takes about five minutes to cruise into the courtroom, so I get plugged in again, but only one ear, so I can hear her. I have to stop for a sec, 'cause the left arm hook doesn't manipulate the earbud, gotta use my right hand. Can you believe how cool an iPhone is? I mean, *come on*! Talk about rad to the max. It's going to be a hoot when the Bluetooth gets really small ear inserts that no one can see. No one will know you're tuning them out for, like, the Rolling Stones and "The House of the Rising Sun." Yeah. That'll get your thoughts cookin' in the morning. That *was* a really cool sunrise coming around that yellow tree.

Yellow means caution.

"You know the Judge hates to be kept waiting, even if this is a pretrial hearing." I'm presenting evidence for my client in what I will call "Case Number Two." My Case Number Two. The Judge is presiding. He's also a patient. It can be complicated.

Lisa twists her head as she walks and gives me a pursed-lip, prune frown. "While I'm talking to you, could you turn off the music?"

"Sorry. Helps me get into the mood." The Judge is a condescending son of a bitch, so I need something. Better than lighting up. Right?

I admit I like a joint every now and then. But nothing beats a bike ride in the Colorado autumn to give you a natural high the rest of the day.

That's when both cases started, three weeks ago.

Three weeks compared to one hundred and eighty seconds is a hell of a long time. But memory can put you anywhere in a heartbeat. Pretty cool.

Anyway, three weeks ago I'd been going at it: riding my bike twenty-four miles at about sixteen miles per, that's thirty songs—give or take. Morphine was pretty good, back in the day, but thirty songs coupled with an endorphin high of exercise? They could cut my chin off with a chain saw and I probably wouldn't care. I know that sounds ridiculous but coming from a guy who's lost a right leg and left arm, you can trust me. Even if I am a bit off kilter.

I was plugged into my iPhone and trying to zen out, seeing, feeling, hearing, smelling, and, as it turned out, tasting the entire bike ride, interspersed with thinking about the case.

The case, you ask?

Yeah. Okay, I'm sorry. Because of my prior injuries, my brain takes a few left turns here and there. But, they all get connected pretty well, eventually. I'm still able to practice medicine, though I chose to do it only part time, and only on an outpatient basis.

Let me go into the first case, first. I'll get back to the bike ride and case two. And trust me: you won't want to miss the ride or case two.

Pretty soon you're going to be asking how the hell I know all this stuff, what all these people did, their thoughts and everything that follows. Like I said, my brain not only takes odd turns but it also wanders around in the air and experiences the thoughts of others. Not everyone and not every thought. That would make me God, not to mention make me a lot of money. But I only connect with a few people, and even then it can be spotty. And, over last year, that connection has been weakening. I'm hoping it means my brain is healing.

Oh, yeah. The other thing is, some of these people have been my patients. And some of my clients are patients as well.

So, if what follows at times seems to be me reading other people's minds, just go with it. I'll be there leading you along, bopping in at odd times with my odd thoughts. It's like a weed trip with a good friend and brownies after.

CHAPTER 2

Case One—The Mirror Reveals

T hat Saturday, three weeks ago, the mirror arrived at Judge Craghead's mountain villa early in the morning and revealed exactly what the Judge had been hiding over the last year, but only to the delivery man. The Judge heard the doorbell and walked to the front door right by the bay window. Blue skies and vast mountains consumed the view from the huge bay window forever, or at least from Fort Collins, Colorado to the limits of the Judge's eagle vision. He didn't care about beyond. He'd been everywhere, seen every idyllic panorama in the world. He breathed deep, the air as bright and clean as the sky.

Outside the front door, the delivery man waited and watched the reflection of the panorama in the mirror and saw much more. When this first started, after an incident in Iraq, he thought he was crazy, as did his brothers in arms. But he came to accept it as his new normal and believed the mirrors. His doctor friend, Var, had a word for it, but he couldn't pronounce it. Var said those mirror visions made sense, considering what had happened to him in the war.

The Judge flinched when he opened the door, surprised because he was staring into the mirror the delivery man had purposefully placed in front of him. He'd unpacked the mirror, knowing that it needed to see, to reveal the Judge's true nature. After all, that was why he was here.

The Judge said nothing to the mousy little man, didn't even notice that his white tee shirt and frayed blue-gray overalls were sparkling clean despite his grimy hat pulled over greasy hair. The Judge only marveled at the beauty of the mirror, or rather the oak frame that surrounded the antique mirror. He'd found it at an auction of an old ranch estate two weeks ago. A deep gash marred the frame on the right-hand side, said by the auctioneer to have been gouged by the original ranch homesteader in the 1860s. Rumor said he'd slashed at his adulterous wife with a huge bowie knife, missing the first time and finding the mirror's frame. As the story went, the mirror did not fall from its perch thanks to a compulsive and careful Mexican housekeeper who'd hung it with sturdy nails beside the fireplace. That, according to the seller, was exactly where the mirror had remained until the Judge bought it.

At the auction, when the Judge had lifted it off the wall, he'd carefully stepped around the dark stain on the wood floor. It was a reflex action. The blood of the adulterous wife was no longer able to discolor his shoes, but, still. … He could not understand why someone had not scrubbed the blood stain out of the beautiful white pine floor, which was a wonderful, glowing beige color, a rare blond pine. Some people did not appreciate beauty enough to clean off a blemish.

Now, to the plain, tidy, quiet delivery man, the mirror reflected exactly why no one had scrubbed the floors. Even as the Judge stood upon his doorstep and marveled at his purchase, the history played on the silvery surface like a movie that only the delivery man could see. It played through hundreds of years in mere seconds. ...

A little towheaded boy cowered in the corner; the orange flames danced in his nickel-sized, midnight pupils as his father screamed in rage and slashed over and over, the hunting knife glinting in the flames, flicking blood onto the walls—Dante's scarlet drops on a Michelangelo canvas. The boy grew up and froze the house in time, a freeze-frame of the moment, everything exactly as it had been—no scrubbing of blood stains, oh no. And he was in charge, since his father had realized what he had done and took his own life right after killing his mother, his hanging rope still hanging. The boy wanted to remember that night every time he looked at the room. Every detail unchanged.

The mousy delivery man could not turn off the mind-video of the mirror. It played out the boy's entire life in fast-forward, a mere pause in present time, as the delivery man lifted the mirror to bring it inside. It showed the joys (grandparents from Gabriel—yeah, the angel), his family (his love pumped their hearts so full they rarely cried), and his stainless-steel sanity, all despite (or perhaps because of) the tragedy. He grew old and lived and, more than that, he cruised through a Cadillac life with ice cream laughter and chocolate love his daily companions on the ranch he'd preserved in a death snapshot.

Until he died. His daughter who inherited the ranch could neither continue the ranching business nor live (if that's what you would call the depressive existence she crawled through after he died) in that house. She sold it all in the auction, the time-stuck ranch with ghostly particulars unchanged from that day: the suicide rope that hanged his father's sorry body still swung from the monstrous support beam where Daddy Dearest had wept his last tears, croaked his last breath, and formed his last vision that accompanied him to Hades: his wife bleeding to death onto the white pine floor.

The mirror-enhanced video seen by the unusually common delivery man flashed forward to the day, the very moment when the Judge bought the mirror two weeks ago: how he'd stepped over the stained floor; how that same frayed rope, hangman's noose intact, tickled the back of the Judge's neck; how the Judge had swiped at the rope, and frowned, even as he continued to carefully step over the blood stain and away from the wall with his prize in hand.

The mirror view went dark. Even though it had only lasted seconds, the delivery man felt like the memories had filled his head into a throbbing, nearly bursting migraine, and now abated into warm and soothing relief.

The Judge stood at his door, still not observing the delivery man, caught up in his own paltry memory, miniscule paragraph of time that it was, of buying the mirror. He gazed across the valley. Dust clouded the sky. The demolition of the ranch house was today. The daughter couldn't bear to have that mausoleum of memory remain on this earth.

A movement drew his attention: the delivery man. He hadn't really noticed him before, except in the periphery, like a tree in the yard or a door in the house. A dirty, black baseball cap covered most of his greasy mouse hair that clung to his scalp and stained the edges of the cap. His frayed, blue-gray coveralls had not a spot of dirt. Calloused, cracked, and stained hands gripped the mirror, firm but gingerly, as if he carried eggs.

The man stood silent, like a boy, his head bowed, seemingly unaware of time or the Judge's scrutiny. The thing that bothered the Judge most: the man never looked at him.

Yet, the unpretentious man, like the shyest boy at the high school dance, *had* watched the Judge, every second, through the mirror. He never, ever looked at any person, except through a reflection—a mirror, or glass, or whatever was handy.

"Hello there. What's your name, son?" The Judge's voice boomed; the only thing lacking was the echo he was used to hearing when he settled unruly courtrooms.

The man did not look up. He could see the Judge's reflection as plain as, or actually much clearer than, any day. "Hollister, sir."

"Surely they don't just call you Hollister. What's your given name? What did your *father* call you?" The Judge drew out the word father, as if he were Darth Vader explaining himself to Luke. Hollister liked that movie. Nothing was as it seemed.

"Robert, sir." To the Judge, the words sounded as pale and colorless and dull as this man who reminded him of Dopey from the Seven Dwarfs.

The Judge stared at the black cap, willing the man to look up. "Robert Hollister ... hmmm. Do I know you, son?" The grease-edged cap never raised one iota. Perhaps the Judge was losing the power of what he considered his Superman Glare.

"No sir."

"I *know* names. I *remember* names." In the mirror the

Judge's reflection tapped his temple with his index finger. "I'll figure it out. I *know* that name."

"Where do you want me to put the mirror, sir?" Robert's head lowered further, like a beaten dog, and he spoke into the mirror, only a quiet reflection of his voice reached the Judge.

The Judge's hearing was as sharp as his vision. He opened the door wide. "Well, Robert, why don't you put it in the kitchen?" He pointed with his long, knife-like finger; Robert was sure he saw the Judge glare into the kitchen, reminding him of God pointing to Adam in Michelangelo's Sistine Chapel. Paintings were so much better than photos. The reflection of an artist's inner self emanated from the canvas.

Robert moved quicker than the Judge would have thought possible and had the mirror leaning on the kitchen wall in seconds. He stared into the tilted mirror while a beautiful woman sashayed down the spiral, balustrade staircase.

Robert loved it when a woman sashays, a wonderful side-to-side movement of hips choreographed with a slight twist of the waist. Human beings are capable of truly lovely movements: a marathoner's effortless run, a bullfighter's flourishing cape, Joe Namath's touchdown passes, and this particular woman's walk.

Robert knew that Var blamed himself for Angela's predicament. He'd said, "If only I could have been there for her when she needed me, everything might have turned out differently." If only Robert hadn't had the unfortunate incident with his beloved Aunt Betty, and the shitstorm in Fallujah. If only.

The Judge bellowed, "Hello, my dear. Our mirror has arrived. Isn't it beautiful?"

The woman smiled at the mirror. She had a delicate nose and full lips. Raven hair weaved the sunlight and bounced at her shoulders with each stair she stepped. Her shirt was white; her teeth were so white and straight that Robert pursed his lips shut. He should have taken better care of his teeth. He should have done a lot of things. Maybe he would smile more if he had.

In the next instant the mirror revealed what Detective C had told him to look for, had sent him to look for. He wished he didn't have to see it. But the mirror had to tell the story—impossible to lie.

Delicate fingers grasped the edge of the basement door: children's fingers. Behind the door, dirty lines of tears traced lovely black faces and dripped onto their nakedness. The Judge slammed the door shut and slashed his wife's throat with a shiny butcher knife. Robert flinched at the blood spurting towards him from the mirror. In that flinch he turned away from the mirror, and out of the corner of his eye the woman's high-heeled feet and taut calves promenaded towards the kitchen sink.

No blood. The Judge's size thirteen Nike's, still huge and white as ever, stood by the front door, on legs sturdy as an oak. The basement door was closed.

It had happened again, as it had countless other times, though this time the mirror's tale had seemed so real Robert had wanted to run. And now another woman and countless girls in the basement were threatened, just as his aunt had been. Just as the woman in Fallujah. But he couldn't do to the Judge what he'd done then. He could feel it beginning, though, the burn in his stomach, the swelling of his chest, his hands gripping hard. Soon the rage monster inside him would burst out of the closet. He had to leave.

"Are you all right, Robert?" the Judge said. He had seen the man flinch after placing the mirror against the wall. He wondered if he was an epileptic? Tourette's perhaps. That would explain his strange demeanor. But the Judge reconsidered, mulling over the replay of what he'd seen. It was as if the man turned away from something he saw in the mirror. Had he seen the Judge scowling at his wife as she walked away and ignored his question? Had he felt the sudden urge—yes, that was what it had been—an overwhelming desire to slice his wife's neck. It happened at the same time he had focused on the gash in the mirror frame.

The Judge forced a smile at his wife. She'd been ignoring him a lot after he'd spoken with her about her infidelities. There was no way he could divorce her. It was her family's wealth that had allowed him to rise from a so-so lawyer to a prominent judge. Once, he had needed that money. And since then, he needed the girls behind the door. He was not the man most knew and respected. But then again, his wife, Angela, was not the woman he knew and respected, either.

Angela knew he needed her girls. Too well.

Yes, but did he need her? If she wasn't there anymore …?

He gazed at the mousy man. Did Robert know what the Judge desired? The black-capped head turned, and words filtered up around the bill toward the Judge. "I'm fine, sir. Is there anything else you would like me to do with the mirror today?"

The Judge squinted one eye at the cap, trying to discern Robert's thoughts. But the blasted idiot would not look at him. He could tell a lot from a man's eyes, had discerned many a lie on the witness stand that way. He relaxed. Robert Hollister was merely a dumb delivery man.

"No. Nothing, Robert. I'll take care of hanging the mirror. Here, take this for your trouble." He took out his wallet, fingered through the bills and pulled out a single one-dollar bill and handed it to Robert.

Robert pocketed the bill without looking at it and shuffled toward the door. He placed his hand on the knob and the Judge said, "Son, are you sure there's not something wrong? I just saw you jump when you looked in the mirror. What did you see?"

Robert turned the knob. "No sir. I'm fine. Me and mirrors sometimes don't get along."

The Judge knew for sure then: Robert Hollister was not only dumb, he was superstitious as well, a combination that spelled H-I-C-K. He probably couldn't wait to get home for his daily six-pack of Bud. "Thank you for delivering the mirror. Maybe we'll call on you again, sometime."

"Yessir." Robert slurred the words together as he took a quick step outside, easing the door shut behind him.

The Judge squinted one eye at the door, a half-masted glare that invariably had made defense counsel forget any objections. Could Robert be more than a hick? He sighed and turned his attention to his wife, who was pouring a cup of coffee. "My dear, Angela, you didn't say anything about this mirror. Isn't it exquisite?"

She glanced at the mirror and forced the words, "Yes … it's … quite a prize."

Then she glared at him, a look of impatience that had

flowered of late. "I'm sorry, dear. I'm not into antiquities quite like you are. I'm running late for business. Is there anything I can do for you while I'm out?"

The Judge stared her down without answering, thinking, *As if you would actually do something for me.* How about bringing back a body bag ... for yourself?

"No, dear," he said. "Give my regards to Pablo." He smiled at her, hoping Pablo would punish her. "Perhaps he will have more," and he glanced at the basement door, "guests for us." At that, warmth infused his groin.

She took a last sip of coffee and stood to leave, her eyes hard, black diamonds. "No more guests coming. And, stay away from the basement, dear." Her words were sharp as flint.

"Will you be home tonight?" he asked, as if it didn't really matter.

"Yes. Of course."

"Wonderful. How does take-out Chinese sound?" He knew how much she hated take-out.

"Fine." The clipped word raked him as she brushed past and closed the door behind her without a sound, as if it were as fragile as the mirror.

The bay window allowed a great view of her lithe body sauntering down the stairs and easing into the Lexus, like a cat into a soft couch. Or could he be thinking of something else? Maybe he was just looking at the car. He loved that car almost as much as she did. Black suited them both, perhaps her a bit more today. He'd always liked her in black.

Before the dust from the Lexus began to settle, he'd grabbed his keys and was in his black Suburban, on his way. He'd wanted to go directly to the basement, but this was important. Besides, waiting enhanced the pleasure.

The delivery man's white panel van was still visible in front of her car. The Judge followed at a reasonable distance behind them both.

At the entrance to the highway, the van turned right, the Lexus turned left. The Judge waited until the van was over the next rise before turning right and following Hollister.

CHAPTER 3

Buddy and the Detective

When Robert Hollister left the Judge's house, he drove directly to the police station, as Detective C had instructed. He needed the drive to allow his stomach to cool, his chest to relax, and his mind to relock the closet door.

Before entering the station, he patted his shirt pocket, making sure the small compact-sized mirror was there. The receptionist behind the bulletproof glass tried to engage his eye. He never looked directly at her, though, only her reflection in the window beside her. She wondered if maybe he was having second thoughts about coming in. Even though he was the only person standing in front of her desk, it took her a moment to realize he was talking to her. "I ... I'm Buddy, uh, Robert ... Hollister ... and I'm here to speak with ... Detective Cromwell." His words halted and hung, pushed out, like this language was alien, or his vocal cords were rusted from disuse. The latter was true, except for the rust. He rarely initiated speech.

He wanted to say Detective C, but felt the secretary needed the formality. When they'd met up again in Colorado, Robert could have called him Sarge, like in the Marines. But now that Cromwell had come up in the world, a real detective, he deserved more respect.

Detective Cromwell was too formal for most times. It'd be like saying Sergeant Cromwell all the time. Robert stuck with Detective C, except when formality was called for.

The receptionist smiled and spoke in her sweetest voice, as if she felt sorry for him, though slower and louder than usual, apparently mistaking his halting words for retardation. "Yes. Detective Cromwell will be right with you. He told me to have you wait at his desk. Do you know where that is?"

Robert knew she always tried her best to be kind, and to do the right thing. Detective C had told him. If her ten-year-old, hyperactive son needed help with his math homework, she was right there, even though she hated math. Yes, Detective C had picked a winner with her. And he never hit on her. He was that kind of guy.

She started to get up to show Robert the way, but he nodded at her and shuffled quickly and quietly down the hall to the large open room with four modern office cubicles, walked into the detective's cubicle and sat on his chair. He swiveled the chair around and saw the receptionist still frozen, half out of her seat, probably wondering how he moved so fast without making a sound. She sat down and frowned at her fingernails. If you didn't look too close you would only see how smooth and even she had applied the shiny red polish. But Robert had seen the chipped edges and frayed cuticles and had felt a little sorry for her.

He sighed and moved out of her vision, where he could inspect the cloth cubicle walls. During prior visits he'd been in and out with only glimpses to whet his curiosity, which was larger than nine cats and their eighty-one lives. Now he would have time. At the prospect, his heart raced, and he felt a bit of joy fold into his chest.

Most of the photos hid behind glass, a fact that massaged his face like a warm damp towel out of the microwave. He loved glass. Glass always told the true story. Clear glass was not as good as mirrors. But it was so much better than naked paper. All glass allowed him to see the real world, the one most people only thought about. He figured it was because glass was made of molten earth, and mirrors had the added element of silver. Silver was special: It could kill werewolves. It also showed him things, things he knew were true.

Everyone thought him weird, touched, crazy. Everyone except Detective C and Var.

Cromwell lived with voodoo, so that's his out. Var? He knew Robert in the Corps. Before he got weird, before mirrors and glass and visions. And after Var got his brain scrambled and said he died and came back to life, and as a doctor, he said Robert had good reason to become what he was.

Robert scanned the gray wall behind the desk. There, hung an eight-by-twelve of a beautiful bayou, moss hanging from dark weeping willows, reaching down into the mirrored water that reflected the snake-like head and neck of a Great Blue Heron. A prehistoric-looking alligator, with its long, plated body, sunned itself next to a rustic cabin.

Beside the bayou photo was a photo of a much younger Detective C with a beautiful young woman, beautiful and bald. Her bright eyes radiated from hollow dark sockets, as if she were excited to be starved. Her smile looked tired. Detective C was not smiling at all. Below that photo hung an old black-and-white, more brown and yellow, of a man with a neatly trimmed, grizzled beard, sitting at a spacious desk, a judge's gavel in one hand and a pipe in the other. He smiled at the camera, only the smile seemed wrong, and as Robert watched, the smile animated and turned into an evil grin. Robert looked away.

To the left of the desk, the wall held a painting of a detective's shield. It was unusual. Robert had seen the shield on many of the detectives in this department, the all-seeing eye of providence, inside a radiating sun, framed in a pyramid. Was it a setting or rising sun? He preferred to think of it as rising. Below the painting he expected to see something like "Poudre County Police." But there was only one word—*Justice*. He wondered if the painting held any secrets, so he took out the small mirror from his breast pocket and viewed the painting through the mirror. The painting glowed golden and shimmered as if it were alive. It appeared as solitary as a stop sign on the moon, only it was a golden triangle suspended in the void of a cloudless blue Colorado sky. The eye winked at him.

Steps sounded in the hallway and out of the corner of his eye he saw someone coming. He slid the mirror back in his pocket, looked at the floor and held in a deep breath, concentrating his wonder at the mirror's gift. He breathed out, enlightened. Buddha would be proud.

CHAPTER 4

O. J., Buddy, and the Plan

Detective O. J. Cromwell walked down the hall, feeling his molars crunching against the crown that covered his one cracked tooth.

He was glad to be walking out of the Captain's office. The Captain had just finished a tirade, scowled over those cheater glasses he thought made him look god-like, or maybe it was the wise look he was after. "I know you're hiding something from me Cromwell, and when I figure out what it is I have a feeling I'm gonna to be pissed."

Right. Something new and different.

Maybe the Captain was finally at the end of his rope with Cromwell and his big-tongue Rolling Stones tee shirts, his blue jeans, his New Balance running shoes, and his ponytail. Cromwell looked down at his dress. The tee shirt and jeans were clean and neat. He just wasn't a tie guy. Change was always hard, maybe worse for those at the top. Hey, the Captain had a great window in his office. It wasn't Cromwell's fault all he could look at was bricks and mortar.

He took a deep breath and let it out slow and felt his jaws relax, shaking off the meeting with the Captain. He saw Robert Hollister standing in his cubicle, and his day jumped into sunshine. Or tried to.

He kept thinking about the last case involving blown-glass balloons. The Captain suspected something had gone wrong, but there was no evidence, no proof. He worried there was some maniac killer still loose, ready to take another life, a situation that could possibly eject the Captain's rather large butt right out of his elected seat. So he wheedled at Cromwell from time to time, like today, and it always served to bring back old baggage, making Cromwell sweat like he was walking through that old Louisiana bayou with a sun so hot it felt like hell was waiting just around the corner.

♪ ♫

Sorry to interrupt, but I told you at the beginning I might be bopping in and out with my weird clairvoyant thoughts. At that moment, I felt O.J. worrying. I knew that bayou case was a nightmare. It forced him to leave Louisiana and come here. I didn't really know much about it, something about him botching evidence and a woman literally getting away with murder, and a gruesome one involving her husband and three kids and some weird torture. O.J. initially had thought the woman was innocent, which caused him to screw up the evidence. Which put him over the top with guilt when she walked.

Then came the case here with the glassblower. It was a weird and difficult case about which he shared little. After the bayou, O.J. was not going to let another guilty woman walk. Initially he'd been convinced a woman murdered a psychopath glassblower. But she turned out to be innocent, and dead because of O.J. Or so he thought. But he wouldn't share why he thought so, not even after I plied him with more Guinness at Jackie's. One thing was sure: he didn't like what he saw in his mirror. Not that he hated himself; he just seemed to have lost a little of his joie de vivre.

Even though that bayou case brought him here, away from his home and kin, I was glad he was here. I didn't like that he still had nightmares about the bayou case, and I wish he didn't feel he was a failure as a detective, because he was damn good at his job.

Detectives are like us all, though, they can't forget cases they think they screwed up.

Doctors do the same thing. And even though I forget them in the daylight, I still wake at night in a cold sweat over a few cases. I'm sure O.J. does the same. I believe that makes me a better doctor and makes O.J. a better detective: reliving mistakes to prevent another.

All of which proves my O.J. is nothing like the O.J. you all are thinking of. Besides, he was a good O.J. long before that other asshole went to trial.

♪ ♫

Cromwell shrugged off the Captain and smiled at seeing Hollister, or Buddy, as he called him because they were friends, and that's what Buddy's two friends in the world called him. Buddy was using his mirror in there, peering at the shield. *Wonder what he sees,* Cromwell thought. He knew Buddy from the Corps and had been on a few other cases with him. Usually Buddy saw things in mirrors that people tried to hide from the real world. Sometimes he saw things the people were unaware of, until later.

After Buddy had his incident in Fallujah, he'd changed. Now he spoke very softly, seeming to mumble, almost like he was mentally deficient. But he wasn't. Far from it. And he'd proven it in the first case Cromwell had worked with him. In that case, the initial investigation pointed to the guy's death as a natural result of his medical condition. He died of a simple asthma attack. But Buddy told a story beyond the simple asthma attack. He'd delivered a mirror to the house and in the reflection had seen the wife poisoning the husband. The guy was allergic to cockroaches and she sprinkled some kind of dust, presumably ground roaches, in his face while he smoked a cigarette. Buddy had told Cromwell he saw it all in the mirror.

♪ ♫

Cromwell grew up in the bayous of Louisiana, so voodoo and weird shit like that didn't faze him. I guess that's part of why we get along so well. He doesn't see me as odd, even though I don't really believe in voodoo. Maybe it's because I once lived in Pensacola, and he grew up right in the heart of it in New Orleans. He believed there was powerful truth in voodoo.

♪ ♫

So, believing Buddy and his mirrors was no great stretch. The trick was convincing the forensics guys to take another look and see if there was anything unusual in the guy's bronchial tree. Yeah, they said, there were cockroach pieces in his wind pipe. So what? The CSI pukes said. He lived in a trailer that hadn't been cleaned since Eve lied to Adam.

The mirror had told Buddy something else: where the wife stored the vial of powder. Cromwell snuck in one night while she was working the corner of John and Jesus and found the vial. Empty. She was brighter than he gave her credit. But he took the vial, just in case.

After a little more digging, it turned out hubby had recently bought a large life insurance policy. He was a plumber, made twice what Cromwell did, but a $2.5

mill policy showed quite a love for such an ungrateful wife. With that info, Cromwell convinced the forensics guys to take another look.

The vial held traces of peanuts, which just happened to be coating every corner of the plumber's lungs. Peanut allergy can be fatal, especially if you inhale the dust. And dirty trailers had no monopoly on peanuts.

So, yes, Detective Cromwell liked Buddy Hollister. But they were more than just friends. They had shared rat stew thickened with a rice cooked in various hovels throughout Iraq and Afghanistan, and they'd covered each other's backs for over ten years. They'd started out fellow grunts, privates at age eighteen. Then Fallujah changed Buddy forever. War can do that to some. Cromwell progressed. Buddy didn't.

Cromwell walked into his cubicle. Buddy's head snapped down and he slipped the mirror from his hand to his pants pocket.

"Hey, Buddy. How's it hangin'? Don't worry about the mirror. It's no big deal."

Buddy let out a deep breath and turned his head towards Cromwell, without eye contact. "I thought it might be someone else."

Cromwell sat and swiveled over to his desk to get some papers. Buddy shifted back and forth on nervous feet.

"What?" Cromwell said.

Buddy blurted a stream of staccato words in a sentence long enough to rival Faulkner, and about as cryptic. "I'm glad it's you Detective C 'cause what I saw this morning was bad: the Judge I delivered a mirror to this morning up on the hill, like you said—I didn't like that mirror anyway—and then I saw him slashing at his wife in the mirror, but it could have been the history of the mirror that was bad with a rancher a long time ago killing his wife and hanging himself, oh yeah, and there were children or young black women in the basement, and they were crying and naked, and I thought you might want to know."

Buddy called Cromwell Detective C dating back to the end of Afghanistan when Cromwell became an MP— respect Cromwell was not sure he deserved.

"Buddy, whoa. Slow down, man. Not sure I've ever heard you say that many words all at once. Or maybe ever." Cromwell stood up and craned his neck to look in the other cubicles. Luckily the other officers were in a sexual harassment training session down the hall and hadn't heard Buddy's weird harangue.

He sat back down and motioned for Buddy to sit. "You seem upset."

Buddy shook his head and kept standing. "Yessir. I'm sorry. I left in a hurry. I was afraid I might …"

"You don't have to call me sir."

Buddy pursed his lips. "You're a detective and I'm not."

Cromwell shook his head.

"Also, uhm," Buddy continued, "I was looking at your shield on the wall and it winked at me."

"It…*winked* at you? Is that what you said—winked?" Cromwell was glad no one was around. This was getting weirder by the minute. He took a deep breath and sighed.

"Yessir. That's right. I'm sorry. Just telling you what I saw."

"Okaaay. I can see how that might upset you. But let's get back to the person you delivered the mirror to.

Who was it?"

"It was the judge who lives up on the hill, you know, with the pretty wife."

"The judge? You mean Judge Craghead?"

"Yes sir. I think that's his name."

The Judge had always struck Cromwell as an asshole, always ruling the way he wanted, even if the evidence pointed elsewhere. Cromwell had some experience with other judges that bent the law—his Cajun grand-daddy and namesake, Judge Oliver Jude Cromwell was crooked as a gator's jaw. He glanced at the photo of the smiling crook with the gavel from hell about to crush another law into the maple desk.

"Did you say I told you to go there?"

"You remember."

"Uh, no. I know Judge Craghead pretty well, and I'm sure I would remember if I told you to visit him."

Buddy turned his head side to side and looked around the cubicle.

"Buddy?"

"You said I should investigate any feelings I had about a bad person."

Cromwell sighed. Yep, that had come out of his mouth.

"Okay. Tell me again what you saw."

"He slashed at her with a big knife and, oh yeah, there was a gunshot and blood spurted." He dropped his chin to his chest and muttered softly, "Everywhere. There was so much blood."

"Shit, Buddy. He stabbed his wife, Angela?" Cromwell felt like his heart dropped into his stomach. A bit of sour phlegm pinched the back of his throat. His reaction was mild, if you ask me. I would have vomited.

Buddy nodded, his eyes wide. Then he shook his head and looked at the floor. "I'm not sure. Like I said, there was a history with that mirror and the rancher's wife getting killed. It all happened pretty fast. I thought I might do something, so I left."

♪ ♫

Cromwell and I both knew what Buddy meant by "something bad." We three were brothers, not by blood, but by more. As Shakespeare put it: "we few, we happy few, we band of brothers—for whoever sheds his blood with me today shall be my brother." Buddy's story with women started when he was in high school with his Aunt Betty. The women in Buddy's life had always been good to him, and his aunt was the best. So, he helped her after her husband died. One day, he offered to help her after school, but she told him no, saying she wanted Buddy to have time for homework. He finished his homework early and went Aunt Betty's place anyhow, figuring he'd surprise her and take the leaves out of the gutters. He walked into the kitchen and found a guy bopping her. He killed the guy with a butcher knife: right through the groin. Except that didn't just kill him. He ripped the knife all the way to his mouth. Aunt Betty lost it and never recovered. There was no trial. The juvie-court judge threw out the manslaughter charge from the local DA citing Buddy was only doing what any kid who loved his aunt would do, though it was never clear to me if Aunt Betty was being raped or just enjoying herself. The guy who'd been bopping Aunt Betty was a homeless dude, or what they called back then, a hobo, and everyone assumed the worst. The judge had been a teacher once, taught Buddy in grade school. After he reached his pinnacle in the county, he judged Buddy's aunt's pepper jelly number one at the county fair. Country judges did things like that. He might have had a crush on Betty. He also judged Buddy not guilty. Buddy turned eighteen a month later and joined the Marines. I always wondered if the juvie judge had made that a stipulation of his dismissal of the case.

Anyway, now you know how Buddy reacts to things happening to women. He is kind of off kilter about the other sex. Then there's Fallujah where the mirrors started. That was much worse, but that's another story.

♪ ♫

The door down the hallway from Cromwell's office opened and Cromwell could hear the mumble of voices getting louder as the other officers started moving to their cubicles.

"Damn. Wait a sec. You said it was in the mirror, right? Didn't really happen?"

"Yeah, it was in the mirror, but it felt so real I ... I didn't look very long." He shuffled two steps towards the cubicle exit.

"Wait." Cromwell swallowed and took a breath through his nose, trying to calm his tripping heart. He stepped in closer to Buddy and put a finger to his lips, then spoke very quietly, "Don't go yet. Did you see anything else? What time of day did it happen?"

"Dunno," Buddy whispered. "Light was faint. Maybe twilight. Felt like it was soon. Maybe today."

"Okay," he moved his mouth to within inches of Buddy's ear. Absolutely no one else could hear this. "Wait a few hours and go back. Think up some kinda excuse to reenter his home. I've got some stuff I need to do, first. I'll meet you at noon-ish. That should give us plenty of time to investigate his home before, well, you know." He had to testify at a court case. Should be in an out quick.

"'Kay."

"When you're in there, though, you watch him, watch him close. And don't do anything … like before. You hear me? If you get antsy again, just book."

Buddy nodded.

"Listen, if you can't do this without coming unglued, tell me now. I need your help, but not if … well, you know."

"I'm okay. I can do this."

"Okay. I'm trusting you." Cromwell grabbed his buckskin fringed jacket hanging on the coat post. He needed to be upscale in court.

Buddy nodded again and lit out like bees were after him.

CHAPTER 5

Buddy's Dilemma

The Judge sat in his Suburban across the street from the police station, waiting. He saw Robert Hollister come out and walk as fast as he could walk without running down the street toward his white van. He never looked up. *For some reason,* the Judge pondered, *that greasy mouse does not like to look people in the eye.* Obviously guilty of something. If you couldn't look a man in the eye, you were ashamed of something. Why would he go into the police station? Guilty men usually avoid such places, unless ... he was a snitch. Could he be spying on the Judge and telling the police? What could he have found out? Not a damn thing. All the doors to the basement were locked. No. He was probably paying a parking fine or something.

Just the same.

He started his Suburban and followed Hollister, saw him park at a McDonald's, pulled over and punched a number into his cell phone: my number, Var.

After three rings I answered, "Hi, Judge. What can I do you for on this fine sunny day?"

The Judge likes me because I treat his gout and keep his hypertension from causing a stroke. I used to like him before he began having bad thoughts about Angela. I guess it shows in my voice. He hates the way I talk to him: chipper with a hint of disrespect.

"Good morning, Var. Do you have some time this week for another case?" After the word got out, even the Judge wanted to have my investigative help. Plus, he liked free.

"Did Angela get another speeding ticket? She's a maniac in that Lexus. I'm surprised she didn't talk her way out of it. Her body language is some mighty powerful juju, don't you think? You're one lucky man." Or at least he used to be.

Luck had nothing to do with it, the Judge probably wanted to say. Instead, he said, "Yes. *My* wife is beautiful." He paused, like he wanted his emphasis of *my* to hit me a little harder. If I wasn't his doctor I'd hang up.

He continued, "However, that's not what I need you for. I'd like you to look up a name and we can meet tomorrow, say at lunch, to discuss your findings. You like that greasy spoon with the big hamburgers on Fourth Street, right?"

"Lou's? Love it. Best guacamole burger this side of I-10. Onion rings to die for. Whose dirty drawers you want me peeling back?"

"Robert Hollister." He spelled out the last name. Like I really needed that.

"How far you want me to go?"

"As far as you can get."

That wouldn't happen. Yet, I wondered if maybe my wandering mind had been sleeping. Hollister had a history. "He threaten you?"

"I'm not sure. Just find out all you can about him, and we'll discuss it tomorrow."

Okay. Robert Hollister, Buddy to me, hadn't gone off the rails. If he'd threatened the Judge, there'd be no doubt—the Judge would not be able to carry on this conversation. "Maybe you should go to the police if you're worried he might come after you."

"I can take care of myself. Besides, he's not a physical threat at all. I'll talk to you tomorrow."

He ended the call.

If the Judge only knew. But I wasn't going to tell him. Buddy Hollister was the worst physical threat anyone could imagine.

♪ ♫

Buddy Hollister drove to the local McDonald's and had some French fries and ranch dressing while he sat in the van and watched white puffy clouds coagulate into darker bunches over the mountains to the west. A scant breeze came through his window, cooling his over-heated head. A black Suburban that had been parked down the road flipped a U and drove off.

Buddy finished the fries and drove toward the Judge's place, soon reaching the dirt road that led to the house. He turned left. This dirt road was like a long bow that curved right and passed a few nice homes and con-tinued around the bend to another entrance from the highway. Hollister liked coming in the front way. The Judge's home was on the right, the driveway a gentle slope up the hill to the huge house. As Buddy turned right into the driveway, dust floated in a low cloud from the back road on his left into his window and made him want to sneeze.

The driveway curved left to the garage. There were no cars in the driveway. He parked and walked to the door and rang the Judge's doorbell. He waited, reflec-tions of the mountains and clouds in the bay window crisp in the noon sun.

The reflection of the road he'd just driven showed no trailing dust from Detective C's car. He thought about what would happen if Detective C didn't show up: plan B. As usual, he had a plan C, too. That's what they taught you in the Corps. So he was ready when the Judge opened the door.

"And what brings you here, Mr. Hollister?" The Judge had an attitude. Not good.

"I … I need to check the back of the mirror, sir. If you don't mind."

Probably an electronic bug back there, the Judge thought.

"Come on in. That'll be fine."

When the Judge closed the door, Buddy looked into another mirror hung behind the door. It reflected an angry scowl on the Judge's face.

Buddy shuffled faster than any mouse to the antique mirror in the kitchen and watched the Judge carefully through the mirror. There he saw how the Judge had followed him to the sheriff's office in his black Suburban and afterwards had taken the back road from the highway. That would account for the dust that made him sneeze. And the Judge's bad attitude. Buddy had to break off his gaze, for the Judge was inspecting him, more than carefully. Buddy had seen his share of people like that in Iraq and Afghanistan, twitchy enough to explode. He would have to be careful. No way he could kill the Judge like he could Taliban. Detective C wouldn't want it.

A stamp-sized brown paper marker, the same color as the back of the mirror, stuck to Buddy's palm, out of sight. It had 57890345$Calahan written on it. One sticky edge was curled up and ready. He gently tilted the bottom of the mirror off the wall while placing his hand behind it and palming off the marker more deftly than that card shark sergeant palmed an ace in Iraq. He hoped the Judge had not inspected the back of the mirror earlier.

The Judge scrutinized Buddy's every move, but all appeared copasetic. Buddy lifted the mirror off the hook and turned it around.

"There it is," Buddy mumbled. He made a show of pointing to the brown marker on the lower left corner of the brown mirror backing. He peeled it off.

The Judge squinted at the marker, thinking, *Maybe he's here legitimately. Maybe he just went to the police department because he had other business there. Maybe he was just a deliveryman and not sent by the police.*

But his suspicions had never been wrong before, and neither had his instincts. There were no maybes. This man was setting him up, he was sure of it.

Buddy held up the marker like a winning number at bingo. "This is our special ID number for this mirror. My boss is upset with me for leaving it. You could get into our computer with this number. Sorry I had to come back."

The Judge peered at the sticker. "May I see that, son?"

Buddy held it out for him to view, but only briefly. "Sorry, sir. Can't let you really inspect the code. Shop computer file secrets, you know."

"I understand perfectly. You wouldn't want a respected judge in your computer, now would you?"

Buddy was not thinking polite thoughts: *That Judge. What a character.* More like: *What an asshole.*

Buddy turned the mirror around to hang it. The Judge's reflection changed from the frown of a concerned man to a leer, his lips an ugly snarl, his eyes black lakes lit with fire that flickered and sawed exactly like the small boy who'd seen his mother bleed to death.

Buddy felt a cold desert snake crawl into his belly. So cold, so very cold and black and evil as oil. And he knew the evil of oil after being a Marine in Iraq. He shivered.

The Judge was so close he felt Buddy's body vibrate, as if someone had plugged him into AC current for a second. In that instant the Judge knew his instincts had been spot-on. He also knew he must lure Buddy, this idiotic, hick deliveryman, somewhere he could dispose of him without the police suspecting.

The Judge pretended to stretch his back. "I guess you're all done with this mirror, Mr. Hollister. Sorry you had to make the trip all the way back out here. But as long as you're here, I was wondering ... My back has been bothering me. Perhaps you could put another mirror up in our bedroom?"

Buddy took a deep breath and let it out. This was not going to work. He made a show of carefully folded the marker in half so it stuck on itself, and slipped it into a shirt pocket, which he buttoned as he would have for the real markers used on many of his deliveries. The story he'd given the Judge was not a total confabulation. But he was sure the story the Judge had just given him was an absolute and total lie.

"Sir, I really need to get back."

The Judge held out a crisp twenty-dollar bill. "Surely, son, ten minutes will be worth your time."

Buddy glanced out the front window and wondered if it was time for plan B. His plan B, not what Detective C would want, but exactly what the Judge needed. There was still no sign of Detective C, and it had already been much longer than five minutes. Detective C needed to be here. Had to be here.

His hands felt slick. Part of him wanted to run. The other part of him started to swell inside his chest like an alien about to burst out and annihilate anything it found alive. Detective C was not coming. In the mirror, Buddy noticed the Judge twisting his head to peer up the stairs. The Judge looked back at Buddy, his pupils large voids, as dilated as a cat pleading for food. Buddy nearly ran when the orange flame in the black hole of the Judge's eyes snaked out and flitted across the room like fire on a wire, hitting the mirror and lancing into Buddy's eyes with a piercing pain that made him cry out. If he did what needed to be done, Detective C would not forgive him.

"Mr. Hollister, are you all right?"

Buddy kept his eyes fixed on the floor. What was he going to do? He knew for sure this man was evil. The world would be better off if Buddy gutted him. But that would make Detective C's life hell.

"Yessir. I hurt my back, too, the other day, and every now and then it grabs me. Like just now. I can't really lift anymore today. The boss needs me back to help with the computer, anyways. I'm sorry I won't be able to help you with that other mirror. Maybe we can send someone else out."

The Judge smiled at the mirror with such white teeth: pointed, gleaming, razor-sharp shark teeth.

The Judge's beautiful wife, Angela, walked down the stairs, smiling at the mirror with teeth as white as the Judge's—a picket fence in the morning sun. It was as if she floated down the stairs in slow motion, her feet not even touching the ground. She had on the same ivory white blouse, but this time it was unbuttoned to her navel. She wore no bra. Her marble nipples rubbed and poked against the blouse with each step, and her eyes pleaded with Buddy, as if to say, "Take me and love me, now, before the Judge kills me." Any second … any second, now, the Judge would reach for a knife and slash her throat and she would die bleeding, just as the mother of the boy had so many years ago. Or was the blood just that mother? He was getting confused.

Buddy had to do something.

"Hello again, Mr. Hollister." She winked at him in the mirror. "I'm so glad that you came back. My husband and I talked about you, and I've been aching for you all afternoon."

In the mirror, she took three steps toward him. Her eyes changed, became the same empty obsidian pools as the Judge's, with a different fire, a fluorescent green that danced and reached for him, freezing his eyelids.

She reached between her thighs, and unsnapped a beautifully crafted, long leather holster. Through the silvery reflection, he saw a slow-motion video, almost frame by frame, of her sliding out a golden, glinting knife as long as her thigh.

He could not move but forced out the words: "But I thought he was going to kill you like the others in the basement."

"Dear, sweet, Robert. I'm not sure what you're referring to. I would never let him kill anyone."

The Judge's face and fiery black eyes loomed over her shoulder, one arm draped around her neck, his hand fondling one of those perfect breasts. "We've been looking for you for a long time, Mr. Hollister."

Buddy laughed.

CHAPTER 6

Case Two—The Driftin' Mug

Hollister is one weird dude, right? Today that's true. But he was different twelve years ago, when he first joined the Corps. Still, he's a guy you want watching your back when the shit hits the fan. Whatever you do, you never want him against you. He and I both like mirrors, too.

The Judge is no Andrew Jackson Taylor, aka Andy Griffith, not by two or even three long shots, even if the guy swished those three pointers. Sorry about the mixed metaphors, but just go with the flow. I love basketball.

That, as I said, is the first case, or at least the beginnings. I will get to Angela. Later.

My vision blurs and my chest tightens. I'm pretty sure ... no I am absolutely positive Angela once loved me just as much as I loved her. We had big plans. Once upon a time. Then I screwed it up.

I fill my lungs with a deep breath and hold it for a second, then let it out.

Now I can move on. I have to tell you about the other case. It started at the same time as the first case, three weeks before I was going in the courtroom. Remember —the bike ride. The two cases were like dueling *a cappella* artists, only one was a black soul sister and the other heavy metal. You could definitely tell who was who, but Jesus! The two were destined for crappy collisions, monstrous zombie fests. Okay, you're right, that was absolutely uncalled for. I hate those zombie shits. Give me a shotgun and lots of shells.

Taking it down a notch, as my psych dude would say, I ran into the other case whilst (what a cool word, huh —like old English mixed with debauchery—she looked into his eyes whilst ... yeah. Forget it.) I biked up some super hills west of town. The great thing about road-biking, not Harley-dude, but Tour de France pedal cruising, is that once you get your feet locked into the pedals and you're warmed up, it's a rhythmic hormonal high that competes and sometimes outdoes any one eighty song. If you can put the two together, the endorphins and enkephalins will make you think you're the only human on the planet, or the universe for that matter (unless you're Stephen Hawking and you'd get lost in your own mind), and it can take a large distraction to interrupt your reverie, like a big dude coming downhill at about forty, right at you, on the wrong side of the road—my side.

This guy was huge. Twice me. And that's a lot of mass to hit head-on. When you already have one screwed up leg and arm, you don't want another one, so you naturally are looking out for any shitbird trying to ruin the rest of your limbs, even if it means coming out of the reverie and those sexy chicks in "Addicted to Love" by Robert Palmer. What the hell was he doing on the wrong side of the road, anyhow? That other bike lane was plenty big—actually, no. Roadwork was taking up the other bike lane and then some. It's amazing what you can see and react to in nanoseconds.

Shit! I clicked out of the pedals at about the same time I steered over to the far right, sure I would end up swimming in the colder-than-penguin-crap reservoir that made for usually great views on this side of the road. If I didn't hit the scrabble of sharp, multi-angular, sharp (are you getting it?) rocks that lined the reservoir, I'd be fine. Even better: stop. Now!

I did. Those custom front/rear bias brakes on the right handle worked well.

He stopped, too, only a bit slower, and a bit clumsily, like a confused cartoon bull trying to end a charge at Mickey Mouse. After all, he had to halt a lot of weight. You see, he'd been a football player, pro dude, for the Denver Broncos. Muscle mass is heavier than fat, and this guy still had it. Probably benched four hundred. I don't want to even guess what he squatted. Anyway, his intensity, fantastic reflexes, and sheer strength allowed him to stop that bike and jump off it, avoiding a fall over the edge like an Olympic diver getting his balance for a back dive.

"Sorry, man." His voice was kind, smooth, and surprisingly more tenor than baritone. Maybe it was just about almost losing it over that cliff. "I was cruising so fast when I saw the construction I just made a snap decision and was over here. Then I saw you coming up and realized I was still a stupid football player."

"No prob. I'm safe. You're safe. Our bikes are good." I tasted a bit of coppery blood on my tongue. Must have bit it. And then I noticed his front fork was bent to hell.

He saw it, too, and sighed. "Geez. Looks like I got to get another front-end alignment." His smile was wide and contagious. Already I liked this guy.

I held out my right hand to shake his. "I'm Var."

"Mug." As he held out his hand, he glanced at my left prosthetic arm and special handle for the bike.

"Your name's Mug?"

"Yeah. It was a nickname I got in college: Driftin' Mug. I kept forgetting my coffee mug in people's dorm rooms when I visited, and I was a little drifty. So it stuck."

When he shook, it felt like my hand got swallowed by an XXL catcher's mitt. I sure hoped he didn't decide to squeeze. And now that I stood up beside him, all I wanted to do was get six-inch lifts in my shoes to at least look at his Adam's apple. The guy was a mutant.

"Var? Is that like Varsity?"

"Zactly."

"Whadja play?"

My turn for the great smile. "Is there another favorite American game? I mean, not to dis the pitcher-home-run thing, but waaay boring."

He nodded. "Don't tell me—quarterback?"

I gave him my best imitation of throwing a forward pass without a ball. "You got it, Mug."

"I'll bet you were pretty good."

Now see, that's when I knew I would not only like this guy but I'd love him. If he was a Jaguar car salesman, he could have sold me two. He saw natural talent and read between my prosthetic lines. That shows you how cool the dude was. Not only did he like riding bikes on hills, but he could tell by my name I was no second stringer.

"I had my moments."

Then he got all embarrassed-looking, squinching his mouth and trying to read the gravel pieces on the ground like tea leaves. "Sorry to put you off your bike.

Maybe I'll see you later." He began walking his bike down the road, holding the crumpled front end up with one hand like he was carrying an iPhone. I swear the guy could have shot put that bike a mile and then had an easier walk.

It was his limp that caught my eye and got my bleeding tongue moving again from its stupid hiatus. "Hey, Mug, hold it right there. Let me call someone to pick us up. You drink beer?"

He stumbled while turning around on his weak leg, caught himself and showed me a contrite face. Must have been a Catholic.

"Nah. You should finish your ride. I can walk. It'll be a good lesson for me to stop making dumb decisions on the road. One of these days I could kill somebody, maybe even myself. I'd love a beer. Another time."

"But you're limping. You must have hurt yourself."

He glanced at my prosthetic leg, and his next look was pure, are-you-kidding-me? "It's an old injury." He took another peek at my leg. "Minor." He waved a hand over his head and walked away.

I got a little momentum going uphill, then clipped in and finished Robert Palmer and went on to Barenaked Ladies, all the while pumping hard up a mile-long killer hill, only wondering on the downhill side if I would ever see Mug again. He was one guy I wished my floating mind would connect with. Never happened.

But I did see him again. His football days were over, and next time I saw him, this time over a Guinness, the whole game of NFL football was threatening to die. A very nasty death. But, it was a contact sport.

CHAPTER 7

RAZR and Football

The only two things in life that make it worth living
Are guitars tuned good and firm feeling women.[1]

Waylon's voice can tell a story like no other. And it so happens that I agree with him. I'm back, ear buds plugged in, waiting in the elevator, on my way to the pretrial hearing, knowing that this one eighty will end before I arrive.

As you will recall, I'm late and using my chair instead of walking. It usually works better to appear wonderfully normal. I especially wanted that in the beginning, those years ago, after the accident. My leg prosthetic had to be hidden by pants, though my arm prosthetic was hard to hide. I tried the natural prosthetic hand look initially, but that stupid thing didn't work for squat. So, now I usually use the more functional hook and, when needed, I flourish it.

At the right time. Timing, as they say, is everything.

But today I'll rely on the chair. The Judge will see me fumble with things, moving the wooden chairs to make room for my wheelchair. I don't use a mechanized chair for the courtroom. No. Even though this is a pretrial hearing with no jury, the Judge is still human, and just like a jury will equate a mechanized chair with wealth. This case is bad enough having a client everyone assumes is a stinking rich pro-football player, so I don't need any more—what did Mitt Romney call it?—class envy, to cloud his judgment about the truth.

That's what's important, right? Truth.

And he definitely needs to hear the truth about this case. Football gets a lot of hype about the money made by guys like that dirt ball Michael Vick, who raised and bet on fighting dogs, or by the God-worshipping Tim Tebow, who did his bent-knee, fist-to-forehead Thinker pose after any good play that brought him closer to victory and the after-game interview with reporters on his way to more sponsorship.

The truth about the game gets blurred in the money and the hype. But the truth is the game is mostly played by guys who work their ass off to climb out of a rat hole of a life and make a living in hard labor that can cripple or dement them for the rest of their lives, hoping to get their families set before they step into a heart attack, stroke, or an early nursing home from brain-traumatized Parkinson's. The biggest ticket they want to cash in on is the playoffs and the Super Bowl, with playoff bonuses, which were once piddling but now have become *suhweet*. And of course there are the endorsements, something that can allow them to make millions on TV commercials while wearing their bathrobe in those later years when football is long gone.

So when drugs that could enhance their abilities were introduced, drugs that could make them stronger, faster, and all-in-all better than their competitors, it was more than just tempting to take them. If they were legal—or at least undetected by current technology—then the players sucked them down quicker than an interception.

Through the early years of the game, before the '70s, play-enhancing drugs were not banned, except maybe in the eyes of those namby-pamby ethical sport conservatives. The players loved them for the power and the feeling of being Herculean; the viewers loved them for increasing the speed and brutality of a sport that was one step closer to the gladiators of ancient Rome; and the owners loved them because—well, duh!—more viewers, more money.

Two months ago this drug was supposedly introduced. RAZR was the name I heard circulating. Cool. Like a razor's edge. But it was a two-sided razor. The bad side was just as sharp. Now it's the playoffs and the effects have been stupendous—more like the pace and violence of the game has become so crazy that it's, as some rock stars put it, just stupid. These guys aren't getting a degree in ethics or how to be the ideal person. They're physical mutants who use force, speed, and reflexes, along with natural eye-hand coordination to overcome most human beings on the earth in a game that despises losers. And now they have an edge that can put them over the top. Every damn time.

Unless everyone uses it. Then the limits of human anatomy, physiology, skin, bone, and muscle are overcome. Injuries skyrocketed. But most players were used to playing hurt in the playoffs, especially since the new rules awarded playoff bonuses only to those who stay off the injured list and play at least one quarter, or the equivalent in time, in the playoffs.

A week ago, something other than injuries started to surface, or at least several team doctors disclosed to some of my contacts that several players got tremors and muscular twitches. A few players committed suicide. Those were put off to the usual head trauma problems, Chronic Traumatic Encephalopathy, or CTE. Initially a media lid was screwed down tight, keeping this from the public. But eventually some trainers and team doctors—"the namby-pamby ethical ones," as the players argued—wanted to ban players who used RAZR. Problem was, the official NFL drug-testing dudes hadn't figured out how to detect RAZR in urine or blood yet. And the Super Bowl is just around the corner. Without a doubt, every player on opposing teams will be using this drug in the next months. Hell, I'm sure players in other sports are already using it in preparation for their own seasons: hockey, basketball, and God help us, that already ugly sport of mixed martial arts.

It seems a bit strange, though, that this drug was introduced at the beginning of the NFL season, and now, only three months later, guys are suicidal. Maybe it's the psychological effects of the drug, maybe it's another drug mixed in, or maybe not. No way to tell this early. Most times it takes a while to prove any drug causes any bad effect, sometimes years. And if that drug makes tons of money? I knew of drug companies who'd paid off researchers to bury any studies that showed their drug had bad side effects. The guy who designed RAZR was undoubtedly making millions, but it would be stupid to make a drug that started killing footballers after only three months of use.

Yeah, stupid. Greed vs. ethics.

Game time.

I put the iPhone and earplugs into my pocket and wheeled into the courtroom, knowing the Judge would be upset at my late entrance, and also knowing he'd probably forgive me. Probably. But, I had forgiven him for taking Angela, and I have offered to help him with Hollister.

CHAPTER 8

Angela and Mug Against the World

I met Angela in my first year in med school, anatomy class, long before she got hooked up with the Judge. I'd been a football star in college at CU, had a few pro scouts ask me to camp. But I wanted to be a doctor. I did well in premed, but I wasn't prepared for med school. I'd read *Zen and the Art of Motorcycle Maintenance* in college and decided to buy a Honda 350 the summer before medical school. I thought about skipping school and riding across the states like the guy in the book, but I had a Navy scholarship, and my dad had worked hard to get me through college, so I half-assed both. Guilt kept me away from riding the mountains too much, and the wonder and joy of being on the bike kept me from studying too much. Doing the bike maintenance myself and zen-caring about it, then floating over the mountain roads afterwards was, well, what can I say? It was addicting. I nearly flunked out of med school after only the first year.

First semester, second year, the Navy informed me that I would have to pay back the first two years in time as an enlisted guy if I flunked out. About the same time, I laid the bike down going around a patch of gravel at barely ten miles per hour, and I'd just been through an emergency room rotation and seen some bikers with serious head trauma. I sold the bike, my grades improved, and Angela and I were really clicking. During my third-year clinical rotation on ICU, I found out something about her that was a life changer.

Her brother, Dale, had a big problem with asthma. Okay, way bigger than big. Understandably, she became obsessed with developing better drugs for asthma.

Angela, as it turns out, was a very appropriate name when she was younger. She was the angel in the family, taking care of her brother most days because her mom developed early Parkinson's disease. After I got involved in the ER and head trauma cases, I suspected her mom got the disease due to being slammed around by Angela's dad, the retired NFL player who'd made it big with the Broncos. He turned his millions into hundreds of millions with restaurants in Denver, Chicago, New York, and LA. He was a pretty smart guy for a football player. But he was an offensive left tackle and they seem to score highest on the NFL smart tests. He also knew how to invest. And how to avoid any lawsuits for spouse abuse.

Anyway, Angela'd been with Dale at the ER many a time when he suffered an asthma attack. But he started to do a bit better, and her mom was doing worse, had developed dementia and needed more help from Angela, too. Her dad wasn't around much, tending to his restaurants, and to other outside conquests, as Angela put it. You get my drift. She hated him.

That's why I was surprised when she actually dated me. Well, not because I was undesirable. Not then. No, because I was one of them: a gnarly football player. Okay, I was never gnarly. Maybe she dated me because I never liked using drugs, at least not back then, or because I wasn't gnarly. Or maybe something else. Who knows why two people hit it off? Though we did more than just hit it off. Bliss would be too weak to describe our three-year relationship.

One night after making love, we were both wired up, so we padded into my apartment kitchen for some ice cream, she in one of my oversized CU buffalo tee shirts and me in my black boxers. I had a pretty good upper body back then, so a little chill on the air never put me in a shirt. I remember sitting across from her, watching her dig out and spoon rocky road into her bowl. Her face changed from a beautiful slight smile on her lips and a sparkle in her eyes—post-lovemaking joy—to a dullness on her eyes and pursing of her lips—a sadness I'd not seen.

"What's wrong?" I said.

She closed her eyes and gave a big sigh and shook her head a little. "Nothing."

"Come on. You look like you just saw someone die."

Wrong thing to say.

She started crying. I didn't say another word but got up and took her in my arms and just held her: warm, soft, and gentle vibrations of her spasms of sadness.

I brought her a box of Kleenex; she wiped the tears and blew her nose and focused her dark eyes on me. "I'm sorry. I guess it's just all the love you're showing me. I'm," she looked at me, "not used to it." She dabbed her eyes again. "It reminded me of Dale."

We sat down at the table, me on her right side. She'd mentioned his death before, but I figured this was what brought it out. Maybe the psych rotation taught me something about grief and the need to talk about it, especially if it had been bottled up for a long time. And sometimes seemingly unconnected things connected. Kind of like my weird ass brain is now.

"About a bad attack?" I said.

She nodded and looked down.

I just waited. That's what the psych guys said. Just wait and something important might happen. I wasn't prepared for what came next.

She stared off into space. "I was sixteen. He'd turned five the week before. What a happy kid. Something about any five year old, when he smiles ... Well he was my brother and his smile made me so happy." She closed her eyes and clenched her jaw. I touched her hand. She withdrew it and held it up at me, like a stop sign.

I waited.

"That night, about 9 p.m., he had a slight fever, I think 100, and was wheezing. I gave him Tylenol and a couple of puffs on his inhaler, and he settled down and I put him to bed. Mom was watching the TV in her room, and I went to my room to do math homework. Not fifteen minutes later I heard his breathless call, 'Angela,' and his cough."

She looked at me. "You remember hearing asthmatics cough, right. It makes you wonder how they can breathe. "I still hear that terrible cough in my dreams."

She took another deep breath and blinked through tears. "When I got to his bed I knew. His lips were blue, his face pale, he wheezed in and out with each breath, and barely had time to take any since he was breathing so fast. It was worse than any of his prior ER visits. It was worse than last year when he had the respiratory syncytial virus and been in the local hospital for a week." She looked at me and smiled. "During that hospitalization, we watched *Rango* so many times we both knew the words. I still remember Rango saving the town with one bullet."

She stopped and looked off into space again. "One bullet."

It was what every doctor who studied serious diseases wanted to discover: one bullet that would wipe out the disease. It was what I knew she wanted to find for asthma.

"I called 911 and gave him a nebulizer treatment. I yelled for Mom, but she never came. I called Dad but got his voice mail. Dale's big brown eyes were wide. He nervously scratched at his eczema on his arms. He frowned and looked from side to side, searching for some way, any way to get more oxygen. I wanted something, anything to give him to make him better.

"The paramedics came, asked for his parent. I told him Mom was out of it, that she'd taken a sleeping pill and had Parkinson's. And that Dad was not answering his phone. They went in and they saw Mom and couldn't get her attention. They hooked Dale up to oxygen, gave him a shot of something, now I guess it was epinephrine. But his frown got deeper, and his wide eyes kept pleading with me. *Please do something.* I didn't think it was possible, but he breathed even faster, he kept up that damn cough and kept frowning at me."

Her eyes were watering. She stretched her neck and took another breath. "The one paramedic guy was pretty nice. He had big ears and kind blue eyes. Initially he wasn't going to let me go with Dale, but I cried and yelled, and he gave in. I got in the ambulance with Dale and the paramedic. We took off, siren blaring. I held Dale's hand. It's all I could do."

She looked out the window. A tear dripped onto her cheek. "It's all I could do."

She paused. "Just before we got to the ER his grip loosened. His eyes closed and his lips looked like purple lipstick. We got there, they hooked him up and ..."

She stopped and bent her head down toward her hands that were clenched tight.

I should have let it alone, but I wanted to know. "What happened?"

She glared at me through shining eyes. "What the fuck do you think happened? He died! I was holding his hand and he stopped breathing and they pushed me out of the room and when they brought me back he was ..." Her voice trailed off and the tears were rolling down her face. "Gone."

I wanted to hold her, to say something to help. She ran to the bedroom and I followed. She was getting dressed. I tried to hold her, but she shook me off. I just stood there.

"Where are you going?" I said

"Home."

"You should stay here. I love you. You need to be with someone."

She slipped on her shoes, pulled on her coat, and stood and looked at me. "I love you, too. I'm sorry, Var. It's me. I have to be alone. You shouldn't be with me. You're too ... good."

And then she walked out.

We kept dating, and she started loosening up a little, at least I thought. But that story never came up again. I had to leave for an internship at Naval Hospital Pensacola, while she stayed at Colorado University in Denver. We swapped emails, called a few times, and finally made plans for a week or two the summer after my internship. Which never happened. The Marines took precedent. Orders to report ASAP as a General Medical Officer on a float to the Middle East. In Iraq I had my accident, and everything fell apart. Maybe it wasn't meant to be. Maybe she never felt the way I thought she did.

No. She did. You know when someone loves you, not just the words, the actions, and there is the heart thing. I know, I'm a doctor, presumed a scientist, so I'm supposed to be objective. I can't possibly think the heart is anything but a pump, right? But there is more to life than science. Much more. And love is the biggest of these things. When two people love each other, science goes out the window. You don't need a hypothesis, a test, a conclusion. Love infuses every pore and you know. Angela and I loved each other.

I blew it.

Back then, the Judge was just getting started in the courtroom, working on medical cases, and Angela dated and eventually married him. He was a sincere guy who wanted to help her. At least, that's what I thought, then.

I finished rehab in Pensacola but got hit by the drunk driver. I lost it. First, my leg, now my arm. I was a mess. I called her, and like the angel I knew her to be, she got the Judge to help me put away the guy who almost ended my medical career.

Yet, if that drunk driver hadn't hit me, I might not be who I am today.

So, I'd help the Judge with Mr. Hollister: I owed him, and I wanted the best for Angela. Maybe I thought if I helped her ...

I looked at the back of Lisa's head as she tried to lead me into the courtroom. Her mom died of ovarian cancer while she was in college. Her dad had a massive heart attack just as she was set to go into NCIS training, so she never went. She had to help with her sister here, so became a PI. Her sister paralyzed in car accident when she was riding with her at age sixteen. And now her sister was getting worse. Plus, all she had done for me since my last accident. Stuck with me since Afghanistan. Thick, thin, and horse-muck times. Hell, she and I had been making love for months and she lived with me. And here I was thinking about Angela. Boy was I a dick.

The drug company's lawyers were there, but not the Judge. Probably got word from Lisa that I was running late.

I bumped into the chairs even though Lisa tried to make room. After the second chair bump, she gave me a sharp look. I frowned at her and moved my eyes toward the defense table. She nodded and her face relaxed. It had been a while since I'd done the wheelchair. It was part of the show. I faced the defense team, and then the small group in the courtroom and gave an obvious, but not too blatant ashamed look at the floor, then wheeled over to the left, waited patiently for Lisa to move another chair out so I could clumsily pull in next to Mug. I smiled at him. He smiled back, and we shook hands. Even when I was an almost pro-football talent, he would have dwarfed me. Now, slumped a little in my chair, vis-a-vis Stephen Hawking's posture, I'm sure the pile of lawyers on the other side saw me as a wimpy guy.

The Judge walked in, his robe flowing behind him.

"All rise." The bailiff had quite the penetrating and respectful baritone.

The Judge flourished his gown and sat, immediately putting on his reading glasses and perusing papers in front of him, as if he couldn't be bothered with those waiting for his acknowledgement.

The bailiff continued. "District Eight of Colorado District Court is now in session. Judge Lawrence presiding. Please, be seated."

The Judge peered over his glasses. "Mr. Mackay Adair versus Salvation Laboratory." He looked at his papers. "Are both sides ready?"

The head defense lawyer from Salvation Laboratory stood. He was the penultimate Wasp with a Millennium twist: black hair in a spiky do, a Roman nose and large brown eyes that I'm sure women would call romantic, and a twinkling diamond in his left ear lobe. His navy-blue suit was well tailored and had a sheen that spoke bank rolls. Big mistake. "Your honor, we would like to settle this out of court, but Mr. Adair," he paused and cast a sideways glance at Mug, "would not settle, so we are—"

"Mr. Turpis," the Judge interrupted, "please answer my question."

Turpis, the dick, sighed. "Yes, we are ready, sir."

The Judge squinted at Mug and he stood. I felt like I was in the shadow of a huge oak tree. "Yes, your honor, I'm ready."

"Proceed."

Mug glanced at me and flipped open his college composition notebook with one huge finger and read in his smooth, slightly tenor voice, "I will show that Salvation Laboratories made a drug, called RAZR and put it on the street to intentionally end pro football, and it ended my career."

"Are you sure you don't want counsel?"

"Yes, your honor."

I turned to see Turpis. He'd just made another mistake. A George "W" smirk was on his mouth, and his upper eyelids lowered to lizard half-mast. That's when I noticed Angela sitting several rows back. She caught my gaze and looked away. My face grew warm, and my chest felt lighter.

Why was she here?

My mind flipped back to Buddy Hollister and what he'd told me about being in her house and her lurid approach to him. I thought it had been to shock him. She'd done that with me in the past. Then I thought about those "black faces" Buddy had told Detective C about. No way would she hold young women captive in her basement. I wish I could see the basement, but my meandering mind was a blank. Buddy's past views in mirrors had been spot on. Maybe he just misinterpreted.

I took a few deep breaths in and out and tried to concentrate on Turpis and his weaselly smirk.

"Your honor, Mr. Belfger, Salvation Lab's owner, would never allow such a hideous use of any drug Salvation Labs produces. As to this RAZR, as Mr. Adair stated, it is not even a drug Salvation Labs makes." He turned toward Mug and smiled. "I'm afraid Mr. Adair is mistaking a professional and competent pharmaceutical manufacturer as a Pied Piper of illicit drugs."

The Judge squinted at Turpis. "This is a court of law, Mr. Turpis, not a stage for you to try out your latest jokes."

Turpis started to say something and the Judge cut

him off. "Do I make myself clear?"

"Yes, Judge."

The Judge looked at Mug. "Okay, Mr. Adair. What's your proof?"

That's where I came in. It all started at a bar.

CHAPTER 9

Mug's Suspicions

About a week after I first met Mug on my bike ride, I walked out of a sizzling hot summer day into the cool A/C of my favorite bar in Fort Collins: Jackie's. I sat in the corner booth, faced the door and ordered my usual, Guinness on tap, pulled out my iPhone, plugged in to James Gang "Funk #49," grooved to Walsh's guitar riff, and started reading the latest *Climbing* magazine about the ten best drills to improve your footwork. They forgot my number one: listening to "Funk #49." It always got my legs moving in the right directions. Sometimes I still felt that missing lower left piece. The server brought the Guinness, and I looked up and saw Mug walk in. I waved at him. He frowned initially, then brightened in recognition, and walked over as I unplugged.

"Hi, Var."

"How's it hangin, Mug? Have a seat. I'll buy you a beer."

He shrugged and sat. The bright look had vanished.

"You look like you just lost another bike."

He smiled. "No. I found out about a weird thing going on in pro football, and I don't know what to do."

I held out my hand. "I never formally introduced myself. My name is Var Lenus, Dr. Lenus to many, and to others, including you, I'm Var, the investigator. I'm a part-time private investigator and part-time doctor."

He once again enveloped my hand in his catcher's-mitt hand, and his smile widened.

"That's right," I said. "You've come to the right table to share the nectar of the gods." I patted the table with my good left hand. "Spill the beans."

His face drooped, and he looked out the window as if pondering a dear uncle's death. His Guinness arrived, and Mug seemed to stare right through the server. I gave her a smile and a thumbs-up and then tapped Mug on his mountain of a shoulder.

"Can't be that bad. Come on. Tell me about it."

He looked back and pursed his lips. "You probably charge too much for me, being a doctor and all."

"I don't charge a thing for my PI services."

He looked sideways at me. "Did you get hit in the head when you, you know…?"

"Yes, I did, and I came back from the dead twice. I am a bit strange, but I don't charge because, well, it's a long story. Maybe after three or four of these molasses cream pies I will get to it. But, for right now, you can be assured I'll give you my all without you worrying about a penny."

"I can pay, you know."

"Of course. But don't worry about it." I paused, some-thing hitting home. Here was a guy who should be a very wealthy football player, now worried about my fees. Hmm. "Now, tell me what's eatin' you?"

He suddenly noticed his Guinness and looked around the bar. I sensed he wanted to tell the server thanks. What did I tell you? Mug is a class act.

"Don't worry. The server'll be back."

He took a sip of his beer and licked the tan foam off his upper lip.

"You heard about football and RAZR?"

"Yeah." I didn't like where this was going. "Hold out your hand."

He did. No tremors.

"Don't worry. I never took it. But the guy who hit me and put me out did."

I sighed. I'd been so pissed at the drunk guy who'd hit me and caused my leg injury, I'd wanted to kill him. Not quick either. I looked at Mug. He seemed pretty calm.

"Okay, so you found out this guy took RAZR and you want damages from him?"

"Nah. I don't blame Jamie Lee. He was just doing his job and trying to impress, make more money. Jamie Lee's got a mom that lives in Birmingham on welfare, has a wife with three kids, one getting expensive treatment for some kind of weird brain disease, and he'd had a bad year, could have been cut if he didn't do something. He found out about RAZR and took it. I probably would have done the same thing had I been in his shoes."

"Okay. So what do you want?"

"I want to prove that Salvation Laboratories made RAZR to purposefully end pro football."

"End pro football? That seems like a stretch. How do you know Salvation Labs even makes the drug?"

"Jamie Lee told me that's where he got it."

I took a long swig of Guinness. Maybe Mug had more head trauma than I ever did. "Look, I know Salvation Labs is a legit business. I heard RAZR was a street drug, not FDA approved. How did Jamie Lee get it? And how could it end pro football?"

"Salvation Labs made the drug and then leaked it on the streets, gave it to several players."

"And you know this how?"

"Jamie Lee—"

"Right. So, how does he know this?"

He hung his head a bit cockeyed. It matched his mouth. "Wouldn't tell me."

"So he doesn't know?"

"He knows. He just let it slip about Salvation Labs when I bought him a few drinks after he walked me out of the hospital. He's a nice guy. Just in a bad spot. I think they threatened his family, too."

"Okay, so let's assume you're right—Salvation Labs somehow got RAZR to Jamie Lee. How can that end pro football? Guys hit harder, and injuries go up, but so what?"

Mug looked at me like I was in need of a psych consult. "You had me hold out my hands. And it ain't just the shakes. You know that, right?"

I did know. "Yeah, but one guy gets the shakes or offs himself is not going to end pro football."

Mug shook his head and sighed heavily like he was trying to keep from punching me. "Var, you have any idea how many guys are taking RAZR now?"

Yep, I am slow sometimes. Here's a drug that elevates a player's game severalfold with no pain of twice daily workouts, no special diets, and no side effects for months. Probably two-thirds of the guys headed to the playoffs were on it just when the major shakes and suicides would start. It would devastate the playoffs, but would it end pro football? This year would be bad, but there was always next year.

Then my brain kicked in. Finally.

"Are there any college or high school players taking RAZR?"

Mug shook his head again, like saying, Are you sure you're a doctor.

"Yeah," I said. "Dumb question. I was even taking some roids in high school, and I was a quarterback. I knew of at least ten other guys on the team that were on em. Got em from a guy whose dad was a veterinarian. The coaches never said anything. We had no drug screening program."

He raised his eyebrows and had a no-shit-Sherlock smile on. "You wanna play with the big boys, you gotta have an edge."

I remember reading a few years back that every year over a million guys play high school football. It narrows down fast to only 3,500 college players in the pro draft pool, which picks a mere 250 to 300 players. I was willing to bet that most of the 300 players that would be drafted over the next three years would have had RAZR at least once.

This was way bigger than me or Mug. But all I had was him and his story. The cops would need some proof.

I thought about trying to prove Jamie Lee had been on RAZR to a civil court judge. Not going to work. I would have to investigate Salvation Labs. And they had to be some nasty players if they were okay with selling this stuff to high schoolers. Yet, I knew about Salvation Labs. Something wasn't tracking right.

"Maybe Jamie Lee is just telling you this to shift the blame onto Salvation Lab. They are a real, bona fide, legit pharmaceutical company."

"I don't think so. The thing is, Jamie Lee liked one other effect of the drug. Made him a sexual Tyrannosaurus and his wife a nympho. But the other side effects were too weird—the suicidal thoughts and shakes. Lots of guys were on the drug and one guy traced it back to Salvation Labs. Jamie Lee even went to Salvation Labs and asked them about it, but they told him to stack BBs —they never made any drug like that. But he had the bottle with their name on the bottom. They took the bottle from him, said it was a drug they'd been testing on animals, and accused him of stealing it. Jamie Lee is good on the field, but he said he started feeling trapped. Thought he would go to jail. They told him never to mention it to anyone, or they would come after him. That's when they threatened his family."

He took a long pull of his beer. I did, too.

Salvation Labs sounded pretty nasty. Why would they want to ruin pro football, though?

"Maybe," I said, "you could get another bottle with their name on it and show the cops."

"I've been trying. Can't find any other bottles like his."

"Okay, so somebody got a different bottle of pills from Salvation Labs, emptied it out and put in the RAZR pills."

"Jamie Lee swears it was labelled 'RAZR' and gave directions and everything."

His beer was gone. We needed a couple more to finish this.

"Okay. I'll see what I can find out."

He smiled. I put my hand up for our server lady. We had another brewski, but I didn't talk much. Thoughts were jumping around my frazzled brain.

If I was going to get any law enforcement to believe me, I needed proof. Salvation Labs was the first priority. This would be tricky.

CHAPTER 10

Salvation Labs Great Adventure

S alvation Labs made lots of great drugs, many of them that helped me through two amputations and the recovery afterwards. Not as good as, you know, that ancient hemp, but still ... After all, I couldn't get any weed in the hospital.

I know you're thinking I'm just some pothead wacko quack who hands out narcs like candy to anyone who wants them. Okay, you got me.

Right. You've been doing more weed than I ever did.

No. I do use a legal bit of MJ every now and then when my thoughts get carried away. It's usually after those thoughts bloom into ugly flowers with just the right combo of explosions or gunfire on some stupid TV show. When I travel out of Colorado, I have to avoid those shows. I have to tell you, cops in Texas are not real pleasant if they find weed in your car.

But, I am trying to learn the techniques of mindful meditation and stimulate my parasympathetic nervous system when the sympathetic one takes over, to avoid using the weed. But it's not easy when weed works so well. And they say it's not addicting.

Anyway, I figured the best way to figure out what was what, was to visit Salvation Labs. Information fuels investigations. It was going to be tough, since they were not a publicly traded company, so they could put a lock on their door and no one could get in without a warrant. But their website said they were open to tours. Salvation Labs was a class act, so I had to dress according to doctor code. I put on my good leg prosthetic, the one that was put together by a genius in San Diego. It had lots of transducers that made it close to the real thing. Close enough at least so the limp was barely noticeable. I donned the suit I'd worn to a buddy's wedding a few years ago. Yes, navy blue with a crisp white shirt and red and gold striped tie. Marines are a branch of the Navy, you know, and one I was proud to serve with. The arm prosthetic was the one that looked like a real hand. It had a few more enhancements that would be particularly useful for this recon trip.

I drove once around the building snapping some shots for Lisa on my Nikon Coolpix camera with 60X optical zoom. They had outside security video cams, but not as many as I would have thought. Someone was being thrifty, or at least at the beginning, before they started bringing in warp-drive bucks.

The PR guy met me at their small but inviting and appealing, amber-lit visitor's center, replete with flowering violets, a small waterfall, and even goldfish in the pond. Quite calming.

The guy walked in wearing a smile I needed sunglasses for, manicured eyebrows, skin with many hours on a tanning bed, and an ironed lab coat as straight and white as his teeth. He wore a photo ID card, name of Roger Tanner. A scatter scan code was on the bottom —for ordering his tanning bed or getting into special rooms.

"Hi, I'm Doctor Tanner, public relations." Perfect

name. And a doctor for public relations. The CEO must be a full professor at Harvard, Yale, and Stanford, with at least one Nobel Prize.

"Dr. Var Lenus. I'm looking to tour your plant for a possible future drug production." Okay, so I fibbed. But I had to get inside and get a lay of the land, before sending in Lisa. You remember Lisa? Reddish hair, yellow-green eyes … Nice. Yeah, way more. She's also extremely flexible and strong and knows a lot about burglary. She worked with the MPs in my unit in Kandahar just before the accident. We became friends. And then after, a bit more than friends. There are some really amazing people in this world, and she's one of them. Quit the service to take care of her sister, Riana. Visited her in the nursing home almost every day. The shits. Since the courtroom her sister had tanked. Only weeks left, she'd said.

Once her sister was gone, Lisa and I … Do I love Lisa? Do I still love Angela? It's hard to get over number one. I gritted my teeth and brought my head back from its crazy wanderings. It was easier to do this each day.

"Okay," Dr. Tanner said. "Should I get my R&D guy down here?"

I thought about that. "Yes. That would be …" I paused for effect. "Excellent." You remember *Bill & Ted's Excellent Adventure*? No? Geez. You must be a baby.

I don't think Dr. Tanner knew it either or he might have thought I wasn't a serious scientist like him.

Lisa had wanted to put a tiny video cam in my tie clasp. But even though she is the licensed PI and I am not, she allows for my opinions. I had an idea that Salvation Labs did a pretty thorough body and equipment search before allowing visitors to enter their labs. And I was right. No probing of body cavities, but it was thorough.

They took my briefcase, which is when Dr. Tanner noticed my prosthetic hand. The metal detector bleeped loud and long about that and my prosthetic leg. I pulled up my sleeve and pant leg, so he could look closely, though he missed me touching a few key buttons on the hand prosthetic while the palm was open to his security badge. We had a brief squinting and frowning and finally sighing session from Tanner and the security dude, and then we went on the tour.

I met Dr. Jong from R&D.

"The compounds I've developed," I began, verbal tap dancing based on conversations with Mug, "are akin to Viagra, but with an extra that Viagra wished they had—desire enhancement. They can be used for either males or females. One reason I contacted you is that I understand your lab developed something similar in the recent past, but the trials were not promising. I'm hoping your past experience will help tune up my compounds."

I paused to let that sink in.

Mug's research on RAZR told me that it was initially tested as just this sort of drug, but then found to have more useful properties for sports other than sex.

"I'm thinking," I continued, "there are other companies wanting to discover this secret, so I'm very interested in your security."

"Yes," Tanner said, "I understand perfectly." He locked eyes with Dr. Jong. I was reminded of the scene from *Spies Like Us.* Doctor. Doctor, Doctor, Doctor ... I squelched a smile.

To my astonishment, Tanner did not say Doctor.

Instead he said, "We've had experience with similar drugs."

Okay, Doctor, you're lending Mug more credibility about RAZR.

"Tell me," Dr. Jong said, "why would you be interested in such drugs?"

I canted my head and gave him my most wan smile. "Well, as you might have noticed, I'm missing some body parts."

He shrugged a bit sheepishly.

"In my recovery, I encountered others who had body image problems and it affected their ability to have sex. Counselling helped to a point, but not enough. After a lot of interviews with the couples, I thought how great it would be for a drug like this. I think I forgot to mention, it has a bit of euphoria that adds to the other effects, kind of taking their minds off their image problems." I flourished my prosthetic hand like a conductor.

Not sure if it was my unusual conductor's wand or the story that satisfied Tanner, but we continued the tour. There were numerous locked and closed doors we did not enter, but I kept tabs of them in my mind. Okay, my mind is not exactly a steel trap anymore, but I think I could give Lisa the layout.

Now came the tricky part. "I'm in a bit of a hurry to market my drug. I know the FDA process is very lengthy, but I heard there might be ways around that, like maybe calling it an herb or vitamin. Also, I've already tested it in macaques and chimps, and there have been no problems. I'll be happy to share those trials with you. Do you have a way to expedite human trials?"

Dr. Jong's eyes widened, and his mouth ticked up on

the sides. Dr. Tanner bit his lower lip. "It depends on the animal results you have. We would need to see those before moving further."

"So you have ways to get this going quickly?"

"Perhaps."

None of their answers were useable in court but coupled with their body language I was pretty sure Mug's story about them making RAZR was solid.

"I will have my assistant get you those results. Would email be okay?"

Tanner pursed his lips. "We prefer paper. It's a bit more secure."

These guys operated like the Taliban. They'd found out we could trace electronics, but putting a real body onto a paper trail took much more work. So, the less electronics the better.

"No problem. It is a thick file, though. Maybe we could get it to you next week?"

Tanner nodded.

We walked back to the secure entrance to the lab. I collected my briefcase, wondering if they had tried to open it. Then I sat with Dr. Tanner for a few final questions in the very pleasing visitors lobby. Violet flowers go well with goldfish and waterfalls. I got up to leave and so did Tanner. He must have tripped on the orange and gold Oriental rug because just as I was passing him, he fell onto my left side. I felt bad at catching him with my hard prosthetic, afraid I was gouging him in the side. It must have strained the connection to my stump because I felt a twinge of sharp pain. He recovered, but his eyes were downcast, lips pursed in shame.

"Are you okay?" I asked.

"Yes. Fine. I'm so sorry. Did I hurt your arm?"

I twisted and flexed the multifunction hand in front of my face. "No. All is well."

His eyes shifted and looked at the floor, then at my arm prosthetic. He sighed. Was there too much regret there?

"Really. I'm just fine." A twinge hit me in my arm, but I shook it off. I had been a football player and almost a Marine. "Thanks for your tour. I'll get back to you."

I walked out of the building. The video camera above the exit whirred and its dark eye followed me to my car.

CHAPTER 11

The Judge's Happy Home

Buddy's laugh at the entire situation—being caught in the Judge's house with Angela flaunting her breasts, pulling a knife from between her tawny thighs, the Judge fondling her beautiful anatomy —was nervous. Not about feeling threatened, but about what he might do. The mirror never lied, and he knew the visions it afforded him were not a present-tense reality and could be mixed in with the bloody history of the mirror. But her words had been real.

He walked quickly to the door and left. Not a word to the Judge or Angela. Outside, the heat hit him like the white phosphorous that killed Sergeant Crum in Fallujah. He couldn't breathe. Sweat rolled down his chest and back, and his heartbeat pounded in the back of his teeth. He gasped for air and ran to his van, jumped in and twisted the key and punched the accelerator. The rear wheels spun and scattered dirt behind him. His door slammed shut as the van shot forward. In the distance he saw another car's dust trail coming toward him—Detective C's crappy gray Honda Civic.

Buddy didn't slow when he neared the detective. He did notice the detective staring at him with wide eyes and raised eyebrows. His head tracked Buddy's van going by like a cartoon character tracking a ping-pong game. In the rearview, Buddy saw the Civic turn around and follow him.

Buddy kept cooking, so fast he had to grip the wheel as the van skated left and right on the dirt road. It was like driving on ice. Once he made it to the tee at the blacktop, he turned right. His wheels screeched. He was breathing again instead of gasping. Now he could really put distance between him and the Judge.

Not again. No, he would not go back there again or he might lose it.

Even though his van had a powerful three-fifty, the Civic caught up to him. The headlights flashed and horn sounded. Detective C waved an arm for Buddy to pull over.

Another five miles down the road, Buddy blinked a few times and felt his heartbeat slow. He let his foot off the accelerator, the van slowed, and he guided it to the right shoulder and eased to a stop.

Detective C pulled around and stopped in front, then jumped out, slamming his door as he strode back toward Buddy.

Buddy unrolled his window a crack, enough so he could hear Detective C, but not so much that his whole face wouldn't be behind glass.

"What the hell, Buddy?"

"I'm sorry, Detective C, but it was bad."

Cromwell knew bad to Buddy meant something especially hideous to most people. Cromwell cooled his jets. "Tell me about it."

He did, getting a bit squeamish about Angela's breasts, but he managed. Cromwell felt even hotter, standing outside the van.

"So, you saw this … promenade of Angela in the mirror. Not real."

"But their words were real. She said she ached for me. He said they'd been looking for me for a long time. For what? I think they wanted me to help them with those illegals in their basement. Or she was coming on to me to get me off balance, so she could cut me open with that butcher knife. Women just don't do that. It wasn't right. That Judge is controlling her like those mujes did their women in Iraq."

"Everything is not like the mujahideen in Iraq, man. Maybe they just wanted to find you, so you could help with some other stuff around the house. Could you have misheard her?" Cromwell paused, blinked, and looked left then right, searching for a sane thought. "Could she have said she ached because she couldn't find you to help her with lifting things?"

Hollister looked through the glass pane at Cromwell, a look that said he was disappointed in Cromwell not believing him.

"All right. Geez, I'm sorry. I believe you. And that's even more reason for you to go back and help me figure this one out."

"No. If I go back, I might ... You go back and tell them you need to see their basement."

Cromwell shifted onto his other foot. Sweat trickled down his chest. "Yeah, I could do that. Of course, they will say no."

"Then get a warrant, right?"

Cromwell shifted to the other foot. "Look, *I* believe you, Buddy. But I'll need real evidence for a warrant. It would take time, and the Judge would already have moved them. The real evidence will be gone."

"You think too much. Just go back and get those girls

out of the basement."

"Yeah. Maybe. What I really should do is get a few guys and watch his house and see if he moves anyone, take pictures, then get a warrant."

"A warrant for the Judge and his rich wife, Angela?"

"You're right." Cromwell walked back to his crappy little Honda, fired it up, squealed its tires in a fast one eighty, and drove back to the Judge's place.

The sun was high and hot and bright when he got out of his Honda and closed the door and walked to the front door. He knocked.

The Judge opened the door. "Hello, Detective Cromwell. What can I do for you?"

"Hi, Judge. Is your wife in? I have another speeding ticket I need to discuss with her."

"Oh, dear…" He sighed and shook his head. "Angela!" He yelled and looked up the stairs. "Detective Cromwell is here about another ticket."

She came tripping down the stairs like a high school ballerina, all quickness and balance and nymphal joy. She wore sandals, tight blue jeans, and a turquoise, pearl-buttoned cowboy shirt. The whiteness and outline of a bra was visible beneath her shirt. A little disappointing, but Cromwell smiled at her anyway.

"Sorry to bother you, Angela, but were you in town today?"

"Why yes. I met my sister for lunch and some family business."

Cromwell gave the Judge a sheepish smile. "Well, an officer at the station says he clocked a black Lexus going about one-oh-five a few miles outside town. He only got a glimpse of the license plate since it scared the bejesus out of him and he spilled his chocolate shake on his lap. But, I think it was your Lexus."

She gave him a very contrite smile. "Probably."

"Since he had no photo and just the first few letters, he can't be sure, so don't worry. If you don't mind my asking, why were you in such a hurry?"

She smiled up at her husband. "The Judge got some new antiques, and I was excited to see them."

"Antiques, huh? From anywhere around here?"

A look of confusion crossed the Judge's ordinarily surly face, but only for a second. "The widow Mayfield's estate."

"You didn't get that mirror next to Mr. Mayfield's hangin' rope, did you?"

"As a matter of fact, he did," she said.

"Could I see it? I've read a lot about that horrible affair but never actually visited the place. The widow wasn't exactly an easy person to cozy up to. And I never would have had enough money to afford anything at her auctions."

The Judge put an arm out towards the dining room and beamed like a proud father showing off his beautiful daughter. "Of course. It's right in here."

Cromwell walked by the basement door, trying to detect a feel, a whiff, a sound from behind it. Nothing. Though he did glimpse something edging out from under the door.

He inspected the mirror with the gash. Just an old mirror.

"Wow! That is an impressive gouge from the knife."

"Knife?" Angela said.

"I guess you don't know. The story goes Old Man Mayfield slashed his lovely wife's throat back in '45 and carried the stroke through to the mirror. Pretty gruesome. Very bloody."

The Judge frowned. "Not what I heard. It was just a missed step coming into the house and it was scratched on the outside stone wall."

"Hmm. That doesn't give it quite the flavor." Cromwell paused and looked at the basement door. "I hear you are a great antiques collector. If you got any in the basement, I'd like to poke around. I love antiques."

Cromwell took a step towards the door.

The Judge stepped in front of him. "Sorry, Detective. We had to fumigate the basement of woodworm we found in one old chair we recently got from Scotland. Wouldn't want you to get sick from the fumes."

Cromwell felt a hand on his lower back, Angela's, out of sight of the Judge. She traced her fingers up and down his spine. Her fingers lingered at the base of the spine, just at the top of the butt crack. Drove him wild. But he had a feeling she was not coming on to him.

"Yes, we wouldn't want to cause you any," and her fingers stopped and flitted around his butt, "loss of function."

At that point, he was fully functional. "Okay," he said, hoping his voice didn't quaver. "I guess I'll be going." He took a step away from her fingers and held out a hand to the Judge who shook it.

Cromwell walked out the front door. First thing he did outside the door was sigh and adjust himself, so he could walk without a painful crimp. *Jesus, what a tease,* he thought. No wonder Buddy panicked. Cromwell loved attention from good-looking women, but that was just crazy. She probably thought she'd distracted him, the way she did Buddy. But, he'd seen something he was sure she probably had seen, too: The reason for the finger job.

CHAPTER 12

Angela's Darlings

T he Judge waited for the sound of the Honda starting, then turned to his wife. "What the hell were you doing playing with his ass? If he wasn't suspicious before, he will be now."

"I was trying to distract him."

"From what?"

"You literally jumped in front of him to keep him from the basement. He surely thought something was amiss. I didn't want him looking at what's under the basement door."

The Judge looked down. "Damn."

Visible at the small space between the bottom of the door and the kitchen floor was a crucifix, or at least the top half of one. It was woven straw, or possibly hemp, with the center of the cross emblazoned with a distinctive blue globe inside a yellow diamond inside a green rectangle: The Brazilian flag emblem.

He reached down and slid a finger under the door and retrieved the crucifix. It had a string attached, and he held it up with the string around his middle finger and the crucifix lying in his palm. He remembered the blue circle represented the globe. The constellation of the Southern Cross was below a white belt crossing the equator, with an additional twenty-seven stars—the number of states in Brazil. The words *Ordem e Progresso* were written on the belt. Order and Progress. The original thought had been an order from an oligarchic dictator to allow progress for democracy. Except, in Latin America, dictator's whims seldom gave in to democracy.

But, the Judge thought, *Brazilian women were still beautiful, especially the young ones, even if they were wily and conniving little bitches.*

He took a step towards the basement door. Angela stepped in front of him.

"No," she said "They are my responsibility. I will make sure this doesn't happen again. They trust me, not you."

She thought, *How could they ever trust a man like him? If only Var had never gone to that stupid war.*

She held out her hand and he dropped the crucifix in her palm. She opened the door, flicked on the bare bulb above the stairs and walked down the painted wood stairs, closing the door behind her. The contractor stairs creaked and crackled with her weight. They were painted white, but worn and chipped, revealing tan, pressed wood in the middle of the lip in three stairs. Spider webs hung under the corner of the bottom stair. Unpainted particleboard covered the basement floor, the glint of brass screw heads lining the edges. The walls, though, were semifinished with unpainted drywall nailed on top of four inches of soundproof insulation, including over every window. Four bare bulbs were the only light, casting an eerie glow onto stacks of chairs and dressers and all his ugly, old furniture and knickknacks, filling all space except a walkway between. When he died, she would haul it all off and burn it. A turpentine and lacquer smell filled the air. She thought about how easily she could burn down the whole damn house. She hated the place, though it had allowed her to do what she needed to do. Once the Judge was eliminated, could she move on? She wanted to.

Other than the minimal creak of her steps, there was no noise. The room at the end of the walkway could not be seen or heard. The Judge made sure of that. He'd contracted a friend to construct a nearly soundproof room. There were eight inches of foam between plywood walls, and two inches between special metal doors. No one could hear the girls even if they yelled or beat or kicked the walls. Though that was only a problem for the first week. Then Angela would have had time to make their lives so much better.

Had Detective Cromwell descended the stairs, he would have found nothing but the crucifix. The room was well hidden. Except, Cromwell was smart. Probably smart enough to be suspicious of the crucifix, though she was sure she and the Judge could deflect any suspicions, maybe say it was inside one of the pieces of furniture and must have fallen out.

Then again, he'd zeroed in on the basement. Could Hollister, the delivery man, have tipped him off? Hollister seemed innocuous, a bit weak in spirit and dull witted. Yet, she had sensed, as had the Judge, that he had some unusual sensory feeler, like a blind man's cane, tapping and feeling things others could not.

But a nagging thought kept coming back to her: How had the crucifix gotten up the stairs and beneath that door?

She wound through the path between antiques and

reached behind the ducting from the heater and pushed the recessed button. What looked like another bare cement wall between two-by-four studs clicked on one side, and she pulled on the left stud and a door opened into a dark hallway. She reached in and flicked a switch on the wall and another bare light bulb lit an unfinished hallway that she walked down to another doorway. She took out keys and unlocked the door and opened it.

Before her was a well-furnished room: flat screen TV, a couch, two wing chairs, an end table with lamp, and off to the right a kitchen with bottom-of-the-line, new appliances. To the left was another locked door. She unlocked and opened it.

On the two beds sprawled seven young women, very young, handcuffed to the bedposts, something the Judge insisted on. "They are a substantial investment, my dear," he said, and though she'd argued, she knew that without them, her asthma research would be dead.

They wore white shorts and brightly colored tank tops that emphasized their dark skin and thin, shapely figures. Two sat and two lay on their sides. Fourteen dark eyes glared at her.

"Hello, my darlings," she said in perfect Brazilian Portuguese.

They were indeed her darlings, each worth about one thousand dollars per night, three thousand for a good client. She gave them food and a comfortable apartment, even if they were not free to roam the countryside.

"We're hungry," the tallest, Maia, said. At nineteen, she was also the oldest and the most desired by men, with a hawk nose and thick eyebrows.

Angela didn't understand the draw that some men

had for the thick eyebrows. It always reminded her of her mother in the morning after a bad night with Dad: thick brown eyebrows, a matt of unkempt tawny hair, bruises on her ribs when she padded around before breakfast in her bra and panties, smoking a cigarette. *What a whore.*

"There's food in the pantry and fridge," she said as she walked to each bed and unlocked the cuffs.

"Please," Maia said, "we need something good. We are tired of baked chicken and fish and vegetables."

"Have you looked in the mirror? Do you not see how lovely your skin is, how perfect your figure? Have you forgotten how fat and ugly your mother and sisters were? Would you like to go back there? Or would you like Pablo's friends to pay them a visit?" Maia had seen what Pablo did to Angela.

Maia pursed her lips and looked away. "No, I am sorry. It is just hard the last week I have been so hungry."

Angela stopped at Maia's bed, unlocked her cuffs and put a palm on her cheek. "I know, darling. But being hungry for a week is better than starving for a lifetime. After tonight you can celebrate. I will bring home a Big Mac and fries, with all the Oreos and vanilla ice cream you can eat."

Maia looked into Angela's eyes and smiled, teeth as white as snow, lips ripe and plump as red plums, contrition and true thankfulness in her almost black eyes. "Thank you, Aunt Angela."

"Now," Angela looked at each of them, "it is time to get ready. Prepare yourselves. Tonight will be special. These men are very wealthy and kind, and will show you a lovely time. All they need is some of your love to forget their boring lives. Be good to them and they will be good to you." She paused and scanned each of their faces. "If I get good reports, we'll go shopping tomorrow for jewelry and new clothes." She focused her gaze on Maia, "As well as your decadent foods."

All their faces lit up. They jumped off the beds like sprites to a woodland dance and hurried toward the two bathrooms. Their lives had been full of dirt and boredom and abuse before she had rescued them. It had taken time and money to get them into shape. But you never make money without spending it. Dentists in Sao Paulo had done wonders with Maia's teeth. Getting the girls shaped up before getting them on the plane was important. They had to look presentable for the false passports, more upper class than poor filth so the customs officials would wave them through without hesitation. It had been tricky and more money than the previous trips with three or four to get all seven here. On the airplane, two well-paid trusted escorts kept them quiet, then helped Angela get them from plane to parking lot, where they boarded a panel van labeled "Mike's Plumbing." It hadn't been an easy trip. But now that they were producing, it was worth every penny. Profit of ten dollars on every dollar she'd spent. And even though the main man, Pablo, got five of those nine dollars, four was a much better profit than her father's pitiful restaurants and stock portfolio.

In the end, she had used only the bare minimum to keep up appearances. Almost every penny went to the new asthma drug research.

She approached one of the other girls, Elektra, who was primping in the bathroom mirror. She was the most deceitful and tricky, but also the most religious. That was a good Catholic for you, ask forgiveness after committing sin and all was well. Angela tapped her shoulder and motioned for her to come out to the living room. Elektra frowned and squinted at Angela in concern but followed her.

"Did you lose this?" She held out the crucifix.

Elektra's eyes flitted to the crucifix then shifted back and forth, avoiding Angela's gaze.

"Yes, Aunt. I must have dropped it. Where did you find it?"

Angela grabbed Elektra's face with one hand and pulled her nose to within inches of her eyes. "You know exactly where I found it. If you ever pull a trick like that again, Pablo's amigos will cut your brother and mother into fish food."

She released her hold. "Look at me."

Elektra glanced up but looked away.

"Look at me, I said." Angela's voice had dropped an octave.

Elektra looked at her.

Angela held the crucifix in front of Elektra's face, broke it in half and dropped it. There was no god. It had taken Angela too long to learn that. There was only you and your wits. Even those you love will eventually abandon you. It had happened with her father, her mother, and—she chewed on her lip—Var.

Elektra let out a gasp and put her palms out to catch the fragments.

Angela turned around and walked out the door, locked it and then went through the next door and locked it as well. She went up the stairs. At the top, she wiped a tear from her cheek then clamped her jaw. She hated what she did to these girls. But it was all for the asthma drug that could save millions. She and Var were over. Done. Past. She had to steady her resolve.

Yet, seeing him on and off this past year had brought back the old feelings. He had been so kind to her. She had loved him. He had loved her. Does love ever die?

As she pushed open the door, she pushed out the thoughts. Get ready for tonight. It was an important night: some business and fun. And the end of the Judge. Then ... maybe ... she could concentrate on Var.

CHAPTER 13

Another Bike Ride

Once I returned from Salvation Labs, I sat with Lisa in my living room and downloaded what I remembered about the lab. My memory wasn't as picture perfect as it had been before the accidents, but luckily it was still pretty damn good. Unlucky as well. The dreams of my accidents are very detailed.

My house is tucked into a northern hill a bit west of Fort Collins, just over the first hogbacks. It's one of those "damn hippie homes," as Mom would say; "green home" is the proper term nowadays. The north wall is composed of old tires filled with hay and buried to the roofline. The south wall is mostly windows with an overhang that allows lots of sun in the winter and very little in the summer, leaving a constant inside temp of seventy to seventy-five degrees. It's built to work *with* the earth and the solar system, rather than tear it down. They have lots of rules about water out here— it's a more valuable resource than oil. You need a permit to collect rainwater, which I got. I use the rainwater on the first pass to drink and cook with, then run it through some filters and do it again, then let it go the third time to water the greenhouse fruits and veggies. There's also a stream that runs through my property, but diverting water from that would require enough legal work to feed and clothe three lawyers and their families for five years. So, I have a backup water tank, which I've filled only once in the last two years since I sold my parents' place and built it. Solar panels and two wind turbines on the roof collect energy, which is stored in a large bank of batteries under the floor. Much to the dismay of the county and city tax men, I'm off the grid completely. Well, almost. I do have cell phones and a satellite dish. The city requires each household to have an electric line to the property. After all, this is a civilized town.

The septic tank is also a great filter and won't ever have to be emptied or changed. Amazing what you can do when you put your mind to it. The thing is, this technology and similar houses have been available, notwithstanding a bit less efficient, but still available since the early '70s. Hence the word: hippie house. My dad could have had one had he not been too busy trying to one-up the Jones's. Oh, yeah, and make a living for me and my brothers and Mom. He did a great job at that and at the age of fifty-four wore himself into a heart attack, which planted him in the ground.

No, I don't really believe that. His heart attack happened the week after my IED because my accident broke his heart. His son, whom he'd taught multiplication tables, the wonders of nature, how to throw a football, how to ride a bike; his son the doctor, who helped Marines, who could have been a pro quarterback; his son, who the doctors said would never walk again. Then, after my second stupid accident in Pensacola, when I lost the left arm, Mom, who had dwindled the year after Dad died while I was in Walter Reed and rehab, got breast cancer. Love for another human being is a powerful thing. She died six months later, despite my full recovery and coming back to Colorado.

War takes so much: my Dad, my Mom, my arm, my leg. I can deal with those, mostly. But taking my daily thoughts and Angela? Every veteran at one time or another thinks about eating a bullet. "22 a day" is the saying. And the statistic for veteran's suicides. One every sixty-five minutes.

But I was determined not to be one of them. I had too much to live for. Angela was still around ... and Lisa. I had to get my head straight about them. If only I could. There is something about your first real love, your soul mate, that pulls your heart like a locomotive. I wished my brain was driving the locomotive. Could the IED have screwed up my brain on love, or was I just born that way?

Lisa sat on the recycled leather and hay couch with blueprints for Salvation Labs spread onto the polished, pine coffee table. Made from beetle-kill pine, the table radiates a cool bluish tint that sooths my half-baked mind. She got the blueprints from the county office—a friend of a friend. She's lived in this area all her life, except when she was in the Navy, and has a lot of friends. She is a beautiful woman and has a beautiful heart that I don't deserve. She is also a valuable asset. With sneaky skills. She proved that in high school where she was a journalist and bugged a pedophile teacher's home. She knew me then, she says. I don't remember her until Kandahar, when she was a Navy security spook. Yeah, I know. I'm a dipshit.

Using her laptop and top-end architectural software, she'd constructed the inside of the Salvation Lab building in 3-D based on my memory and the blueprints. I also had digital photos from the palm camera in my prosthetic: photos of Tanner's security card and bar code.

It took about an hour to finish. Afterward, we made some security cards with the right codes. Now we needed to ponder our next move. But we needed a break, and Lisa hadn't done her daily workout, something she never missed. She said it was her antidepressant. She also managed to get me to do it with her as often as possible. I'm no psychiatrist, but I'm sure she believes it helps keep me out of the dark corners of my mind.

We've always found that biking gets our blood moving through all the right neuronal tracts in the frontal cortex, and right now we needed all the thinking power we could get. She grabbed her Soma road bike, me my Trek, and we walked the bikes to the end of my dirt road and mounted them at the black top and were cruising. Lisa was good at letting me do my thing. She didn't hover.

Soon we were peddling beside Horsetooth Reservoir, a long lake with a road beside it that travels up and down hogbacks and hills, the lake and distant mountains and plains always in view—a biker's nirvana. Thanks, Dad. Without the proceeds from the house he'd paid for, I'd never have my house this close to great biking. Sometimes I tune in to the sounds and feel like I'm floating: the gentle hum of the tires, the *zhzh-zhzh* of rhythmic pedaling, the occasional *tic* of a rock under a tire, wind in my ears along with the constant, high-pitched ringing: tinnitus has accompanied me everywhere after the explosion.

Soon we could talk without huffing and puffing between every two words.

"It won't be easy," Lisa hollered back at me as we reached a more level stretch.

"That's why I have you."

A yellow-bellied meadow lark welcomed us into the next meadow with its flute-like *I see-you, triddlie-doodlie, triddlie-do.* A pair of ravens flipped and twisted with each other in aerobatic antics on the way over a cliff, then recovered a few feet from the water. Our tires rumbled over a cattle guard signaling free range and the opportunity to dodge cattle.

There were no cars behind, so I pedaled faster to get abreast on her left. "All you need to do is photograph bottles with the RAZR label like Mug said or computer files about development."

"Yeah, right," she said, quickly turning her handlebars to dodge a patch of gravel. "What we need is the email files and an actual bottle with the RAZR pills inside that we can chemically analyze or use on some test animals with our own unbiased experts."

"Yes. That would be quite … excellent!" Not sure if she got the "excellent!" She can be hard to read sometimes.

"I figured a good way to get in and out quickly."

"Yeah?"

"Should be in and out in under fifteen minutes."

"Think that'll be enough time?"

I felt it first, then saw a truck coming up behind us, so I slowed and got behind her on the narrow biking lane. Around here most drivers give bikers their space. But occasionally you run into ones that don't like bikers taking up any space on *their* road, even the bike lane. This guy initially gave us a wide birth, then punched the accelerator, blowing out a cloud of black diesel smoke. Clouding, they call it, intentionally obscuring the biker's view and filling his lungs with diesel fumes. He swerved into the bike lane narrowly missing Lisa. While keeping my right hand on the handlebars, I twisted my left-hand prosthetic, which unclipped it so I could stick it in the air at the guy. It had the effect of giving him the finger. Lisa had slowed, and I caught up to her.

That truck? Had I seen it recently? The guy driving? I wasn't sure.

I swung up beside Lisa.

"You okay?"

"Yeah. What an asshole." She glanced at me. "You know who that was?"

"Looked familiar, but I can't place him."

"Could it be someone from Salvation Labs?"

"No. Can't be." Yet I knew it the second she said it—the briefest glance from the side showed the brilliant white teeth bared in a semi-smile against the tan face. Why the hell was Tanner up here tailing me and Lisa and trying to run us off the road?

She glanced at me again. "Did you tell them where you lived?"

"No way." But it wouldn't be hard to find. No matter how you try as a doctor, keeping your home address a secret is almost impossible. Between the hospitals, insurance, fire stations, ambulance drivers: any one of them had either called or even picked me up at my home. They had friends, too. Some at bars, the best word-of-mouth advertising business in town.

"They apparently don't like you."

"Yeah. It usually takes a bit longer." I felt a slight burn

in my left arm stump and remembered our parting at Salvation Labs. Maybe he was smarter than I gave him credit for.

She was quiet for several seconds. "I'll have to go in tonight or they'll have time to increase security. Even now, they'll likely have taken precautions. My estimate of fifteen minutes will have to be trimmed."

"How can you find anything in less time?"

"It all boils down to knowing where to look. I have some pretty good ideas."

"Maybe we should head back in case he turns around," I said.

She sped up. "I'm not cutting my workout short. He comes back, I got a little surprise for him."

Angela was like that, too—determined, not willing to let others control her. Yet I'd left her, and everything changed. For her. For me. The world. The Judge seemed so controlling. He had to be, remembering his court actions. Maybe if I got back with her, she would be her old self again. I knew she didn't like the Judge, or at least I felt it. Divorce him, get back with me? Would she do that? We would be our old selves again. I looked down at my prosthetic arm and leg. Could she accept me as I am?

I watched Lisa pump and speed up in front. I knew Lisa accepted me. More than that, really. I was lucky. If I made the right choices. I wish I could let go of one of them. All it took was a conscious decision. That's what I told my patients addicted to cigarettes. Sometimes it worked, but most of the time they stayed in their comfort zone. The mind can be a horrible thing if it becomes addicted to drugs or sex. Or love.

And then there was power, the ultimate heroin for

the wealthy. I thought of RAZR and big pharmaceut-icals and pro football. The drug could not only kill pro football but all professional sports and maybe human-ity. But, wow! Would the owners and fans love the end run, and Dr. Tanner and Salvation Labs would make huge companies like Pfizer a mere speck of an "Ace Hardware Ford" in Tanner's "Costco Ferrari's" rearview mirror.

I let Lisa take the lead and I enjoyed the view.

Ah, geez. I need to get my mind out of the gutter. I sped up and joined her.

She looked over at me, smiled and pumped harder. She either wanted me to watch her shapely butt or she wanted to challenge me. Probably both. She'd helped me with therapy from day one and been more than a friend. Hell, she lived with me most of the time. She put up with my thing with Angela, whatever it was.

Her limit might come soon if I didn't make up my mind.

CHAPTER 14

Trafficking Humans

Cromwell drove down the dirt road from the Judge's place and turned right onto the blacktop. He thought about what he'd seen: a straw crucifix under the door with an emblem at the intersection of the cross. At first the emblem reminded him of an eye, a solid blue circle. But there was no black pupil, only a white strip across the middle. Maybe some cult's symbol for light splitting an eye? Could the Judge and his wife be running some kind of cult in the basement?

He shifted into fourth and turned the air on. Ever since that time in the bayou last year—the dead father and kids—heat gave him problems focusing. He wanted an ice-cold Fresca. The squirrel running the Honda thumped faster and louder; the air started to cool him, and other things about the emblem came back.

The blue eye with the center white strip was inside a yellow diamond shape that was inside a green rectangle. And there was something else about that blue eye. Some kind of white spots below that white strip —like it was maybe old and had some of the blue paint wearing off. Maybe someone had been rubbing it with their thumb like a rosary and worn off some of the paint. And the white strip had some green writing on it. Or maybe it was just some kind of tarnish.

Whatever it was, it confirmed Buddy's vision of somebody in the basement. Whether they were young women was hard to say. But there was something going on, that was for sure, considering the way the Judge jumped in front of him and Angela played his ass like a sex piano. They were both trying to keep him from going into the basement. First Angela threw her sexuality at Buddy, and now at him.

He had to get into that basement.

He pulled up to the police department office, sandy brick two-story, parked, jumped out and jogged into the front, pushing through the side door rather than going through the revolving door. He threw his keys, badge, gun, and phone into the plastic bin and walked through the metal detector. The desk officer buzzed him in as he collected it all and stuffed his gun into his chest holster.

First, he needed a cold Fresca. He stopped at the breakroom fridge. After the Marines he'd had it with coffee and anything with caffeine. Made him jittery. Var had initially suggested Fresca. And Cromwell found he liked the taste of carbonation and grapefruit. Sometimes he had Squirt, sometimes a generic. But it worked for him. He didn't want diabetes and high blood pressure like his mother and brother.

He popped the top on one and guzzled it down, burped loudly, finished it and got another for the office. He walked quickly around the mayhem of open modular cubicles of those of lesser rank, many with papers and laptops and photos in disarray. In his semiprivate cubicle, he glanced at the photo of his grandfather on the wall, stuck his tongue at him, and sat at the computer. What he really wanted were colored pencils to sketch out the emblem while it was still fresh.

He googled *yellow, green, and blue emblems*, and while the little working circle circled he opened his lower-right drawer, thinking he had some colored pencils from another case, one for which he'd drawn lots of diagrams of plumbing and ducting and electrical and gas lines—a different color for each to keep them straight when they needed to blow a hole in a wall. The drawer held folded and printed papers, a box of evidence gloves, a half-empty package of blank printer paper, some stray manila file folders, and, in the very back, a box of colored pencils. He snagged the box, grabbed a couple of clean printer sheets, and closed the drawer. He started sketching—the outside in green, the inside in yellow—and was filling in the blue circle when he glanced at the computer.

What do you know? The very first thing that came up looked almost exactly like his rough sketch. It was the Brazilian flag. What the hell was a crucifix with a Brazilian flag emblem doing in the Judge's basement?

Buddy's story about some pathetic brown-skinned girls in the basement was looking more and more credible. Just like that plumber's wife.

Cromwell had to find Buddy. He crammed the colored pencils back into the drawer and closed it. They had to figure a way into that basement. Soon.

He hit the *Print* button and googled Brazil and illegal trafficking to the USA and found an article stating human trafficking in Brazil was up 1500 percent in 2013. It was a country ripe for trafficking, with lots of poor, desperate people and a corresponding percentage of rich assholes ready to pay and take advantage of the poor. Sex trafficking was the most common international type of human trafficking, and 99 percent of its victims were women. The most common runners of illegals were women, either relatives or friends of the illegals.

Cromwell wondered about Angela and the Judge. Did they have any connections to Brazil? He remembered something about Angela's mom. Var would know. Cromwell was pretty sure Var had dated Angela for a while.

Cromwell picked up the phone and dialed.

CHAPTER 15

Oh, the Pain

"You are kidding, right?" I said to Cromwell. "Angela and the Judge sex trafficking illegals from Brazil? You really hate the Judge, don't you?" I heard nothing from the other end. Maybe the cell coverage had died. But I knew it wasn't that. Cromwell probably didn't like my answer, but the story he'd just fed me seemed out there, even for the Judge and Angela.

I'd answered his call while sitting in my living room, pouring over the blueprints of Salvation Labs. I kept looking at Lisa, her concentration on the blueprints allowing my close observation. She had this little mole in front of her right ear. Sometimes she picked at it when she was serious, like now. I didn't really want or like her breaking and entering Salvation Labs. It was too dangerous. I mean, I was grateful, and the thought of her going in and doing this for me was ...

"No, I don't," Cromwell said. "Not really." Even while thinking mostly about Lisa I could tell Cromwell's voice sounded a bit off kilter. He lied poorly.

I needed to get him straight. "You know what Angela did after med school right?"

"She's a doctor?"

"No, she quit med school after her third year when ...

uh … never mind. She devoted all her time to research for an asthma drug. Where have you been?"

"Well, for one thing, I didn't grow up here. Remember?"

"Yeah. Right." I paused. "You know, I can't really thank you enough for all your help in P'cola. The therapist you got me was way radical and helped me get where I am now."

I thought I heard him sigh, like he knew all this and didn't really want to hear another thank you. "Angela?"

"Right. She found some new drugs for asthma. Her brother died of an attack when he was only five and she made it her life's ambition to save other kids."

"Your point?"

"For a detective, you're a bit dense. Look, if she were that interested in helping kids, why would she start trafficking girls for sex? It's incongruous, ludicrous, ridiculous, injudicious, outrageous—"

"All right. Geez. Enough with the twenty-dollar words." He paused. "Maybe I'm not the greatest detective in the world, but you know Buddy is usually right on, and the emblem, the way she and the Judge acted, and Buddy's story all add up to plausible, despite all your fancy words. Besides," I heard him ticking his tongue on the roof of his mouth, "didn't I hear something about her doing another kind of research on a drug to help her conceive when she and the Judge couldn't, you know, have a kid?"

I remembered. Yeah, and now I remembered where I'd heard the name of Salvation Labs, besides my drugs and Mug's case. Angela's research company to develop a fertility drug was a subsidiary of Salvation Labs. And what I hadn't told Cromwell was that she had left med school the same day I left for my internship. We'd had some words; I had my Navy obligation, and ... I left. God what an idiot I was.

"You still there, Var?"

"Yeah. Listen. I'll get back to you. You might want to do that stakeout of their house you were talking about."

"Wait!" he said, but I ended the call and looked at the ground, wanting to think this through without having Cromwell yapping at me. Angela and drugs to help conceive had turned a bit sour, as I recalled. It had sidetracked into a drug that enhanced sexual pleasure for women. Several of my male patients had a hankering for testosterone, thinking it would boost their sexual prowess. Women wanted on that bandwagon, too. There was a female hormone replacement paired with a testosterone derivative that was supposed to enhance women's sexual drive during their "autumn years," whatever that was. Seemed to me very few of us wanted anything to do with "autumn years." We wanted summer, summer, summer, followed by a quick end at age one hundred. The so-called rectangular aging curve. I preferred to call it the Beemer and babe over the cliff: keep perfectly healthy and feeling like you're twenty-five until you drop dead at a ripe old age, hopefully while having great sex with a babe or boy toy.

I think Angela got into a sex-enhancing drug that has aspects of testosterone, a muscle-building hormone that could enhance athletic performance. Sounded a lot like RAZR. If I would have been there for her, none of this would have happened.

Lisa had collected her bag full of tools. She leaned

over and kissed me on the cheek. "You better watch out for Angela. She's no angel." She started walking toward the door.

"Wait. Let me get someone else to do this. I know a guy—"

But she cut me off. "I'm ready; I'm going; I know how to handle myself. Get over it."

I raised my eyebrows. "Okay. Be careful."

She walked out the door.

Ever since I'd known her, she was tough. Could be a product of dealing with her family problems or could be the assault in Kandahar. After that, she'd taken ju-jitsu, qualified expert in pistol, and kicked ass on a few sailors who tried to overpower her on a night of liberty. She'd been doing surveillance since high school, found a way to convict the asshole who was responsible for paralyzing her sister, not to mention was accepted to NCIS. So, my words "be careful" were empty. She knew how to burgle without being caught, and she knew how to take care of herself. I was beginning to realize how much she really meant to me.

But I had other problems right now.

I dialed Mug.

"Hi, Var. Did Lisa get in?"

"In a few hours. Hey, listen, you said RAZR had sexual enhancing abilities, right?"

"Yes. That was another thing guys loved about it. Once the game was over, they could pop another one and last all night."

"And it helped women as well?"

"Oh, hell yes. Jimmy, you know my linebacker friend, he did that first off, 'cause his old lady ... sorry, his wife kind of, uh, lost the desire. He was one of the good guys that didn't jump into another woman's sna ... uh ... bed when things didn't work out with his wife."

"And? What happened?"

"I think he said something like, 'We burned the sheets off the bed that night.'"

"That good, huh?"

"Well, kind of."

"What's that supposed to mean?"

"He was all bragging and smiles until after the first beer, then I got the real story. He said they couldn't have sex for a week afterwards they were so sore."

"Wow. Still sounds pretty great."

"Nope. He never used it again. He assumed he'd had great sex from the way he was so sore, and the way his wife talked, but he never remembered it. It was like a double roofie. He could have done anything to his wife but didn't remember. I don't know about you, but one of the reasons I like doing it is the memory. Makes you want more. Like anything that feels good. But if you're just sore for a week in a place you want to be having fun, well that kind of turns you off."

"Yeah. I get what you're saying. But it seems like the guys remember the power and speed it gives them on the field."

"Yeah. True. But the sex part, not so much. Though it affected his wife differently. She was pretty sore but kept begging for more drug."

"Thanks, Mug. Hey, I'll let you know in the morning what Lisa finds tonight. Rest peaceful. We're gonna get these guys."

"Thanks, man. Talk to you in the morning."

I clicked off and thought about RAZR and how it could make a woman a sexual maniac. Sounds custom made for a sex trafficker. Though, if it made her sore for a week, that would probably be a drawback.

There was something I was missing, but it kept floating away.

The pain started where my left wrist should be. Felt like a hot, vibrating knife stuck in my forearm. Not good. Then pain began to consume every brain function. I couldn't think.

They call it phantom limb pain, but there is nothing ghostly about it. Unless you're thinking of the Keymaster in *Ghostbusters*, a wicked, huge, bear/dog, as real as Mug, that would eat me alive, starting with my left arm, if I didn't find a mirror and plug into my music. Like, now. And that meant I'd be out of it at a crucial time, while Lisa needed me on the network while she burgled Salvation Labs in a few hours.

I really wished she'd hung around a while longer. I could use her help now. But I was on my own.

I pushed the earbuds into each ear one at a time, grabbed the iPhone, gritted my teeth and stumbled to the bedroom. This attack was a real doozy. And I don't do pain meds after that little problem I had with the Ides of Morpheus.

My therapist in Pensacola taught me that when the phantom limb pain comes, all I have to do is sit in front of the mirror over the waist-high dresser and flex my right hand. My brain will think it's my left hand. It has always worked. Unless it was a doozy. Then I needed music as a catalyst.

It was a simple thing I had to do: flick my finger across the iPhone screen, find the music icon, and get something playing.

But now, it was not so simple. My hand trembled and

didn't want to respond. I forced the pad of my index finger across the screen. Too hard. The phone slipped out of my hand and tugged out the earbuds. My hands moved in slow motion trying to catch it, but it slipped away like a muddy football in a rainy game just before I crossed the end zone for a touchdown.

The sound of the phone hitting the wood floor was like a distant echo in a gymnasium. I watched it bounce and felt hope bounce away with it.

Fireflies flitted about my peripheral vision. A mad kettle drummer pounded in my chest and sent nasty elf kettle drummers into my blood. And they really knew how to crank up the amplitude in my temples, my eyeball, and though I only had five fingers, it felt like those mad elves were smacking all ten fingernails.

I went down on hand and knees and groped for the phone. Then everything went black.

CHAPTER 16

The Real Buddy?

Cromwell hated that I'd hung up but realized the reason was going to help him. It had to do with Angela and those illegals, he was sure of it. Then I got the pains and lost track of Cromwell's actions until later. Either that, or my mind was losing its ability to meander in and out. Which could be a good thing. Only, in this instance, I wish I'd known what he was doing when he was doing it. Maybe things would have turned out differently, but this is what he told me happened:

Cromwell remembered something from a recent briefing on sex trafficking about the deep web, or dark web, or something like that, and sex trafficking and the FBI using an unusual web crawler that could get into the deep, dark web and find out a bit more. Buddy was just the man to help. Him and computers were like a sheet and blanket in the winter, never far from each other and completely molded to the other's whims.

He called Buddy. Ten rings, then, "This is 667-2221. Please leave a message."

"Hey, Buddy. I need some computer help, getting into the dark web. Give me a call. It's about this thing with the Judge."

Where the heck was Buddy? The last time Cromwell had seen him was hours ago on the road after Buddy's visit with the Judge and Angela. If Cromwell would have seen the same vision Buddy had seen, he would have gone straight for the Jack D. But Buddy didn't drink alcohol. Couldn't take it after Fallujah. His stress release was video games.

Cromwell patted the Smith and Wesson in his shoulder holster. What a great feeling, knowing the gun that had saved his butt many a time was right there. He walked quickly out the door of the office. Buddy's double-wide was at the edge of town.

♪ ♫

Buddy was cranked into Mirror's Edge on his Xbox, running as the warrior woman, Faith, when his phone rang. It was a plain ring, like the old phone on Aunt Betty's farm, familiar, cheerful, right. The phone sat next to the Xbox and computer on his uncle's old office desk. He let it ring and go to voice mail.

Sitting in the one straight-backed oak chair next to his bed in the small and familiar bedroom, playing his favorite video game for the last hour, he'd finally relaxed after that tight spot with the Judge and his sexy wife. He wanted her, and he thought she wanted him, too. Detective C was going to put her away, he knew that. But Buddy didn't want that. He wanted to help her ... and a small part of him wanted her for himself. She was beautiful and there was something so vulnerable about her. Doc Var had a thing with her, too. So maybe he would just help her. He didn't deserve her, anyhow.

He put the game on hold, picked up his cell phone and listened to Detective C's message. The dark web: it was used for good, and extremely illegal. Over 95 percent of information available on the internet was in the deep web. The dark web was a subset of that where only those logged into special search engines could tool around. The engine kept your searches anonymous for whatever "stuff" you watched. Detective C must be thinking about those dark-faced girls in the Judge's basement. Were they prisoners? He thought of Angela's comments being offered so nonchalantly after he'd told her he suspected the Judge would kill her and the girls in the basement.

He remembered her words, *Dear, sweet, Robert. I'm not sure what you're referring to. I would never let him kill anyone.*

How could she stop the Judge? Or was she in with him? No, that couldn't be. She was too beautiful. She needed Buddy's help.

He started playing the game again, running as Faith over rooftops, climbing walls, kicking those black warriors in the head. What kind of name was Faith for a warrior woman who got a tattoo on one eyelid? He thought about that as she jumped onto a rope and slid down to the next rooftop. Faith was the ultimate hope, like not just hoping something would occur, but believing it would. Believing you could overcome all obstacles, including bad men. Faith was a woman pitted against all those male warriors, and she won most of the fights. He could have used someone like that with him in Iraq. But the women he knew in the service were all too weak. He could take them out with one fist to the head. Down, unconscious, maybe even dead, depending on where he hit them. So why was it he liked playing this warrior game as a woman?

He wanted to help Angela. That's all he knew.

He put the game on pause, turned off the Xbox and flicked on his computer.

In a minute he had entered the deep web. Then, using a specific program similar to Tor, he entered the dark web where his IP address was lost in servers all over the globe—untraceable is what they said—though he knew better. Human beings could always find a way. Time, energy, knowledge and luck: they always worked. But for now they might think he was in the Netherlands or France, not sitting right under their noses. He knew Memex, a search program developed by DARPA and used by the FBI, could find human traffickers in the dark web. They had the time, energy and knowledge. He had to find Angela's site and what her plans were before they got lucky.

He typed in *Angela in Colorado* and got two thousand hits. Too broad.

Angela's girls in Colorado. Better, only five hits.

He looked at the various sites and one struck a chord: *Angela's Judgment Day.*

He couldn't find the IP address either, but the name fit.

He went into a message board on that site and followed the information back a few weeks and found what he wanted. He knew if he could get the information, Memex and the FBI could, and Angela would be in jail by midnight today if they found out what he'd just seen.

He exited, erased the history, grabbed his phone and walked toward the door. He should call Detective C. They had both been eighteen at Fallujah in 2004, in the Corps nine years after. Detective C had become an MP, but Buddy's problem in Fallujah kept him a grunt. They'd been together at Var's accident. That ended it all for all of them, over three years ago. Buddy had lost some edge since then, but Detective C was still sharp. Buddy should get his help. Especially going where Angela was going. Buddy didn't really know the lay of the land there.

The late afternoon sun streamed through the west window onto the old couch in the living room, sparkling off the polished brass handle of the side table. Soon the sun would sink behind the mountains. He walked to the side table, opened the drawer, and pulled out his Glock. Hadn't used it on a person in three years, but he cleaned it every week. And target practice with Var every month proved Buddy had not lost his eye. He'd never lost his nerve. Yeah, he'd run from Angela and the Judge, but not from fear of them. He knew once he got started with them, he wouldn't be able to stop.

Maybe he would call Var instead of Detective C?

No. Var had a history with Angela.

He picked up the clip, checked that it was full, and pushed the clip home. Then he closed the drawer. He stuck the gun into his front pants pocket and headed for the door. He would not get Detective C's help. He was on his own tonight. He would just have to control himself with the Judge. All those people would be around. He couldn't believe Angela would get in the way, but if she did, well, she was just a girl. Buddy would be gentle and still save her.

CHAPTER 17

Fallujah

"Hello, Buddy," Cromwell said, feeling guilty for cornering him.

Buddy had just opened the door of his double-wide. The late orange sunlight shone in Buddy's eyes, but he didn't blink or squint. He actually looked directly into Cromwell's eyes for longer than two seconds before glancing away. It reminded Cromwell of the Buddy of old, before the killing. Cromwell saw sadness, surprise, and panic there, all things he expected. But what he also saw was anger. What could Buddy be angry about?

"Why are you ignoring my calls?" Cromwell said, standing his ground at the door, not letting Buddy by.

"You called?"

"Cut the bullshit, man. We go back too far."

Buddy's eyes squeezed tight. Cromwell knew what that meant.

"You can't avoid this by going into your little brain room where you shut down. I need your help to get the Judge and An—"

Cromwell stopped speaking. Buddy's lips were puckered hard together like he was trying to press a nail into a two-by-four using only his lips. And Cromwell was pretty sure he knew what the two-by-four was.

"It's okay, Buddy. Angela is not the girl in Fallujah. She's—"

Buddy's eyes opened wide and his face took on a snarl. "What do you know about her? He's going to kill her."

"Maybe the mirror was wrong."

"It's never wrong."

The color of the sunlight, the way Buddy said it, the look in Buddy's eyes: all of it brought Cromwell back to that fateful day in November 2004. Fallujah, Iraq. The Second Battle of Fallujah. THE battle. The biggest urban Marine battle since 1968 in Hue City, Vietnam.

The yellow-orange dawn, the sun almost up in the scalding desert. Day usually turned Fallujah into a thriving city by the Euphrates River. Usually peaceful, too. Quiet. Kids running in streets playing soccer. It wasn't thriving now. Most of the 350,000 people were gone. And peace had been shattered all night with shells exploding building, tracers etching death across the dark. The city of mosques, teardrop-shaped orbs, bulbous reminders of the infiltrative nature of religion. It's like any Louisiana or East Texas city Cromwell knew: churches scattered sometimes every other block. But here there were no bars next door.

Old and new buildings intermixed and lined narrow streets making it hard to maneuver a vehicle; everything gray and tan as a desert should be except the odd smattering of green from palm and poplar trees and green-painted mosques. From IEDs or US mortar fire, piles of bricks, dirt and detritus of broken buildings littered the roads. It was war.

The dawn breaks. The thing that's missing today is the musical call to prayer over the loud speakers. A bell tolls. Yelling from mujahideens: "Allahu Akbar. Grab your guns. The infidels are coming."

The music that had been blaring since 2 a.m. starts again. The bell tolling starts the song, followed by a guitar riff then the screaming voices of AC/DC in "Hells Bells." The heavy rock sounds blare from a pile of huge speakers in the Marine courtyard. Not as classical as "The Ride of the Valkyrie" from Apocalypse Now, *but this is a new war, a new battle, though the soldiers are still young, and they appreciate the lyrics.*

> I'm rolling thunder, pouring rain
> I'm comin' on like a hurricane
> My lightning's flashing across the sky
> You're only young but you're gonna die
>
> I won't take no prisoners, won't spare no lives
> Nobody's putting up a fight
> I got my bell I'm gonna take you to hell
> I'm gonna get ya, Satan get ya![2]

They hoped the PSYOPS of loud, demonizing hard rock and heavy metal would work, demoralize and drive the mujahideen crazy. But what if the mujes loved hard rock and heavy metal? They weren't cave men.

Days pass. The popping of hundreds of guns, bullets fly everywhere. A woman screams; Buddy runs into the building; the same one he had been in many times over the last two weeks. She gave him peace in a world of chaos. Cromwell is in the same unit as Buddy and has been joking with him the last week about his new woman. Now he runs in after him; Marines help their buddies. Besides, Buddy's only eighteen.

Cromwell sees mirrors on the walls reflecting two visions, though in the dust and dim it's hard to tell which of the visions is real. A dark-haired mujahideen with a large knife is cutting the throat of a woman, Buddy's woman. Her screams become gurgles as she chokes on her own blood, pouring onto the tile floor, the splatting sound like water from a pitcher.

Buddy fires his M-4 all around the room, his animal shriek of anger continuous behind the cracking sound of the gun. Mirrors shatter on the south and east walls. Cromwell dives behind a couch as bullets thwack all around him.

Buddy's scream and firing stop. He says something like "Yeah," in a low voice, and there's the click and smack of a new clip going into his gun. Cromwell peeks over the couch and sees Buddy standing over the prostrate muj next to the woman, the woman Buddy had loved lying in a pool of her blood. Buddy fires one bullet after another, pausing after each, into the knees and elbows of the muj. The man is still alive and jerks and screams after each bullet. Cromwell starts to get up to tell Buddy to stop, but then sits back down, his vacant eyes staring at the bullet-pocked wall as he shakes his head. There are some things war is good for—one of them is punishing the wicked. He sits and stares at the wall and hears it all. Shot. Scream. Groans and struggling sounds. Shot. Scream.

Cromwell eases up again. The muj begins to pray, and Buddy fires a burst in his heart, silencing him.

Buddy kneels by the dead woman and weeps. Cromwell watches and cannot move. Guys don't comfort guys. Warm tears run down his cheeks.

Two days later Marines all over Fallujah cheered and jabbed fists in the air. This was the best way for a Marine to celebrate 10 November, the Marine Corps birthday.

The best way.

Everyone knew why Buddy lost it after that. No one knew exactly why he could only look at people through a mirror, though Cromwell thought his theory was probably the best: the view through mirrors showed the true nature of people, even those who professed to love God.

Cromwell stood in the doorway and watched Buddy drop his head and go for the mirror he always kept in his pocket. Only Buddy didn't pull out his mirror. He pulled out a Glock.

CHAPTER 18

B&E

I awoke on the cool hardwood floor of my bedroom, a burning pain in my left arm. I was in front of my dresser. The light was different, but how ... I couldn't put it together. The pain was definitely less than when I lost consciousness, but ... it was taking over again. It dawned on me: It was twilight, just when I needed to be my sharpest for Lisa, and I still felt fuzzy around the edges. God damn that pain. I fumbled my good hand around, only getting the occasional glimpse of my phone through the narrow tunnel the sparkling hoard of fireflies in my visual field allowed me.

Finally, I grasped the cool rectangle with the earplug wire coming out one end, sat up, and put it on the dresser, then, using the dresser as support, pushed up and flopped onto the chair in front of the mirror. Lucky for me the good left leg balanced my good right arm. My breathing was ragged. My head felt like my heart was nailing it with each beat. The pain was getting worse. It burned all the way up to my shoulder now.

I shakily pushed one ear plug in each ear, steadied the iPhone on the desk, and, this time, gently swiped a finger across the screen. A few taps and James Taylor was playing "Fire and Rain" in my ears. I looked into the mirror through the small cone of vision surrounded by flashing lights, saw my right hand as my left, flexed it and wiggled the fingers. The pain eased. My vision cleared. I did it again and the pain eased some more, now pulsing instead of burning.

Sweat cooled the back of my neck and dripped down my back. A chill ran through me. I watched in the mirror as I plucked a nearby Kleenex from a box on the dresser and wiped it over my face, my right hand disguised to my brain as my left, telling it everything was okay. I wanted a Guinness but knew water was my best friend right now. The iPhone digital clock read 6:53. I'd been out for two hours. Lisa would be at Salvation Labs in seven minutes.

A few deep breaths, another flex of the fingers, arm and forearm in the mirror, and the burning pain completely left, though the throbbing ache remained. Not normal, but I could work with it. It seemed safe to get up. I unplugged and stood. Once again, mirror therapy had worked for my phantom limb pain. I remembered a phrase from a friend who always crammed for finals in med school on the last day, "There's no minute like the last minute."

On shaky legs, I limped to the kitchen, ran water from the faucet until it was cold, filled a glass and drank the whole thing. Then another. I dashed cold water on my face. Life was good again. Sort of.

I sat at the kitchen table and took off the left arm prosthetic, hoping for nothing. I shivered in sweat dripping down my neck and chest. A red area on the stump I had been nursing along with moleskin and lotion massages was now covering the whole end of the stump and the center was broken open with crusted yellow-white drainage. Damn.

So the pains I'd felt were not completely due to phantom limb. This had triggered it. Infections of stumps were of two types, benign and bad. Okay, there were the in-betweens, but to an amputee those were benign, too. Now I knew why I'd been sweating yet cold. This infection had spread to my bloodstream. I might lose more of my arm. How the hell had this happened? The redness had been so miniscule this morning before I visited Salvation Labs. I remembered Tanner falling against my arm and the twinge afterward.

Could he have stuck something in my stump? Who would do something like that? Someone who already knew why I was there. Someone who almost ran me and Lisa off the road.

Lisa was in real danger.

I went to the sink and ran warm water over the stump, soaped it off. Oh, yeah. That felt better, but in the process I could feel a fluctuant liquid underneath, likely pus under the skin that needed draining. I tried to remember if I had any leftover antibiotics from past uses. Hopefully they hadn't expired. There was a sterile scalpel somewhere, though the way I was feeling I didn't know if I could lance it without local anesthesia. I couldn't remember if I still had lidocaine with epi. It had been such a long time since the last infection. In the bathroom, I rummaged through the medicine cabinet. Nothing. Then the drawers under the sink.

My cell phone rang. The caller ID read *Lisa.*

I walked back to my computer, plugged in the earbuds, and clicked the mic. "Hi. Are you in?"

"A few minutes. Testing the comm lines first. Is this clear?"

"Five-by-five on your voice. But, wait a sec, Lisa. I just

found out something that leads me to believe you're in a lot more danger. You need to get out of there."

There was a pause. "No. I have to do it tonight, or we'll never get anything. I'm going in."

She was right, but this felt very wrong. "Lisa, please."

"All right, I'm going in without you."

"Wait. I'll help. Let me get to the computer for video." She had a GoPro and transmitter strapped to her head. Not the highest tech, but when we'd splurged on my hand camera it was the best we could do. Her PI business wasn't that lucrative, though she'd made some good investments with her Dad's life insurance money.

"I thought you'd have already been on video."

"That was the plan. Something came up." I sat and clicked into her video feed. "Try to look at one area and not move your head."

The grainy, infrared picture flickered, then steadied. She was at one of the side doors to Salvation Labs, behind the dumpster, the west side, as I recalled from my recon views.

"Okay. Give me a view of the cameras and the different sides of the clinic, but slowly."

Salvation Lab's outside video camera was just visible at the southwestern corner, allowing one camera to get shots of both sides, though not all at once. Thrifty, as the Scots would say. Cheap was my term. Once they were rolling in the dough they should have updated with more and better cameras.

The camera was rotating away from her, toward the southern side.

"Okay. I'm ready." My stump throbbed. I remembered where I'd left my infection-treatment supplies:

in the trunk of my car. I'd forgotten to bring them in last week after my visit to Walgreens.

Yeah. Lisa's sister was nearing death, she'd probably not gotten much sleep for days, could be killed any second, and I was thinking of myself.

The video picture danced and blurred. But it wasn't me. She must be running to the door. She had a red headlight strapped on below the GoPro and it shone on the door lock. Her hands worked in the view screen; a few clicks and she opened the door. She was good. I pressed the timer on my watch. She said it would take fifteen minutes. I hoped it was less and that no one was waiting.

She closed the door behind her, then flicked off the night view and turned the headlamp to white light. There were no windows where she was going, no worries that someone would see her light as she moved through the building. She moved carefully but quickly, the video screen bright, clear, and smooth. The heart of the lab was through the door ahead; at least that was our supposition based on the schematics of the building, which showed tons of electrical and large ducting. We figured it was probably for refrigeration, outlets for lab analysis machines, and ducting for a venting hood.

Her light shone on the security card reader at the door. She took out the security card we'd made that morning and slipped the bar code under the reader. A needle-thin red light scanned it, the door lock clicked, and she went in.

CHAPTER 19

Going to the Show

The Judge required only the occasional taste of the wares. And of course to share in the profits. Angela was tired of sharing money and sex with someone she loathed. The research for an asthma drug had drained her family's wealth, and she had become dependent on the Judge's money. But this new enterprise had ended the need for his capital. Even if it hadn't, she couldn't stomach him any longer.

She drove the rented black Suburban, and he sat in the back with six girls. Maia sat in the passenger's seat. She wanted the girls to feel pampered on their drive to the Stanley Hotel in Estes Park. The oil men from wells in northern Colorado worked hard and had asked for a relatively private hotel in a small town.

The road wound like an anaconda up the Thompson River canyon, the headlights offering a mere glimpse of the canyon walls, trees, and a few houses. The girls' airy giggles mixed with the Judge's baritone in the back. Perhaps it was his hands that made them giggle. Though he was not rough, none of them enjoyed his overtures. They knew what he wanted. And he had it whenever he wanted it in the basement room. Another reason to get rid of him. He was making them want to run.

This was her first trip with the girls to Estes Park. Angela had picked this exact time of the autumn to avoid the usual summer road construction. Everything about this trip had been planned with precision. Handy having the internet for all kinds of things. But she couldn't allow her name to pop up on any lists, so she used a search engine called Tor in the dark web. It allowed private, discreet and untraceable searches, and provided much more than Google: charter flights from Sao Paulo, under-the-table dentists, and road construction timetables. Summer over, the construction crews were working extra hours to get it done before winter set in. Construction would have meant stopping the Suburban on occasion and that would risk a girl escaping. They probably wouldn't and even if they did, they couldn't go far, but it would be a pain to round them up. The vehicle had child locks on the doors and darkly tinted windows, which reduced the chance of problems. Angela was thorough. It was in her training as a physician and researcher.

Well, almost a physician. If only Var hadn't left. The future had looked much different three years ago when he'd left for internship. He'd been the only man she'd ever loved, and when he'd gone, days of black, empty, cornerless rooms with nowhere to hide enveloped her and took her deeper than she'd been since the first day her father had hit her at five.

But the research had saved her. And now the sky was the limit, provided she could rid herself of her husband. And this hateful use of women.

She thought of Var and her chest lightened and she smiled. Maybe there was a future with him. She had often ached for the love they once had, sometimes crying after making love to that oaf the Judge. Hope. That's what she needed. And his love again.

But he had a new girlfriend, some PI who helped him. Could Angela hide what she'd done from Var? Could he love her if he found out all she'd done?

The giggling got louder, and the Judge was laughing. Had he swilled some of his Chivas before coming?

"Darling," she said, "you didn't bring liquor for the girls, did you? You know they must be on their game tonight."

"Of course not, dear. We just enjoy each other's company."

Angela made eye contact with Maia, then turned her head and eyes quickly from Maia to the back twice.

Maia twisted around and looked in the back, then looked back at Angela and shook her head, indicating there was no alcohol. Angela had a special connection with Maia; it had been that way from the start. Respect and something more. Angela never forced their love making. It just happened. And once Angela and Maia were on the drug, they needed the sex, sometimes too much. RAZR kept the girls going full bore long after their male companions were spent. And the next day they knew they'd had fun, though they weren't exactly sure what had happened. A great drug in so many ways. Too bad it eventually killed them. Angela had stopped taking it two weeks ago, but she still wanted it. Desperately. The feeling it gave her was like being super-human.

Maia grabbed the bottle of water in the drink holder, popped a capsule into her mouth and chased it down. Angela looked at Maia and noticed her eyes jumping, her hands quivering when she reached up to brush a lock of hair from her eyes. The downside of RAZR. The others had not yet begun to show the side effects, but it wouldn't take long. Angela would have to get more girls in three or four months. Maybe she would use her connections in Utah. Some men preferred white girls. Could be Mormon girls would last longer than the Brazilians. And, she smiled, their religion, or cult, or whatever Mormons really were, had been teaching threesomes and more for years.

She glanced at Maia. A shame. Just when she was getting used to her. And maybe ... Angela gritted her teeth. Sex, yes. But love was out of the question. Not with one of the girls. What was this drug doing to her? Yet, she did love Maia. Like the child she never had? No. Like a sister? No. The sex ... Her mind and heart crashed into darkness. *Get by today. Just get by today.*

Houses along the river were mostly in shadows now and soon gave way to riverside resort rooms and cabins. Estes Park was just over the next hill. A cramp in Angela's hand made her drop it from the wheel, fast so Maia wouldn't be able to see the tremor. Angela had stopped RAZR once she started developing the tremor, not to mention the crazy thoughts of blowing her brains out. She still had the residual cramp and tremor in her left hand. Not getting worse, but her thinking wasn't right.

Salvation Labs knew about the suicides, but also knew no one could prove it was their drug, so the drug kept coming.

She had a large stockpile of RAZR, though she might not need it. From what she'd seen in previous girls, the effects on football would be devastating in another month. By then, Salvation Labs should have her asthma drug finished and she could get out of this ugly business.

Get by today. She sighed as she crested the hill and saw the lights of Estes Park just beyond Lake Estes. The sun had dipped below the far mountain peaks.

"We're almost there. Please make your final preparations, my darlings."

She glanced at Maia and noticed her swallowing another pill. If one was good, why not two? In the rearview the others did the same. The Judge caught her eye in the rearview and gave her a wan smile as he groped one of the girls.

Yes, she thought, *you can smile, dear. Now.* She decided she might need more muscle tonight, so she also popped a RAZR. It's showtime.

CHAPTER 20

The Meet Up

Cromwell backed off a step when Buddy pulled the Glock.

"I didn't want to bother you," Buddy said, holding the gun by his side, pointed at the ground, "but now that you're here, we can do it together."

He'd quickly explained to Cromwell what he'd found, and they jumped in Cromwell's car and sped toward Angela's house. Cromwell pushed his crappy little Honda hard. Its engine whined in protest. Buddy sat in the passenger seat. Once Cromwell saw the dirt road spur that led to the Judge's home, he slowed and parked the car behind a slight rise with clumps of sagebrush hiding them from anyone who might drive from the Judge's home to the blacktop. Cromwell reached behind Buddy's seat and pulled out from the seat pocket a hand-sized set of binoculars. He got out and walked up the hill, stepping carefully between sage bushes, hoping for no rattlers. This was the worst time to be out in the sage. Warm and full of rabbits and ground squirrels —rattlesnakes loved them.

Buddy followed.

At the top, Cromwell peered through the binocs at the Judge's house. Angela and one teenaged dark woman were getting into the front seats of a black Suburban, the Judge in the backseat with what appeared to be more girls. Cromwell took his eyes from the binocs and looked at Buddy, who was frowning in concentration at the Suburban. He'd probably seen the same thing, just not as magnified. Everyone was there. He'd been right.

The metallic sound of the Suburban doors slamming echoed across the foothills. Cromwell looked back into the binocs. Angela was driving and didn't fool around. The black SUV cruised towards Cromwell like a locomotive. He motioned at Buddy and ran down the hill, cringing and jumping to the side when he heard a distinctive rattle.

They made it to the Honda and jumped in. Cromwell breathed fast, and his heart was popping. If Angela turned left onto the pavement she would easily spot the Honda. The Judge would recognize the car even if she didn't. The Honda would be no match for the Suburban and they'd be gone.

Angela turned right. Cromwell breathed easier and waited until the red taillights were almost out of sight, then gunned the Honda for all it was worth, hoping he hadn't waited too long. The red lights disappeared over the next rise and Cromwell pushed hard on the accelerator, but it was already jammed on the floorboard. The engine whine missed a few beats. It had been a great car, but the old engine could throw a rod anytime with this stress.

Angela must have been staying within the speed limit, because he got closer to the Suburban, close enough for Buddy to use the binocs. The Honda chugged and spit. Cromwell gritted his teeth and kept the accelerator down. Buddy peered through the binoculars and nodded, indicating it was the right car. Cromwell felt his body relax and eased off the accelerator. The Honda settled back to a safe distance, purring in thankfulness.

Cromwell followed them up the Big Thompson road toward Estes Park, though traffic was scant. He was the only car behind Angela, so he lagged uncomfortably far behind, hoping she wouldn't turn off at a side road when he lost sight of her car around each bend. Finally, a car pulled out of a riverside home and drove between them. Cromwell sighed and his grip on the steering wheel relaxed.

They made it to Estes, turned right before the main street, and sped up the road to the Stanley Hotel. Cromwell had driven to the Stanley for a detective's conference in 2011, but that was in the winter. All he'd wanted then was to get inside to the warmth, the heater in his Honda marginal even in lower altitudes. This was the first time he'd really studied the outside of the hotel, and the first time he'd seen it lit at night.

It was a long, white, rectangular box with two large cubes attached on either end as wings. A slanted, terracotta roof topped three stories of windows, the wings three separate windows wide on each story. Columns on the first floor held up a second-story balcony. The building felt thick, solid, built to last. The roof had a central cylindrical bell tower with a spire atop flying an American flag. Two gabled dormers symmetrically spaced occupied both sides of the bell tower, and one gabled dormer sat on the roof of each wing. Yet another dormer stood to the right of the bell tower, asymmetrical, like an afterthought. Strange.

He could see how Stephen King would think it a

perfect hotel for a spooky tale, the central bell tower being lit like the central white horn of a demon with the multiple dark windows on either side as eyes and the large, central square entrance below the white horn a yawning mouth giving access to the inside's lighted, fiery innards.

Cromwell's car window was open, and he heard music playing from the left side of the hotel. Shapes moved in the far-left wing windows—the ballroom where they'd had lectures and dinner for the crowd of detectives. Old-time rock and roll played loud, sounded like Bon Jovi. People were dancing and having a good time. Cromwell's hair, scruffy beard, and Stones tee shirt would fit right in. Buddy's jeans and a black moon tee shirt with a howling white wolf would do, too. His greasy baseball cap would be out of place, and he might balk at going into a huge room full of people, but they'd cross that bridge ...

The Suburban pulled into the parking lot. Angela and several girls spilled out.

Okay, Cromwell thought. Buddy was right about the women being at the house, though it could be some of Angela's friends. Had to make sure.

The Judge stayed inside the SUV. The others entered the building through a side door.

Cromwell parked and wondered how he was going to go in with the Judge watching.

"Go to the other side," Buddy said.

The hairs on the back of Cromwell's neck prickled. Buddy was a little spooky sometimes, the way he seemed to read your mind. He'd been that way even before the killing in Fallujah. It had saved their asses more than once. Now, coupled with the haunted feel of the hotel, Cromwell wondered if he should wait and call for backup.

But he put the car in gear and drove to the other side. Cromwell had no proof of anything. Any of his friends who would trust him would take at least and hour. It looked like this was going down right now.

"Reach behind my seat," he told Buddy, "and get my hat. You're not going in with that greasy thing on your head." The hat was a black curved-bill baseball cap with the New Orleans Saints trident on the front and *Saints* printed on the side of the bill.

Buddy frowned, but took off his cap and replaced it with the Saints cap.

Cromwell parked the car and gave him the once-over. "Suits you."

He cracked his door open, wondering if Buddy would come.

Buddy opened his door and got out. They shut their doors and walked inside.

Cromwell flashed his shield at the double doors to the auditorium—the never-fail entrance ticket to any game, concert, or dance. It even worked well into backdoor illegal parties in New Orleans, provided the greeter knew you were the dirty cop keeping out the bad boys. Another reason Cromwell liked being away from the Big Easy: It was too easy for police grift.

He and Buddy wandered to the right side, opposite and as far as possible from the band. They stood behind a large column and leaned on it, keeping the room in view, but their faces almost hidden. Buddy held his mirror down by his side reflecting the entire scene from a different angle.

At the center table, two men sported white moustaches and cocked-back dark cowboy hats and had two women by their sides, thin, tanned, and wrinkled. All four observed the writhing, dancing crowd, with a look that said, *Damn I wish I was that young.* A banner hung from the bottom of the table with large letters in black: *Third Annual Frackers of Colorado.* Below that was smaller lettering in red: *We Do It Deeper and Sideways.*

A round table set up to the right of the band offered champagne bottles in ice buckets and a large lazy Susan with meats, veggies, fruits, and deserts. Every table was lit with candles and full settings of dishes and silverware. A handful of dapper men in tuxes sat at a table, some in animated conversations.

Cromwell began to feel like he and Buddy might stick out. But then he looked around the room and saw a lot of other guys in tee shirts and jeans. The guys in tuxes must be special. Reminded him of that stupid show, *The Bachelorette.*

O.J., Buddy, and Var had once watched that show, just for grins after a few beers, maybe more than a few. It was the first night Var came back to Colorado—kind of a reunion. God, those guys in the show were dumb. The babe wasn't so smart either. Good thing they had all those *Bachelorette* TV goonies helping them through the rough spots. The dumbest people of all were the ones watching the show, believing it was all actually unrehearsed and unrigged. But maybe it was the closest thing most Americans got to "reality." A commercial advertised *Survivor,* the show touted as the "ultimate adventure." "Yeah, try war." Var said. They turned off the show.

Cromwell noted the guys in tuxes seemed to be waiting for a party with Angela's women. Who would be

Bachelor Number One?

Cromwell tapped Buddy on the shoulder and shifted his eyes toward the men. Buddy already had a bead on the table with his mirror. Cromwell and Buddy moved to the right, putting the column between them and the men.

Buddy put the mirror in his pocket and held his cell phone by his thigh, looking at the digital screen of the camera app. *A good man to have around*, Cromwell thought. Buddy adjusted the zoom to get some close-ups and started clicking off photos.

One of the men stood and the rest followed suit. Angela flowed in with her women. There were six of them, besides Angela, by Cromwell's count. No, seven. The last one straggled in about thirty seconds later, gesticulating with long thin arms to Angela in what appeared a profuse apology. Nothing could be heard over the rock and roll band, but the anger on Angela's face at the late woman could almost be felt. This was Angela's show. At least the women knew it; every one of them kept their eyes on her. Meanwhile, the men picked their dates for the night—two argued over one. Angela stepped in, smiled, pointed and held out her hands palms up in a gesture of *plenty to go around*, and one of the guys broke off to the woman Angela proffered, not looking very happy. The woman gave him a pouty look, then reached around his neck and kissed him long and hard, her body tight against his. The guy was probably happy now.

They all sat down to eat, drink, and be merry. Cromwell thought about calling for backup again. This was going to be a big job. But he still had no proof that Angela was using illegals as whores. He also wondered where the Judge was. Why hadn't he come in? Was it because he was too well-known? Surely, he wouldn't sit out there all night. Could he be with another girl in a room already? Maybe Cromwell should send Buddy back to check on the Judge.

The music pounded, now hitting the familiar guitar riffs of *Kansas*; Cromwell made his way to the food and drink table a few times, gathered cheese and crackers, and hunted for a Fresca, settling for a Sprite. He brought food and a Sprite to Buddy, who had shuffled around the dance floor a few times to keep from looking too conspicuous as a watcher.

Cromwell munched and swigged Sprite and thought about the Judge some more. One man stood up at the center table, took the hand of his chosen partner, and escorted her out of the room. Cromwell started to walk after them when a woman from the dance floor stepped in his way.

"I love the Stones." She was middle-aged, darkly tanned, obviously artificially endowed and staring at him with hungry eyes.

"Yeah? Ever see them in concert in London?" That was a line that usually ended it for any comers. Not many had ever been to a London concert.

"I saw them in the UK a few years back." Her eyes glazed over and the amber liquid in the glass she was holding almost dripped out the top. Almost. She was good at balancing.

Great, he thought, *a drunken, middle-aged groupie. The worst kind.* In the future he would have to think of a different line for women of that era.

"I wish I had," he said. Out of the corner of his eye he saw Bachelor Number One and his wonderful date walking up the balustraded staircase. They would be out of following range in thirty seconds.

He glanced at Buddy who'd brought out his mirror by his hip and was perusing the winners table. Cromwell took a step toward him and poked him with a finger. "I'm going upstairs."

Buddy smiled at him, patted him on the shoulder, and gazed back at the mirror.

The Stones fan sipped her drink and gave Buddy then Cromwell a studied look over the rim of her glass. "Are you gay?"

Cromwell shrugged.

She did a great John Wayne walk away from him. Smooth. Very smooth. Didn't spill a drop.

Bachelor Number Two got up and led his wonderful date by the hand the same way number one had gone.

Cromwell moseyed after them, making sure his walk was nothing like John Wayne, thinking, *The Duke was probably the only guy who could pull off that walk without attracting other guys. At least he didn't attract guys in his movies. Who knew what happened offscreen?*

CHAPTER 21

Was RAZR a Lie?

Lisa was out of Salvation Labs in thirteen minutes and twenty seconds. My timer beeped long after she'd closed the door and turned off the video feed of the darkened exterior of the building, her footsteps walking away, her lips sighing in the microphone. It was not a sigh of satisfaction.

What the hell were we going to do now? She'd found no bottles of RAZR. No telltale labels like the one Mug had described. I was pretty sure he wasn't lying. He just didn't seem like he had it in him. But had his buddy lied? The one who'd crippled him—what was his name? Jamie Lee?

The first rule of private investigation: everyone lies.

Time to meet this guy—way past time. Should have met him before we risked a B&E. Chalk one up to inexperience as a PI. Sure, I'd spent time with my dad and learned a lot of tricks of the trade. But he'd always wanted me to be a doctor, feeling his job as a PI was too sleazy for a son of his. So I'd forgotten another rule: talk to everyone involved. Everyone. You have to ask them the hard questions, look in their eyes, feel their emotions, watch their body language. Then and only then can you decide if they are lying.

I thought about Mug's conversation again. I'd been

watching his body language. He wasn't lying. I'm not sure he would or even could tell a lie. Right. He's human. But he hadn't lied to me unless he was someone completely different than he appeared to be.

I called him and when he answered I said, "Hey, Mug. Lisa found no RAZR bottles or anything even the least bit incriminating."

There was a long pause.

"Mug, you still there?"

"Yeah. Geez. I thought for sure ..."

"Yeah. So, I need to talk to this Jamie Lee who said he found the bottle of RAZR."

"I don't know—"

"Sorry, guy. I know you didn't want me to get him involved, but something's not right and he seems to be the key to the kingdom, here." Literally. If we didn't get the right info, we were out of this show, and the kingdom of pro football might fall, the pieces never to be put back together again.

I waited for him to say something. Those huge mutant brain cells must take longer than most to crack the whip.

"Mug, listen. I know he's your buddy, he's got family problems, grew up on the wrong side of the tracks, yadda-yadda-yadda. But he could have lied to you for all of those reasons. Do you think he lied?"

"No. Not a chance."

"You seem pretty sure."

"That's 'cause I am. Absolutely sure." His voice was deadpan. Gave me a little chill.

"Mug?"

"Yeah."

"What are you not telling me?"

"He wrecked my career."

"Mug."

"Trust me. He didn't lie."

I wanted to get in his face, but that was hard to do on the phone. So I changed tactics. "Come on, buddy. How can you be so sure?"

His heavy sigh sounded like a 747 taking off. "I held him by his ankles over the side of a tenth-story balcony."

"Okay. That's not so bad."

"He was naked."

"Okay."

"And I let go of him."

"What?"

"I didn't mean to. My hand was sweaty, and he'd put on weight after RAZR."

"So what did you do with the body?"

"Huh?"

"If you let go of him, he fell ten stories and became a pile of unidentifiable flesh and bone."

"No, I caught him with the rope."

"The rope?"

"Yeah, the one around his ankle I tied to my other hand."

"So he's okay?"

"Sorta."

"Sorta?"

"The rope was a little too long and he banged his mouth on the balcony rail below. Broke his jaw and most of his teeth out."

"Can he talk?"

"Yeah. I paid for the oral surgeon and the implants. Almost good as new." The 747 had landed and sounded like it had a flat tire.

"You sound unsure."

"He probably won't want to talk with anyone I send by."

"Yeah. I can see that. But I still need to chat with him."

"Really?"

"Yeah."

"Okay. Maybe if I went with you."

There was a long silence. Thoughts. Consideration. Concerns. "That could work."

He called Jamie Lee, and we went over.

CHAPTER 22

What the Heck?

Cromwell left Buddy to watch the winners table and walked behind Bachelor Number Two and his jailbait date, just out of sight as they jogged up the stairs. They were in a hurry for something. Cromwell was pretty sure it wasn't *The Dick Van Dyke Show*. Cromwell waited at the edge of the hallway and watched them walk by the fateful room 217—the room in *The Shining*, the book, not the movie—and go across the hallway to 218, insert the security card and go in. The door closed behind them.

Cromwell decided it was time. He'd first call for backup, then round up the Judge and Angela and cuff them in the Suburban. Once backup arrived, Cromwell would knock on the doors, starting with 218, and gather all the bachelors and their dates together for questioning. He took out his phone, turned around and took a step down the stairs. He saw the top of the Judge's head as he was coming up the stairs.

A gunshot came from the hallway behind him. Did it come from 218?

The Judge looked up, saw Cromwell, initially got that slight smile and I-know-you look, then frowned and got the wide-eyed, holy-shit look and bolted back down the stairs.

Another gunshot. This time Cromwell was sure it came from 218. He wanted to run after the Judge, but he couldn't exactly ignore gunshots. ... He stuck his phone in his pocket, ran to room 218, and pounded on the door.

He heard a man cursing.

He raised his fist to pound again and the door opened. Bachelor Number Two stood there, a head taller than Cromwell. His unbuttoned tux shirt revealed a very white and hairy chest; black, curly hairs; broad, thick shoulders; and a pot belly. He was a big guy who'd done some work in the oil field and swilled a lot of beer. His eyes were wide, and his lip quivered like he was about to cry.

Cromwell held out his badge and took a step into the room.

"I didn't do nothin'. She killed herself." The man pointed at the bed.

In one glance, Cromwell took it in. On the right, the girl lay on a king-size bed. Across from her was dark brown cabinet with a flat screen TV playing a porn movie with lots of panting and groaning. The girl on the bed lay on her side, head canted up, sightless eyes staring at Cromwell, one temple gone, the other with a neat dark hole in it. The bedspread under her head was a dark mess, and a few blobs had made the carpet. The gun was still in her hand which was cradled in the crook of her neck. The barrel wasn't smoking.

Her other arm jutted out at an obtuse angle, lying over the side of the bed. Her black dress with spaghetti straps was still on, one strap off her shoulder. One foot still had a stiletto-heeled, red shoe on, the other shoe on the floor.

The girl's eyes were wide, her face in a grimace like she was on the verge of screaming in fright. But there had been no screams that Cromwell had heard. And why had there been two shots?

"Okay, sir. Please step away from the door and sit down in that chair." Cromwell flicked his eyes at the far table and chair.

The guy looked at the girl, looked at Cromwell. "I didn't do nothin'. My boss is downstairs. He'll tell you." His white-knuckled grip on the door was like he was going to rip it off the hinges. Or smash it into Cromwell's face.

"Sure. I understand. It looks pretty obvious you didn't do anything. The gun's not smoking, but I've never seen that happen except after a major firefight with a lot of bullets fired. Not just two. And I can tell you're upset. But I'm a deputy sheriff with the Thompson County Sheriff's office, and this is a crime scene and I have to question you. Please step back over to the window and sit in that chair."

Sweat dripped down the guy's neck and chest. He looked about thirty, so Cromwell didn't think he'd have a heart attack, but he was so damn stressed he might do something stupid.

Cromwell drew his shoulder gun. "Get over there and sit the fuck down. Now!"

The guy let the door go and did a little half jog and slammed into the chair so hard it rocked back and came back down with a thud.

Cromwell caught the door and eased it shut. He shoved the gun back in the holster and took out his phone, touching the number for the dispatcher. A woman answered, and he told her the situation and the need for a crime scene unit. The Estes police didn't have one. She said she would take care of it.

"Tell Johnny to come up. I need his help, here." Johnny occasionally helped when Cromwell wasn't working alone, which he decided was not a good thing right now. The dispatcher said she would tell him and disconnected.

He wished he had Johnny here now to get Angela and the Judge. Soon there might be a crowd of gawkers, and surely the hotel staff would arrive. Where the hell was Buddy?

Cromwell looked at the body, then at the guy sitting with his head in his hands. A little bald spot showed on the back of his head.

"So, what's your name?" he said.

The guy looked up, his eyes glazed, his mouth parted. "Jackson. Jackson Reudi. I gotta puke."

He stood and held a palm over his mouth. Cromwell took a step back and lifted a hand toward the bathroom.

The guy ran to the toilet and slammed the lid open so hard a piece flew off. His groan sounded like it came from his toes. The chunks that splashed into the water would not have been pretty on the carpet. Though, Cromwell glanced back towards the bed, by the time the crime scene guys were done, the carpet cleaner would have a lot of work to do.

There was a knock on the door. Good. Probably Buddy or someone from hotel security.

He opened the door.

Buddy was there, but off to the side of Angela, who stood in front of Cromwell. She had a small handgun aimed at Cromwell's chest. Buddy held her other hand, smiling at Cromwell's shoes.

CHAPTER 23

Jamie Lee's Women

Though Jamie Lee had come up in the world, his house reflected the tarnish of recent money lost. The neighborhood was swanky, surrounding a lake. White and yellow and red and blue ski boats blinked chrome on many backyard docks, reflecting the yellow sodium dock lights. Most of the houses were thick and solid, brick, with large picture windows. Ranch homes spread out over two lots. The rich needed lots of room.

Jamie Lee's house was stuck at the end of an inlet, a two-story with brick veneer up front and peeling paint on the trim and siding. The apple-green Cadillac Escalade parked on the street had a big dent in the rear left quarter. In the driveway, the sleek white Lexus GS 350 suffered a spider of cracks on the windshield. The fence around the backyard seemed to be missing a few teeth.

I parked in the driveway beside the Lexus. A yellow light lit the front door, probably colored to avoid bugs this close to the water. Mug got out and limped to the door. I was right behind him. A bass woofer thumped inside the house, powerful enough to make the front picture window vibrate in the reflection of the streetlight but not overwhelming. I thought of the movie *Jurassic Park* and the T-rex and the puddles of water vibrating. This beat would have the T-rex doing a jig.

Mug rang the doorbell, probably a good idea; a knock would be well disguised by the music. We waited for a good minute without an answer. Mug leaned on the doorbell a bit longer.

The deadbolt clicked, and the door opened. A bright inside foyer light downlit a handsome black guy. With a glass in one hand, he stood and gazed at us, his shining black eyes under frowning brows. He wore an orange tank top with a big white number eighty-seven on the front, and baggy, black knee-length shorts. On his feet, flip-flops. He was close shaven, both face and scalp, and as tall as Mug but probably sixty pounds lighter and every bit muscle. His head and neck bobbed for a few beats of the woofer before he smiled, bright white and genuine. The dental work looked great. He took a step forward and hugged Mug. "My man! Good to see you. What goes round?"

Mug didn't strike me as the hugging type, but I was wrong. He not only hugged Jamie Lee but lifted him off the ground. "Oh, you know. The world and my head!" A little weird for someone who'd lost his teeth after being hung off the balcony. But they were football players. A little like soldiers. You forgive the little things in a fellow warrior.

Jamie Lee's glass tipped and spilled amber, whiskey-smelling liquid onto my shoes. Mug put him down, still grinning at Jamie Lee.

I guess Mug's friends all thought that because Mug left his coffee mug in various training rooms, that also meant his head spun. Or maybe it was another inside joke.

Mug put Jamie Lee down and swung a massive paw

toward me. "This is Var. He's helping me with the RAZR case."

Jamie Lee stuck his tongue up under his upper left lip, swirled the drink in his hand, the ice clinking, and eyed me, his gaze lingering on my bad arm. I proffered my good hand and he shook it.

"Now you know I don't have no balcony in the back." His black eyes twinkled, and he smiled again. Quite infectious.

I chuckled. "No, I'm not here to help lift you. Mug can do that pretty well all by himself. Just a few questions about RAZR." I paused and raised an eyebrow at him. In response, he looked back and forth from me to Mug. "If that's okay with you?" I added.

"Done is done. Right?" He shrugged and punched Mug in his massive chest.

Mug and I walked inside, and Jamie Lee closed the door. I heard the deadbolt clack shut again. A careful and protective guy. I wondered where all of Jamie Lee's millions had gone and whether someone was coming to get the rest.

"What can I get you?" Jamie Lee said, motioning toward the built-in bar in the sunken living room. A bank of large windows looked out onto a pool and the lake, though the inlet was dry behind his house.

Mug and I took diet colas and sat around a glass coffee table on a comfy faux leather sofa. Jamie Lee freshened his drink straight from a bottle of Makers Mark, pouring two-thirds up the tall glass. He had spilled a bit outside, after all.

"Tell me about this medicine bottle of RAZR you got with instructions and warnings on it."

Jamie Lee frowned again, took a drink, swallowed,

puckered his lips and shifted his gaze up to the right of his eyebrows, as if searching for a long-lost memory.

"Bottle with instructions? Warnings?"

I looked at Mug. He glanced at me. We both knew someone had gotten to Jamie Lee, or maybe he'd developed a bad case of Alzheimer's in a month.

"Man, you told me ..." Mug said.

"Yeah, I guess I've said a lot of things I don't remember lately." He bounced an open palm off the side of his head. "Too many helmet-to-helmet interceptions, you know?"

He smiled. "But I do remember all those touchdown interceptions." He took a large swallow and looked out onto the lake.

"Salvation Labs has been here, haven't they?" I said.

He kept staring at the lake, then shook his head. "Hey, I'm having a party on Saturday. Ya'll come on over."

Down the carpeted stairs to my left a thin, olive-skinned woman with thick eyebrows and a hook nose came walking, or rather sashaying, wearing a gold bikini—barely.

Jamie Lee put his drink on the table and stood. "This is Bianca. Bianca this is Var and my good friend, Mug."

"Allo," she said in an accent I couldn't place. She offered a sexy smile and walked around the open side of the living room toward Jamie Lee, showing Mug and I all of her long legs and butt, all skin except a thin gold sliver between her cheeks. "I'm going in the pool." She glanced at Mug and me, "Join me?"

Jamie Lee, for the first time, looked unsure of himself. "Go on out, baby. I need to talk to these guys a minute."

She stopped at his chair, bent at the waist, offering the whole estate to me and Mug, and kissed Jamie Lee long and slow, with lots of tongue. They parted lips with a sucking sound, and she put a hand inside his tank top and he winced. "Don't take long," she whispered loudly enough for us to hear.

She turned her head, gave me a sly grin, and then went out the sliding glass door.

The door shut, and I took a deep breath, squeezed my eyes shut, then opened them and looked at Jamie Lee. He had a wan grin on his face and was still watching Bianca, as she strolled around the pool.

"What happened to your wife?" I asked.

Jamie Lee came back to me slowly. He took the last of the Makers down in one long swig. "She left."

"Bianca is nice. Is she foreign?"

He stood up. "Are we done here?"

Mug stood and glowered at Jamie Lee.

I tapped Mug on the shoulder and started walking to the front door. "Yeah."

I heard Mug sigh and his steps sounded behind me. I expected Jamie Lee to be right behind us, but when I got to the door and turned around he was still in the living room, pulling off his tank top. I reached and turned the deadbolt, and heard him say, "Shit," under his breath. I turned and saw him jogging over to us in bare feet and the baggy shorts, his upper torso rippling with muscles.

"You forget something?" I said, knowing full well why he was at the door. He wanted to make sure the deadbolt hit home. As if his fence would keep any collector out of his backyard. As if he had more than two brain cells left from RAZR.

"Nah. Ya'll have a great day. Come by this Saturday for the party."

There were no hugs at the door. Mug and I stepped onto the porch. I didn't ask what time the party started. The door slammed, and the deadbolt clacked shut. Safe and sound. Yeah. Jamie Lee had some major money problems and major people coming after him. I was surprised he didn't answer the door with a gun in one hand instead of a drink. Then again, he was Jamie Lee.

Once we were in the car, I looked at Mug. His face was about as downtrodden and sad as any I'd seen.

"You think he got some more RAZR for the babe?" I said.

He looked up, one side of his mouth puckered in and his eyes accepting. "Yeah, probably."

I started the 4Runner. "Where do you think she's from?"

He shrugged. "Mexico, maybe?"

I backed out and drove off and remembered her accent—probably a bit further south. My meandering mind had kind of shut off. I needed to call Cromwell.

CHAPTER 24

The Trap

C romwell answered on the fourth ring, "Var, we're in trouble."

"You're right, there." I paused. "Angela?"

I could hear a crowd in the background, people talking—and a man was crying. I pulled over to the side of the road and pushed the warning flashers button.

"Yeah. And Buddy. He's gone off the reservation again." He paused. "Way off."

The man's crying became an angry shout, "I don't know! I had my head in the toilet!"

"Where are you, O.J.?" I asked. I used O.J. for endearment, to keep him close when I sensed real trouble.

"I'm at the Stanley Hotel in Estes Park."

"Sounds like you're off the reservation a bit, too"

"Still my jurisdiction."

"Where are Buddy and Angela?"

"They're gone. They took the body with them."

"A body? Jesus. Who was killed?"

"Can't say right now."

"Did Angela or Buddy kill this unknown personage?"

"Not directly. Listen, the Estes Park police and the Park Rangers are here. There was a frackers party. Angela, some girls, the Judge, Buddy ... It's complicated. I have to clear up a lot of crap. What you could do is go to the canyon road and look for a black Suburban. They left about ten minutes ago, so you should see them in about thirty. Angela has a gun and Buddy is kinda with her. You know how he is with women. You got anyone with some beef who can help you?"

I looked at Mug. "Grade A, corn fed." I paused. "Buddy is with Angela?"

"Yeah, I told you it's complicated. I didn't tell anyone else about him. I'd call backup, but I don't want to get Buddy into trouble."

"What do you want me to do?"

"Follow them back to the Judge's and once they're there, keep them there. If you have to, cuff Angela and the Judge. I don't think the girls will give you any trouble. They're kids, really. Jesus, this stinks. If Buddy's in this, he'll fry. You have cuffs?"

"Girls? What the hell is going on?"

"I can't explain now. Oil guys, frackers, Angela, Buddy. And I gotta hell of a headache. That bitch. Shit! There are seven girls ... uh six, now. Skinny and young and ... God damn it! One's dead, probably in the back of the Suburban. So you'll need that many cuffs and one for Angela. I don't know if you'll need to cuff Buddy. Oh, and the Judge was there, too."

A muffled woman's voice sounded and Cromwell said, "I gotta go." He disconnected the call.

Mug had one eyebrow raised at me.

"Pop the glove box," I said. "See if there is a baggie with plastic ties."

He popped it and found the clear plastic Ziploc bag with the black Plasticuffs inside. Looked like about twenty. Plenty.

"Good. Keep them out. We're going looking for a

friend of mine. And a judge. And his wife. It sounds like there was a murder, too. And there might be a body."

I gave Mug an apologetic look. "Are you okay with this?"

"A body?"

I whipped a U-turn and headed west to the Thompson River canyon entrance. It took about ten minutes. The road curved right, going north up a hill. It was wider here, and I accelerated to sixty. In a minute the road descended and curved left. Ahead on the right was the Dam Store sitting above the river, overlooking a dam, though it wasn't really a dam but a diversion. I heard they had great tee shirts I thought about pulling into their small parking lot, facing the car out, and waiting there. Maybe they were having a wet tee shirt party. Maybe my loopy brain needed to get back in the game.

"What kind of car are we looking for?" Mug said.

"Black Suburban."

"You said it's your friend, and some others?"

I didn't want to tell him *the* Judge, the very same guy who was handling his case. But Mug was no dummy.

"Just a lady I know, some women, and a guy."

I turned us around and headed back south up the hill. A right turn ahead led to a ranch, but only two bare posts on either side of the "Side-Bar Ranch" sign could possibly provide coverage, and while it was a nice sign made of iron, Angela would see my car and know it right away.

"Who are the women?" Mug said.

I glanced at him. This was going to get complicated fast. If we had to detain Angela and the Judge and nothing came of it, Mug's case with Salvation Labs would be toast.

"Let me find a place to park and we'll talk."

He shrugged and shook his head, like he was used to people dismissing his opinions.

"It's complicated, Mug. Let me think about this for a few minutes."

"Okay."

The road went downhill and curved left. There was a knife-making shop on the left, but it, too, sat close to the road. The road curved right, then around a big bend to the left. There was a right turn to Carter Lake, the way to Cromwell's place. But without trees or buildings, the intersection offered no place to hide. I didn't turn. The road straightened, passed over the Big Thompson River. A funky Bohemian restaurant sat on a slight hill to the left. Looked like a Quonset hut displaced in Hansel and Gretel: bright white and pastel with gingerbread shutters. I'd be afraid to eat there. Might be the main course. Also, no cover to drive out from easily.

The road wound right. Tucked back into trees was a motel with camping spots. Across the road was a saddle-maker's shop with lots of surrounding trees. I turned into the saddle shop parking lot and pulled a hard left, curling around a big cottonwood and nudging in as close to the huge tree as I could, still allowing room for me to open my door if needed. I turned off the lights and waited. The 4Runner faced up the canyon, hidden from the road by the five-foot tree trunk on the left and the saddle-maker's shop on the right. I could gun the car and be on the road in a heartbeat. Perfect.

This was one of the few places trees remained after last year's thousand-year flood. The saddle maker had been here for decades, survived pretty much intact at the hundred-year flood in '76. But 2013 had wiped out his shop, and he had to build again. Lots of locals helped him with labor and money. They liked him, needed his shop. Plus, that's how people were around here. They helped out when their friends needed them.

I had a good view of the road for about a hundred yards up the canyon. There were no streetlights on this side and the shop blocked most of the headlights from those cars coming down the canyon.

"Okay," Mug said.

"Yeah. Umm. I may have to drop you off."

"I though you needed my help."

"That was before I thought it through."

Mug scratched the right side of his face and sighed. "The judge in the car is Judge Craghead, isn't he?"

I felt my lips pucker and I looked at the ceiling. "Yeah, and if you get into this, and we have to detain the Judge, and then he's released, your case with RAZR goes out the window."

"Wasn't that a cop you were talking to before?"

"Yeah. O.J. Cromwell. Deputy O.J. Cromwell of the Thompson Sherriff's office.

"So these people in the Suburban—the lady, some women, and the Judge—are breaking the law, and may have murdered someone?"

"Yeah. Possibly. I don't know. O.J. was a bit vague on the details."

Mug looked out the window. "Is Deputy Cromwell usually right about things?"

I thought of the case with the broken glass, the hooker, the glass blower, and how O.J. stewed about it. "Usually, yeah. Let me put it this way: Lately he's obsessed with getting things right."

"And he's your friend?"

I nodded and glanced at my watch. The Suburban should be driving by any minute.

Mug gripped one hand over and over. "Lisa found nothing. Jamie Lee forgot everything. I don't have a case anyhow. I'm staying to help you."

I didn't like it, but there was no way I could physically put him out of the car.

So we waited.

And waited.

CHAPTER 25

Buddy and Angela

Before Buddy smiled at Detective C outside hotel room 218, he'd been downstairs holding the mirror down by his waist, tilted toward the center round table. The band was playing Alan Jackson's "Here in the Real World." Angela looked beautiful through the mirror, but Buddy also saw she was not a nice person. He hadn't seen all of what Angela had done through his mirror, just the parts about using the girls. Not nice, but none of us were, when it came down to it, at least in his experience. Yet there was bad and there was worse. The Judge was going to kill her, and he had to stop that. Had to. So when Detective C followed bachelor number two up the stairs, he figured it was time to make his move.

He pocketed his mirror and dashed over to the round table, stopping right up beside Angela, close enough to feel her body heat. He wanted to look in her eyes but only glanced at her face. A normal person would have sensed him and backed off a step. She merely looked at him, unflinching, as if daring him to touch her. He glanced away, stared at her hands. "You are in danger, Angela."

Her hands clench into fists. "What ...Who ... Oh, Mr. Hollister, what are you doing here?"

The band ended the song. There was a lull in the room, as if all the guests were tired of small talk. Hollister's Aunt Betty once told him it was like that at times in a crowded room, even at square dances she used to go to, out at her father's farm east of Greeley. It was a raucous event with laughing, stomping, and country music that could make your heart sing. But there would be times when the music stopped, and everyone would stop talking. That was the time to say the most important thing. Like when Uncle Joe had popped the question to Aunt Betty.

Buddy looked up at Angela, into her eyes. They were dark eyes, full of mystery and wonder and undeniable hate. "The Judge ... He's going to—"

A gunshot upstairs shattered the silence. He stopped and looked at her legs: Long, brown and smooth. He looked away. Did she still keep the knife there?

"Mr. Hollister, can you come with me? I'm worried that might be one of my girlfriends."

"Sure." What else would he say? She needed help, that's what he was here for. He had a gun and could probably best anyone out there with one.

She motioned for her other girls with a hand to the exit. "

One of the men stood up and held the arm of his date. "No you don't. I paid my money, and this is my night."

Angela walked up to the man, causing him to step back, but she kept close and stuck a handgun in his belly. "You remember the rules. Anything goes wrong, you may have to forfeit your night. No refunds. These are not ordinary girls."

"But ..."

She pushed the barrel into his belly.

"Okay, okay." He shook his head, let go of the girl and sat in his chair.

"Go to the car," Angela told the girls. "I'll be there in a minute." She took one of the girl's elbows in her hand. "Nowhere else. The car. Do you understand me?" Buddy could tell she didn't want to leave them. Maybe he could take them to the car.

The Judge hurried into the room. He frowned at Angela. "It's room 218. Maia." He paused and eyed Buddy. "And Cromwell is here."

When Buddy saw the Judge and heard about Detective C, he wanted to run. He took a step away, but Angela's hand gripped his forearm. A vice grip of manly strength. All his muscles froze. He needed to help Detective C, but he couldn't move.

"Take the girls to the car and bring it to the side entrance. I'll take Mr. Hollister with me. He'll help me, isn't that right Mr. Hollister?"

Yes, he would. Of course he would. How did she know?

He nodded and her grip on him loosened.

The band started up again: Meatloaf's "Bat Out of Hell."

The Judge left with the girls. The men around the table started talking to each other.

Angela tugged Buddy's arm. "Let's go."

He took out his mirror as they walked up the stairs. She kept her gun in her hand at the side of her thigh all the way up the stairs. She knocked on door 218 and raised the gun.

Detective C opened the door and all Buddy could do was smile. Smiling didn't feel right to him, but it just happened.

Angela peered around Detective C. What she saw made her grit her teeth. "Move." Buddy had never heard a woman use that tone—like a marine sergeant at basic getting him to do more sit-ups. She motioned with the gun for Detective C to go to the bed. His face twisted in a mass of confusion. He must have believed Angela was in no mood to argue because he did what she said and stood beside the bed.

She raised her gun high and came down on Cromwell's head. Hard. He dropped to the carpeted floor with a muffled thump and didn't move. Buddy flinched. Cromwell would be okay. She could have killed him. He had to help Angela.

Buddy did what she ordered and hefted the body of the dead woman on the bed down the back stairs. The girl was much lighter than any girl he'd carried before. He walked out into the dark and gently put her into the back of the waiting Suburban, then hopped in the middle back seat beside all the young women. The Judge drove them down the canyon.

Angela sat in the front passenger seat and arranged the rearview mirror to observe Buddy and the girls. Buddy sat in the middle seat, two girls on his left and four in the back seat. He watched Angela in the mirror and the mirror gave him a preview of where they were going and what they were going to do. He looked at the back of the Suburban, knowing he should be helping Detective C, knowing he could jump over the back seat and open the back door and be out on the highway in less than ten seconds. But he didn't move. Couldn't. She was a woman who needed his help.

Except for the girls' occasional murmur in some foreign language Buddy could not fathom, the only sound was that of the engine gunning at times after slowing for turns. Angela turned around once when the murmurs became louder, eyes flashing at the girls, and they shut their mouths for the rest of the trip. The Suburban's headlights shown on the right canyon wall, the road, and the left canyon wall as they snaked down the canyon. The SUV didn't exactly take the downhill curves like a sports car, but the Judge wasn't a bad driver, so the tires didn't squeal at the turns, and Buddy had to brace himself only once to avoid falling off the middle seat.

He kept an eye on the road. After they passed the Dam Store on the left, then followed the road through a few curves until the Judge turned right at the Carter Lake road. They were going toward Detective C's house. It was a country farmhouse he rented from a local rancher. Cromwell had helped find his runaway daughter the year before. He liked the place because it was quiet and no one was around. Since Afghanistan he'd slept better away from people.

The headlights lit the straight paved road. In the distance, a few sparse lights shone out from infrequent homes—an area where acreage had been bought up twenty-five years ago to those lucky few. Two miles down and the Judge turned at a dirt road on the right, Detective C's road. Buddy wanted to grab the wheel and turn them around. He kept his cap bill pulled low but watched Angela through the mirror. He saw a mind video of the past: Angela stood over a man with a shovel. Dirt flew. Bodies in black plastic bags were dumped. Dirt was shoveled over the bodies. No words were spoken.

The Judge turned off a quarter mile before Detective C's home. The road wound northwest into a thicket of trees, then southwest down a scant hill. The Judge stopped and made a three-point turnaround, the Suburban's headlights sweeping across a meadow. They were about three hundred yards from Detective C's house.

The meadow was enclosed in pine trees on the south and west and a rock outcropping on the east. The road curved in from the north, then swept west again. The Judge backed the Suburban into the hidden pocket on the north side of the meadow. Some of the pine trees had died over time and prevailing westerly winds had toppled them into the meadow, making backing the Suburban any further than the small pull-in impossible.

The Judge stopped and turned off the SUV. The lights went out.

"Come on, Mr. Hollister," Angela said as she opened her door and got out. "I need your help."

She opened his door.

Buddy sat very still, feeling the hardness of his Glock in his front pocket, wondering where Angela's gun was. Could be she'd put it in the small of her back. He could end this right now. Shoot her and the Judge, then call Detective C. He would know what to do.

No. Not Angela. She was like Faith in the video game, as were all women to him. The hope of the world. Angela was a bit more special, since he feared the Judge would kill her. He couldn't shoot her.

"Please, Mr. Hollister." Her voice had changed to less authoritative. Not meek, but weaker.

The Judge had turned in his seat and eyed Buddy. Did he have a gun, too? Would Buddy be another corpse in their long line of murders?

He got out. He couldn't kill her. Was it the fearful pleading tone of her voice? Or knowing what he'd seen in the mirror that first day at the Judge's house, knowing he would slash her with the knife and watch the blood spurt? No. It was more than that. It was deep inside him. A belief, a faith he'd had since childhood, since Aunty Betty. Even though he knew what she wanted, he had to help her. They had stopped at this spot many times before, knew exactly where to go, he was sure of it, and he still had to help her.

She had a flashlight that played nervously around on the ground like she was confused or had some kind of nerve problem. The beam steadied, and she moved it in a straight line, back and forth toward the rear of the Suburban. "Grab ... her," she said with a hitch in her voice as if she'd been crying, "and follow me over to the field."

He wanted to say, "You don't have to do this." But he grabbed the girl's body and hefted it onto his shoulder as he had in the hotel. The girl was so light, he judged her barely over a hundred pounds. Angela reached around him, her lithe body firm against his hip, and felt under the backseat. She pulled out a shovel, shut the back end, and shone the flashlight beam onto the ground in front of him. She was so polite. It was a moonless night and he was thankful for the beam.

He had no trouble carrying the body, though he took big steps over the deadfall of trees. Buddy wasn't big, but he'd always been strong. Maybe it came from working on Aunt Betty's farm. And he certainly hadn't grown weaker hauling seventy-five-pound packs over mountain deserts in Afghanistan. At least, not in his muscles.

He trudged beside her about twenty yards and felt the earth give way to a soft loam under his feet. Reminded him of a field after plowing, ready for seed. He stepped in a firmer patch and the smell of fresh cow patties wafted up. A few open-range steers and cattle grazed around. He wanted to wipe his foot.

"Wait." She played the light over the ground in searching arcs. "Twenty feet to your right and put her down."

He liked the way she didn't say "the body" but instead, "her." It was only one of many things he liked about Angela.

In the distance a coyote howled, and his brothers joined him. He thought of Detective C and Var, and the muzzle flashes and pops of hundreds of guns on another moonless night. But it hadn't been on this planet. Couldn't have been.

He walked twenty feet to his right.

"Good. Put her down there. Gently."

He did. Gently.

"I will dig first, then you. It won't take long. She deserves better than this..." Her voice weakened and trailed off. He wanted to put an arm around her.

Then she cleared her throat. "But it has to be."

She put the flashlight down, put gloves on, and in the roving bits of light he saw her tears glistening upon her cheeks. She started to dig, but he took hold of her arm and clutched the shovel. He dug and tossed dirt over and over. In twenty minutes, he'd finished everything and was patting the dirt down that he'd shoveled over her grave.

He stood and stretched his back, thinking she should

say something over the grave. He started to turn and ask her when he felt the hard, cold nub of a gun in his back. Angela patted his lower back and his pants and found his gun. She started to drag it out but her glove caught and stopped it. He moved to the side and she was able to pull it out.

"You stay here," she said. "I have to get my husband." Her voice was no longer meek, but hard as granite. He couldn't see her face, but he was sure the tears were long dry.

This felt bad. Was she going to kill him after all? Or maybe she was going to kill the Judge.

The flashlight beam bounced across the field toward the Suburban. He followed her, not making a sound.

CHAPTER 26

Plan B

Boy, right about now I could use my mind flying around and finding Buddy and Angela. No dice. I leaned forward and looked hard at every dark, boxy, SUV-like vehicle that passed by. Not many. Mostly trucks and crossovers. Then, after checking my watch and beginning to think all was over, I saw it: a cruising black form similar to all the FBI Suburbans Harrison Ford drove in, in *Clear and Present Danger*. I waited for it to pass and eased out, keeping my head-lights off and letting it get a few hundred yards ahead.

"I don't think so," Mug said.

"Whadya mean?"

"Get a little closer so I can make sure we're following the right people."

"I don't want to get too close. They'll—"

"I need to see the license plate."

"I saw green." I was pretty sure it was a Colorado plate. But, then again I was looking more for the shape and style of the vehicle. I should have asked O.J. for the plate number.

We cruised around a curve to the left and my head-lights were off to the right of the SUV. The road straightened, and I got close enough to see.

"Montana. Damn," I said. I let up on the gas a bit and

checked the rearview, hoping there was not another SUV behind me. Murphy's law predicted that after waiting so long for a Suburban to come, another would follow right after.

Mug was quiet, the kind of polite person who doesn't say "I told you so." No one was behind me, so I turned left into the Cowboy Church, wondering at marketing religion to cowboys, and got back on the road going west, back to my hidey-hole at the saddle-maker's shop. There, I turned in and waited. Again.

After twenty minutes, I started to wonder if I'd missed them, which I doubted considering Mug's sharp eyes. Maybe they'd turned off somewhere before they got to me. Or maybe they had not been going to the Judge's house.

Mug fidgeted. He'd been patient, *more* than patient. He hadn't asked anymore questions. But I knew he was thinking the same thing I was and wanted to be done with waiting.

I waited another ten minutes before trying O.J.'s phone. Unfortunately, we were out of cell phone service unless we drove another curve or two east, closer to the town of Loveland. I started to pull out, then saw O.J.'s crappy little Honda come cruising around the bend. I flashed high beams, and he pulled in parallel to me. I buzzed down Mug's window.

"You miss them?" O.J. said, his arm resting on his window, casual.

"We've been here the whole time. They must have gone somewhere else."

"Maybe," he paused and rolled his neck. He put a finger in one ear like he was cleaning out a lot of wax, then looked dead at me. "I'm going to the Judge's house to see."

"You want us to come?"

"Nah. I can handle this. I thought about it on the way down. Buddy's too far gone this time. I don't need two civilians getting shot. I'm calling in backup when I get cell service."

I agreed that Mug should go home. But me? "Maybe you should talk to him first." Buddy was, for all his weirdness, a great guy and had always been good to me and O.J., especially in Afghanistan.

He stared at me around Mug's huge frame.

"We're not in-country anymore. This is the USA, and just because he has a thing for women doesn't mean he can help them with illegal trafficking, and possibly murder. It just doesn't flush."

My leg stump itched. I remembered Buddy and Fallujah, and his continued vindication of women in Afghanistan after I arrived. It was one week after Buddy killed yet another asshole who'd slit another woman's throat. Probably the beginnings of ISIS. Those guys loved their knives. Things like that can sometimes drive a man so wacky that he forgets who his friends are. Not Buddy. That fucking IED blew, the Humvee landed on its side, and I would have been a crispy critter if not for him. He had a great smile, kind eyes, and strong arms that pulled me from the burning Humvee. And he acquired some ugly scars from the burns.

"Yeah, well maybe Angela is being forced into a bad situation by the Judge. Buddy told you that, right? I think he deserves the benefit of the doubt," I said. "If you don't call him, I will."

He scratched his temple and squeezed his eyes shut like he wanted this to all go away. Then he opened them. "Yeah. I hear you. I'll let you know when I get to the Judge's." His window went up before I could say anything else, and he sped out of the parking lot onto the road toward Loveland, magnetic police flasher on top, strobing red and blue.

I buzzed up Mug's window and followed O.J. for a mile, but he was cruising fast and I didn't have a police flasher, nor was I legally helping him, so I slowed and looked over at Mug. My house was another five miles. He lived about ten miles away. "You mind crashing at my place? I'm toast. If I drive you all the way home, then—"

"Sure. No problem."

I called Buddy and got his voicemail. "Buddy, please, call me. You're in a world of shit. I can help you. Call me."

I drove on, wondering if Buddy had finally split with reality. As a physician I had often wondered about the intricacies of the human mind and how it coped with disasters. The only conclusion I reached was this one: Everyone is different. Buddy hid behind mirrors. But it was more than that. Something had twisted inside his brain, and he could see things others couldn't. Cromwell told me he had a smidgen of future-cast even before the woman bled out in the room of mirrors in Fallujah. Afterward, that smidgen had ballooned into a mountain—and he'd saved our asses many a time.

I should just ignore O.J.'s order, drop off Mug and go find Buddy.

"Who's Buddy?" Mug said.

"A guy who saved my life in the war."

"I figured you were in Iraq."

"He was there with Cromwell many years before I

met them in Afghanistan. We were all together for almost a year."

"What happened?"

"A lot of shit. A lot of very bad shit."

"Sorry."

He pushed the switch and his window went down again. Cool air rushed in. It felt good on my forehead.

"Who's Angela?" he said.

"A woman I used to love. But she's changed."

"It happens."

"Yeah."

I thought about Lisa and Angela. Lisa might still be at my house. Why was I still even considering Angela? Because I loved her first? Because her photo kept me going even after losing all my shit, and an arm and a leg? Because I thought the Judge was bullying her? After all, the Judge had that reputation. But what if Angela was actually helping with this trafficking of young women? Lisa had her head on straight. And she had been there with me since the IED. I knew it, but since coming back and seeing Angela, I'd stuffed it away, the fact that Lisa more than just put up with me.

Mug was a big boy. He could stay in the spare bedroom. Lisa was with me. If I stayed.

I hooked a left and drove north on the Masonville road. It was a nice night, other than all the shit that had happened. Kept happening. But that was the way life was. You had to enjoy good moments when they arrived. The stars were out, no moon, and the air was cool enough I could sleep with the windows open.

"You got any food?" Mug said.

"Sure. Tons. Might even have a steak or two. I got an extra bike that might fit you, too. Maybe we could take a ride in the morning." A friend of mine had been long-legged and gave up road biking for mountain biking, so I kept his road bike in my basement. I made sure to keep air in the tires so they didn't dry rot like one of my bikes had done.

"Sounds good," he said.

"My girlfriend, Lisa, might be over tonight, and she rides, too." There. I'd said it—my girlfriend.

"No problem."

I crested a rise and my cell phone rang. The caller ID said Angela. Oh, man.

"Hello, Angela. What's going on? Are you running illegals? Where's Buddy."

"Var, I need your help. The Judge has been killed. Buddy Hollister did it.

I slowed down. "What?"

"He just shot my husband in cold blood. I don't know what came over him."

"Where are you?"

"At home."

"Good. Detective O.J. Cromwell will be there soon."

The line disconnected.

I called back and got her voicemail.

Man, come on brain, do your traveling act. Nothing. Not sure if I liked getting back to normal.

I tried again with the same result. What the hell was going on? I was right. Buddy shot the Judge because he *was* bullying Angela. Or worse. Maybe the Judge tried to kill her. No way in hell would Buddy let that happen.

I called O.J. and also got voicemail. I said, "O.J., call me. I just got a call from Angela saying Buddy shot the Judge at their house. I'm on my way."

I ended the call and put the phone down in my drink

holder.

"Looks like we won't be having that steak," Mug said.

"Yeah." I turned the car around. "You want me to drop you at your house? We'll be going pretty close."

Mug peered over at me. "Are you kidding? I'm not leaving you. This is great!"

Great. Yeah. The woman I loved most of my adult life and my friend who saved my life were involved in a murder, or two, and my other best friend who had a hard-on about getting things police-right was about to arrest them.

Just great.

I kicked the 4Runner into overdrive.

CHAPTER 27

Where Is Buddy?

T he door to the Judge's house was open, a mirror in the interior foyer reflected Cromwell's headlights as he eased his crappy little Honda up the driveway. Dread crawled and twisted in his gut. The garage door was closed. There was no Suburban outside.

Cromwell had tried to call Buddy on his way, leaving a message to call him. But he got no call back.

He put it in park and cut the engine. Everything pitched into black quiet, an absence of light and sound most city people had never seen. It was like falling into a rabbit hole of black cotton. He called Buddy again, same result. But he didn't hear his phone ring outside. Maybe he put it on vibrate.

His phone buzzed and lit up and alerted him about my voicemail. He found my message, cut down the volume on the speaker and listened to it while he watched the front of the house and acquired night vision. Message over, he put the phone on the passenger seat and tried to think things through.

There was no sign of Angela or Buddy. If Buddy were still here and thinking clearly, he would have the situation tied up in a nice bow and hand it over. But if he was scared and gone batshit and inside waiting, or out in the sagebrush somewhere looking in …? Cromwell strained his eyes and tried to force his vision to adjust as he peered out at the dark splotches of sagebrush. If Buddy was out there and feeling threatened, Cromwell might be toast. Buddy wouldn't kill him, but he could easily shoot him in the leg. Crap.

So the light wouldn't come on when he opened the door, he flicked the overhead light switch to off before he eased the door handle up. There was a slight click, and he swung the door open. The door hinge creaked as soft as a weak cricket. Crouching behind the door, he peered around it at the gaping hole where the front door should have been. There was just no nice reason it was open.

No shots came. Two egg-shaped boxwood evergreen shrubs stood on either side of the entrance porch like portly guards. The one on his left was in front of the picture window—poor cover. He ran toward the one on the right and slipped into the spot between it and the garage wall. Not safe, because a bullet through the bush would still get him, but at least covered.

But no bullets came.

He waited, caught his breath. A breeze was picking up, cooling the sweat on the back of his neck. "Buddy," he yelled, "it's me, O.J. All I want to do is talk."

A gust blew, and the door knocked against its stop. The place felt empty. Had Buddy really killed the Judge? Could he have finally lost it and killed Angela and the girls, and left in the Suburban? Maybe the Judge, but not the women. He hoped. Buddy's mind was not the most stable. He might do anything.

He breathed in and out twice, easy, then made his decision. He ran to the front entrance, reached around to the inside, felt the foyer light switch and flicked it on, but stayed outside, taking cover behind the doorjamb.

Nothing.

"Don't shoot me, Buddy. I just want to talk."

He did a couple of peekaboos around the jamb. No one. The interior looked neat and undisturbed. The mirror he'd seen in the headlights had a gash over the frame: the same mirror Buddy had told him about from the ranch. That mirror had a history. Seeing it, O.J. felt his guts twist tighter. Maybe Buddy had killed himself, too.

Where *was* Buddy? Had Angela's call been a ruse to get him here while she and the Judge fled with the girls?

The sound of a car engine whining in the distance behind him made him look back. Headlights were bouncing and what looked like a small SUV was traveling fast over the road toward him.

Fucking Var.

♪ ♫

Fucking Var. Yeah, I knew that's what Cromwell was thinking, though, at this point my mind didn't allow me to read his thoughts. I just knew him too well. He'd known, and now resolved in his mind the reason I was coming. I owed Buddy. Though so did Cromwell. So did our whole squad back in Afghanistan. That's why I knew Cromwell would probably not have called for backup. He owed Buddy that.

I pulled in beside his crappy little Honda in the driveway, saw him standing beside the front doorway, and killed the 4Runner's engine. The headlights died. I opened the door and pulled out my Glock. I had been on the verge of sleep not twenty minutes ago, but now I was adrenaline hyped. My pupils must have already been dilated from the adrenaline because night vision came fast. There was a slight buzz in my head. I would have to be careful aiming the gun—my hands were shaking.

I whispered, "Stay here, Mug."

"No problem," he hoarsely whispered and held out the flashlight.

"Nah. I'll just use O.J.'s." I couldn't hold it anyhow in the salute-shaped prosthetic hand I was wearing.

I opened the door.

"You shouldn't have come." O.J.'s Louisiana drawl seemed too loud. My ears were on hyperalert.

"Hey, O.J. What's the deal?" I whispered.

"The door was wide open when I got here. I don't think anyone's here." He didn't bother to whisper. Cool as the night.

"Fucking Angela," I said a bit louder, feeling calmer. And I'm sure he was thinking the same thing—she lied.

"Yeah."

"Where's your backup?"

He ignored me. "I'm going in. Probably no one here, but cover me just the same."

He ducked low and ran into the foyer.

I squinted into the light and aimed over his shoulder. My gun shivered, and not from the cold. I took a few deep breaths and concentrated. The gun steadied.

No shots sliced through the silence. No sound at all except the quickstep of O.J.'s shoes on the wood floors. I stepped in behind him and was glad I'd put on good running shoes with relatively new soles. The traction on the floors was great. Hardly a limp as I crossed the foyer and took the two stairs to the living room and kitchen.

O.J. had turned on the lights to the kitchen and

stopped at the door to the basement. I sensed he knew the answers were there but was hesitant to open that humongous can of worms—a Judge and his wife as sex traffickers—that can of worms might eat up the county. This was not Miami or Tijuana. Something like this would bring in the Feds and the national news. He'd left New Orleans to get away from all that. But with this, his quiet little job in a town with less than one murder a year would be over. It seemed he was a shit magnet.

He stepped forward and tried the door. It opened, and he stepped inside. The light went on and I could hear his steps on the stairs. The can opener had been applied, only these worms had come from tremendous cans. I envisioned the huge sand worms from the movie *Beetlejuice* invading every newsroom in Fort Collins. Yep, I was feeling less stressed. Sure.

I followed him, scanning the kitchen and living room. There were no empty cups or glasses or plates anywhere. The kitchen's stainless steel and tile sparkled. You could eat off that floor, even if you weren't a Marine who'd eaten bugs and dandelion salad.

I didn't go down the stairs, but stayed in the kitchen, looking around. If someone was setting us up, I didn't want both of us trapped with Mug outside waiting to be shot. The door to the garage was closed; stairs with handrail led up to a dark second floor. It was deathly quiet.

From downstairs came a bang.

I jumped.

"Shit!" It was O.J.'s shout. Had someone shot him? Though, thinking about it, did that bang sound like a gunshot.

Steps came back up the stairs.

I aimed at the basement door, the gun shaking again.

The door opened and O.J. walked into the kitchen. "I gotta get a warrant. The door is locked down there; couldn't kick it open."

That was good, right? No big can of worms yet.

He looked at my gun and frowned. I lowered it and sighed heavily.

He eyed the door to the garage, then glanced at me. I nodded. It was the obvious place.

In three big strides he was across the kitchen. He flung the door open and turned on the light to the garage. In several quick steps, I was right behind him with the Glock.

The black Suburban's engine ticked. Long pauses between ticks indicating it had been off for at least ten minutes. Angela's black Lexus was long gone.

The smell of gasoline and exhaust registered at the same time I saw the windshield. I gritted my teeth and felt sour acid coat the back of my throat. The driver's side windshield was splattered from the inside with blood and gray matter and whitish bone splinters.

God, I hoped those were not Angela's or Buddy's brains on the windshield.

CHAPTER 28

The Hidey-Hole

Angela drove just under the speed limit through Loveland on Highway 34, picked it up going north on I-25, east on Highway 14 to the Purcell road, then found the back, dirt roads. She held the wheel with her right hand, her left had started to cramp and shake again. Her headlights were like lighthouse beacons cutting through the darkness ahead. Sagebrush and wheat fields and the occasional lone cottonwood loomed. The damn dust and muddy potholes were anathema to her beautiful Lexus. She winced at each ping and cracking sounds of a gravel and rocks. That better be under the car and not on the paint. *As if that really mattered now.* This was not what she'd hoped for tonight, but she was ready. The trailer was east of Nunn, secluded and far from her home in the foothills. She'd inherited the land from an aunt ten years ago and soon realized a better purpose than rental housing for oil men. The trailer she'd bought with her remaining cash would keep her and her girls safe when needed. Like now.

The girls whimpered in the back. A controllable level of emotion. Occasionally Angela adjusted the rearview to study them for signs of RAZR overuse. But none of them were getting hysterical. Why had Maia done it? Probably she'd hated what she was doing so much she'd taken extra RAZR each time to give her the nerve. The extra dosing must have sent her over the edge. If only she had made it past today. Maybe Angela had pushed her too hard, but she couldn't think about that right now. Tears blurred her vision and she swiped them away with the back of her hand. She swerved to the outside of the dirt road and her tires spun. She turned back onto the middle of the road and gritted her teeth, forcing the tears back.

She had to think positively. She was free of the Judge. He would never threaten or abuse her or the girls again. Surely Var would agree with the end of the Judge's hold on her. She did still love Var. Would he come back to her? Should she even try? Would he even take her after all ... this?

She stretched her left hand in front of her. The shakes and cramping were gone and she gripped it into a fist. She felt cheated over the years she'd spent with the Judge, but worse, she despised how easily he'd fooled her. Her anger welled in her and helped clear the tears. How stupid she'd been. Just like her mother, she suffered a blind spot and weakness for abusive men. The Judge hadn't beat her like her father. But thinking back on it, his psychological abuse had gradually escalated, especially after the girls. All she had ever wanted with him, was to love him like Var. Then she had tried to have a child, thinking it might help. RAZR was supposed to help that, but it only screwed her life up more. She'd become another statistic, a woman like the women she'd seen in ERs in med school. Abused children became abused women—and not by just one abuser but by multiple abusers, over and over. They would even beg to keep the abuser out of jail. She'd always wondered how that could be true.

She glanced in the rearview at her drawn face and wanted to find a cliff and drive off it. She was such a loser. She shook her head, trying to get those thoughts to go.

This crazy world she had got herself into—the trafficking, the sexual enhancement, the secrecy, the panicking at possibly getting caught—it had started for a good cause.

The vision of her tiny brother in the ICU with tubes and IVs coming out of him like some alien torture would never leave her. His face filled with pain, fear, panic—all things he suffered too many times at home while her mother was crapped out after a fifth of rum. Or after Angela's great NFL star father had beat her mother senseless. It was necessity for Angela to always be there for her brother.

But the last time she could not save him. They told her that dying of asthma wasn't unusual. They told her it happened in cases like his. They told her they could do nothing more than they had. Children still died of asthma every damn day. But she was so close to helping stop that. All she had needed was more money. Initially the Judge had helped after her inheritance ran out, but she'd soon realized how fowl his stench, so it had been up to her. The infertility and sex drugs were there, so why not use them?

Now it was shot to hell.

Or was it? Maybe she could turn this around. If she got the Judge's life insurance that should be enough. But Buddy had to take the fall.

A loud drumming of a cattle guard sounded under

the Lexus and her headlights shone in the vast cave of nothingness ahead, lighting the white-tan road ahead, like the Yellow Brick Road. Or the River Styx.

The girls murmuring had gotten too loud. "Shush, my angels," she said in Brazilian Portuguese. She had to get it together. This was a crucial night. She could not be caught, and if she got the girls delivered, that deep pain that had been clawing at her gut since the first time her father had abused her, maybe it would lessen. It had to.

"We will be there soon," she said as soothingly as she could.

They quieted. The engine purred, gravel dinged the frame, and she wished she hadn't done this to Hollister. Buddy. Var's friend who had saved his life. A kind soul, despite his craziness. But it was her only way out. Insanity could be his plea.

Oh, Var. Why did you get bit by the patriotism spider? The poison filled you with more desire for your country than for me.

That was that. Then was then. Now was now. It would all work out.

She pressed on the accelerator. She would make it work out.

Another twenty minutes and they were at the trailer. The closest farm was about ten miles. The trailer had well water, propane, and a relatively quiet generator. There was enough gas in the shed out back to run the lights, fridge, and heater, if they needed it, for the next several days. She had also stocked up on kerosene lamps if she didn't want to run the generator. The girls were used to that, or at least had been before coming to the States. They might have to get used to it again, if her plans for the night failed.

The trailer was a tan-olive color that blended in with the surrounding plains, and every window was shaded and curtained. She pulled the Lexus twenty feet from the front door and turned off the engine but kept the headlights on.

"Let's go," she said, authoritative again.

They all piled out, six girls and her with the flashlight. She opened the trunk and pulled out three bags of groceries full of canned and packaged goods, snacks and pop, and gave one each to three of the girls. Then she slung her strapped hand purse over her neck and one shoulder and walked to the front door of the trailer, unlocked and opened it and moved aside for them. "Put the groceries in the kitchen. Open the windows to freshen it up. Don't bother with the bedroom on the left. That's my room." She touched the shoulder of one of the girls without groceries, the one with the long neck. "Taygeta, take this." She opened the drawer of a stand by the couch and got out the butane candle lighter and handed it to her. "Light the lanterns over there and in the bathroom. Then you take the first shower. And don't stay in very long. We need water for all." She had to have every trace of evidence down the drain. And they had to smell great for what she hoped would get started tonight.

The three girls with groceries put them in the kitchen, then joined two others opening the windows. Taygeta lit the lantern in the living room and then trotted to the bathroom. After the last few months, they knew Aunt Angela only gave instructions that were important. They did as they were told.

After Angela had bought the trailer, she had it towed

out here without the Judge's knowledge. It had taken weeks to furnish but was reasonably comfortable now. There was even a DVD and CD player. The generator had to be started once a month, which she managed. They were off the grid, except for cell phones, and she usually used burners. She'd disabled the GPS in her personal phone. There really was no way for anyone to trace money or bills to this place. Pablo had showed her similar places he'd used in New Mexico and Utah. It had worked well there, too. In Utah, particularly, where men and girls were so obedient. Hopefully she would not have to test the Mormon girls.

Maybe she'd go back there after this was all over. But she was sure Pablo wouldn't let her go. She had to get out from under him, another abusive man.

No. Not yet. She would be fine. Continue the ruse that she would stay here indefinitely. Could that work with Pablo? But she needed just another hundred thousand for the asthma drug and Salvation Labs would start production. The profits from what she had planned next would get her by for a few weeks until the insurance money came in from the Judge's death. If all the puzzle pieces fell into the right place, Mr. Hollister would be accused of the Judge's murder, and she would be back in her house within the week. Would she be able to put Pablo off long enough to leave? What about Var? Would he come with her?

She felt another pang of guilt at what she'd done with Buddy. He seemed so simple and devoted to her. The police would arrest him right away, especially Cromwell. He knew about Buddy's prior manslaughter charge after his aunt's death. A jury would not convict Buddy, she felt sure. No. They would see him insane, just as he had been after his aunt's death.

But, she didn't want to hurt Var, even though he *had* left her. She did forgive him, didn't she? Could he forgive her?

Her thoughts kept popping around her head like hot grease. Disjointed. The RAZR from earlier.

She went outside to the opened trunk of the Lexus. The Judge's shotgun barrel glinted on the right side, as did another flashlight for the girls' room behind the cargo net. She eyed the ten boxes full of RAZR. She grabbed six bottles out of the open box, one for each girl, and put them in an empty Walmart bag. She took another bottle for her, shoved it between her breasts. No telling what the next hours might bring. She might need the extra strength. With the flashlight and Walmart bag in her left hand, the shotgun in her right, she elbowed the trunk closed.

Inside, she surveyed the living room. The mattresses made it crowded on the floor, but better than six feet under like poor Maia. If all went according to plan, the girls would only be here a few more hours. Six girls left —six pro football teams. Six teams that were the most likely for the playoffs. Each girl for one key player. The players were already hooked on RAZR, and from the girl's reports, they were already having tremors. Just one or two playoff games and it would be all over. Doing this to pro football was worth all the problems. She hoped her father would roll over in his grave and never have peace. What was she thinking? He was writhing from flames in hell. Hopefully her jolting pro football would save some other wives or daughters from her fate.

She went into the bedroom at the end of the

hall where two girls bustled about, making beds. She dropped the flashlight on a bed and walked across the hallway to her bedroom and propped the shotgun behind the door. The girls were talking again, their voices more animated with happy notes. She sat on the bed and put the bag of RAZR next to her.

Angela pulled a burner phone out of the drawer of the bedside table, punched in a number on her cell phone, her NFL connection, a guy who bet a lot of money on the teams she had targeted. He had been anxious to get more RAZR and another girl, and was glad she'd called. She made him happy, then dialed five other equally desirous middlemen and sated their salivations. Then she arranged travel for each of the girls. Each would be gone in the next few hours: one each to Denver, Cincinnati, Charlotte, Boston, Green Bay, and finally Phoenix. She also called another minder to get them to the airport.

Everyone would be gone except her. Then it would be time for Var.

After she was finished, she took the bottles of RAZR and walked into the living room. Three girls were out of the shower and drying off, two dressing, two nude on either end of the couch, and one by the easy chair. They had no shame, nor should they. They were beautiful, sexy, and ready. She was ready, too, and wanted to pop a RAZR. The bottle pinched between her breasts.

She called Taygeta over and gave her the six bottles of RAZR. "Distribute these to the girls. You'll need them where you're going."

Then she sat on the couch, took the bottle from her Brazilian breast pocket, and opened it. She shook out two pills out and put them in a side pocket of her purse,

then stuffed the bottle between the couch cushions.
   She called Var on her personal phone.

CHAPTER 29

Buddy's Dilemma

Buddy wanted his gun back. Angela had taken it, but not his phone. Despite the moonless night, Buddy's vision accommodated quickly, just like it had in Afghanistan. He surveyed the meadow and its dark mounds of what he knew were freshly dug earth, some with new grass. Was he always going to be with death?

His phone read *No Service*. Coyotes yipped and howled, and a breeze whished through nearby pines.

He fingered his left upper arm, the sore shallow scrape where the bullet had grazed him. He'd been lucky. He picked his way over the deadfall to the road, took a left and started walking towards Detective C's house, thinking about what had happened after he'd buried the girl and followed Angela back to the Suburban. He'd been ready to kill the Judge. The knife strapped around his calf had done the job many times in the past, and the Judge was just an old man, not an Afghan mujahideen who lived and breathed and worked in conditions that made him stronger and faster than most American soldiers—Buddy had been the exception they hadn't counted on. He'd enjoyed dealing out his form of justice to those men who had no respect for women. And he would have kept doing it for years, but the Marine Corps had become too PC. They were the ones that let the women in, not him. And they thought *he* was nuts.

He'd just about got the Judge, but Angela had seen him first, shot at him, and winged Buddy's arm. Must be he'd lost more of his edge than he thought. He had run, and the Suburban had peeled off. And now Buddy had to figure out his next move. He stopped and looked at the road, saw the silhouette of a dark rectangle with a pointed cone in the middle: Detective C's house. It had phone service, but maybe making a call was a bad idea. His prints were all over the shovel Angela took. Yet, he'd been to Detective C's house many times before —a good reason for his prints to be found there. If he called from here, though, they'd know he'd been here at this moment. He should have disabled the GPS when he got the phone, but it had been a gift from Doc Var, and this was the USA, not Afghanistan. He shouldn't have to worry about being tracked here. But with his history from the Corps, and a little research from a wily law-yer on his aunt's death, no one would believe he hadn't killed the Judge.

The worst thing, the thing he kept coming back to, was how bad this was going to look for Detective C: All those bodies a quarter mile from his home. Con-venient, private, and him being a cop and prior Marine Corps would make those who'd never had to uphold the law or defend a country salivate at the irony and high drama. Great headlines. Especially with all the recent bad cop press. And the girls were kidnapped, underaged, looked like Mexicans. Even being innocent, the detective would need a great lawyer and probably years to clear his name. And just when he was recovering from his stint as a New Orleans detective.

No, Buddy would not make the call. But he would need some stuff from Detective C's garage. He started walking again.

He'd been there so many times he knew all the weak spots for entering and where Detective C kept almost everything. Breaking into the garage was a cinch, thanks to a broken window in the side door. Buddy thought about Doc Var and his partner, Lisa. Why had he chosen her to help him in his PI business? He knew Buddy could do anything she could do much better. Doc Var was just a sucker for women. Buddy shook his head. Weren't we all? And, Lisa had been there for Doc Var through it all. Even though she was a Navy puke, she'd been excellent as an MP investigator for the Marines, good enough to get accepted to NCIS. Doc Var deserved something good. He'd always been good to Buddy. He'd been the one who'd suggested Buddy carry around a mirror in his pocket. It had made all the difference in being able to function and get a job. A little odd, but at least he could work. He felt useful again. The Corps paycheck had vanished, along with their trust, but he still felt useful. He wished Doc Var could help some of his other friends. Without work they just floated in a sea of garbage.

Once inside, he reached for the light switch ... and paused. Would anyone see a light on in the garage after midnight on a weekday? Probably not. He turned it on.

Detective C kept most of his outdoor stuff in one corner. He found an old backpack and started stuffing it with necessities: a hatchet and rope, multi-tool, water filter, rolled-up plastic drop sheet. He found spool of twine under the workbench and cut a length for lashing a sleeping bag to the outside of the pack. He put on work gloves lying on the workbench, grabbed the pack, and opened the door to the kitchen. The clock over the stove read 12:31. He grabbed Granola bars, a jar of peanut butter, a box of graham crackers, two cans of beans, several protein bars, toilet paper, and two bottles of water, stuffing it all into the backpack.

The gun safe in the hallway stared at him. He needed a gun, bad. Getting into the safe would be no problem, but stealing Detective C's gun ...

Nope. Not gonna happen. He'd have to find one somewhere else.

He thought about leaving a note, but he'd leave something better, something only Detective C would know about, in case someone was with him.

He glanced at the stove clock: 12:34. Three minutes. Not bad. He turned out the lights, went through the garage, surveyed the area one more time to make sure he didn't forget anything, and clicked the light off. On the way out, he picked up one piece of broken glass inside the door and placed it outside the front door.

In Iraq and Afghanistan, a piece of window glass placed outside a door by the mujahideens inside let them know if someone was coming in. Buddy figured that out the first time he stepped on it and they all got away. After that, he'd removed the glass and his squad became known as the Ghost Squad. The mujes never knew they were coming.

He shrugged into the pack and walked toward the foothills. Detective C had shown him a place about two miles in, next to a small spring. It was dark, and Buddy stumbled a few times, but he soon found the spot surrounded by spires and boulders and trees and completely hidden from the outside. Detective C said only he knew about it. Buddy doubted that because Var had been up here, too. But he figured he could at least sleep there until morning.

He got out the drop cloth, smoothed it onto a patch of level grass, and laid the sleeping bag on top. Once snuggled inside, he was asleep in a minute.

CHAPTER 30

The Setup

My palms were wet as O.J. opened the Suburban passenger door. It became clear whose brains were on the windshield and driver's window. The Judge lay sideways, his left side wedged between the steering wheel and the driver's door, forehead with a neat, dark hole surrounded by powder burns. He must have been looking at his assailant. Cromwell's words about Fallujah came back to me: *Buddy looked that muj right in the eyes as he blasted him with the final volley from his M-4.*

Buddy, Buddy, Buddy.

O.J. had already searched the front seat and was in the back carefully running over the front row of backseats. He hadn't found the gun yet, and I was sure he wouldn't. Buddy wasn't stupid.

O.J. grunted.

What?" I said.

"There's brass under the front passenger's seat." He held up a pen with the casing helmeted on it. He looked into my eyes. "Nine-millimeter."

We both knew Buddy owned a Glock, and from what O.J. said, Angela had pointed something a lot smaller at him in the hotel. But there were tons of other nine-millimeter handguns out there. We would know soon enough, if they found the slug in the wall. Rifling on a Glock was distinctive, and the ballistic lab would figure it out quickly. But there were tons of Glocks out there, too. You had to match the rifling to the specific gun. If Buddy did this, his gun would be long gone.

O.J. checked the rest of the SUV, including the rear. Nothing. He told me to stay out of the garage and go back to the car with Mug.

"I could help you."

He frowned at me. "This isn't a job for some private dick, Sherlock. Please."

Okay, okay. I rolled my eyes and said, "Really." That's what everyone says. Well, used to say. I guess once you pass twenty-one you can't stay cool. Wait, that's kewl. I put my gun in my pocket and went back to the car.

I sat in the driver's seat and thought about leaving, but knew O.J. would be Mr. By-The-Book for this one.

Mug yawned and said. "What's going on?"

"Someone's dead." Why didn't I want to tell him? The Judge had presided over Mug's case and handed down more guilty verdicts than any other judge in the history of Poudre County. There would be some hoorays in the local jails and prisons tomorrow. I guess I was right there with them. No. I think not. No one should be murdered. I guess I didn't want to believe Buddy had done it and I didn't want to see Mug celebrate it.

"I knew that. Anything else happen?" I hoped Mug was assuming it was the girl we'd discussed who'd died in Estes. He wanted the skinny—another rubbernecker on the highway after an accident. But he was involved, so I could see it.

"Sorry. The body we were talking about earlier, a girl, is not in the Suburban, but there's another one. And this one's likely a murder."

Mug sat there, patient, or maybe just too tired to process. I could feel my muscles getting rubbery, my eyelids scratchy, and my concentration waning as well. My adrenaline surge far gone. I stared at the closed garage door, blinking like an automaton, wondering what the hell was going to happen to my friend Buddy and how O.J. was going to manage to arrest him. It was going to get tricky.

Mug sighed in an exasperated manner. "Who was killed this time?"

He would find out eventually. "The Judge."

"You mean *the* Judge?"

"Yeah." I studied Mug to see if he'd do an end-zone dance with his face, his eyes, or any other part of his body, but he didn't. I had underestimated him. What a great guy.

"Who did it?"

I didn't answer.

Mug stretched his tree-branch arms in front, almost touching the windshield, then laced his sausage fingers and cracked his gorilla knuckles. It sounded like cracking walnuts at a Christmas party.

"You think it was Buddy?" he asked.

"No, *I* don't. But there is some evidence that points that way."

My phone rang. I blinked hard a few times in the hope of better concentration. The caller ID said "Angela." Oh boy. My heart tapped a fast dance in my temples, and I could almost feel my adrenals being squeezed.

"Hello, Angela."

"Var, thank God I got you. I need your help."

Right. She has a car full of illegals she's been trafficking, and one of them is dead. I was tempted to walk my phone in and give it to O.J.

"Where are you?" I said.

"You were hired by my husband, is that correct?"

Technically, she had me. "Yes."

"Well now he's dead, and your negligence killed him. You were supposed to investigate Mr. Hollister and prevent this. So I think you should help me. Don't you?"

"Wait a minute. I asked the Judge if he thought Hollister was a danger to him, and he said no. I told him to contact the police, and he wouldn't. There's no negligence there."

"That's not what he told me. He said Hollister gave him the creeps. He even started carrying a gun he was so nervous. If you check his coat pocket, you'll find it."

I was beginning to see how she could make things bad for me. It wouldn't take much for a lawyer to find out I knew Buddy was dangerous and had gone off the rails before. Her word against mine, telling any listener about a crazy guy who I knew was unstable. And if it came right down to it, I wouldn't say anything against her on the witness stand. I would have gabbed on for hours against the Judge, but not against her.

"Okay, what do you want?"

"First, I want you to swear to me you won't tell anyone where I am."

I shook my head and thought of a few choice Marine words. "Okay."

"Just so you'll know, I'm recording this conversation."

"Angela, are you crazy? I know what you've been doing."

"You only know what Mr. Hollister and the incompetent Detective Cromwell told you. Are you with Cromwell now?"

"Yes, we're at your house."

"Good. Look behind the garbage can, and you'll find Mr. Hollister's gun. I hit his arm with a shovel before he could fire it at me. It bounced on the garbage lid and went behind it. Hollister ran off into the night."

"You hit him before he could fire his gun at you."

"Yes. I thought he was going to kill me."

"And he ran away?" Buddy, running from a woman with a shovel. I tried to imagine that and got a blank screen.

"Why'd he run?"

"Because after I hit him with the shovel, I pulled out my own gun. I shot at him as he ran away and may have hit him."

It could have happened that way. Maybe Buddy was losing his edge. "So what do you want from me?"

"Just tell Detective Cromwell what I told you. I'll be in touch. And Var, I still love you. I always have."

I wanted to ask her where she was just so I could keep my promise not to tell anyone. But she'd ended the call and I remained safe from temptation.

I wished I had Lisa here to trace the call with one of her gadgets. I wished I had Lisa here to kiss me and pinch my cheeks and tell me to forget that woman. What I really wished for was a do-over in college—skip the Marines and go with Angela. Would I ever move forward? Maybe my brain was healing as far as the meandering about, but the emotional part had a permanent scar when it came to Angela. If I'd only skipped the war.

But boys freshly painted in manhood have gone to

wars since the beginning of time. And those war experiences color their entire life. Forever. Why should eons of tradition and evolution make me any different?

Mug looked like he was constipated and needed fresh air. I agreed.

I got out and trotted to the house. I had to tell O.J. I changed my mind at the last minute and continued to jog around the house, amped up and needing to clear my head and get rid of nervous energy.

It was obviously a setup. I felt it in my bones. Cromwell would know it soon I hoped. I was sure they'd find Buddy's prints on the gun and brass. And when they did, I was going to have to have a sit-down with O.J.

I stumbled on a rock and slowed, rounding the corner of the house. Right now there was nothing I wanted more than to help the woman who'd left me for a man who was dead in her garage. They were right when they said my head was screwed up by that IED. How the hell could anyone as dumb as me get through medical school? Not only is love blind, it's dumb.

Another lap around the house, and I decided. It was way past time for me to wise up.

CHAPTER 31

Crime Scene

O.J. was perusing the kitchen when I finished my lap around the house and stepped in the front door. I wasn't breathing hard, but my pulse was still hammering. The biking had paid off for the lungs, but Angela still affected my heart.

I told him what Angela had said. He looked at me like I was a bit off—even more off than usual. "Right. She got the jump on Buddy." He looked me straight in the eye, sarcasm flaring. "You remember that catch-the-fly game he played?"

I raised my eyebrows and shrugged. Buddy could snatch a fly out of Afghanistan's camel-dung fetid desert air at will and throw it against one of those adobe walls so fast it was DOA.

O.J. gave me a wan smile. "How many guys did he kill because he was so quick?"

I nodded. "Yeah, you're right."

"She hit him with a shovel and he ran?"

I could feel the redness coloring my face. "That's what she said."

"Right here in the garage."

"Yeah."

"Where's the shovel?"

"I don't know."

"Well, I haven't seen it."

I shrugged. Another boulder to add to my pile of numb nut rocks of trust for Angela in my head.

"So, you think Angela left Buddy here, and he is out there?" He glanced out into the sage-covered hills.

"I guess so."

He puckered his bottom lip as if to say, *Possible,* but he said nothing and started back inside the garage.

Yeah, I knew it, too. *If* Buddy had been clobbered by Angela, and *if* he was out there, no way was he going to be found by us or anyone else. I wanted to stay and help O.J., but with his current attitude, I would just piss him off.

I turned and made it to the front door, was reaching for the doorknob, when I heard O.J.'s "Fuck!" echoing from the garage. He must have found the gun. Then he said, "That bitch has it all figured out. This is just like the fucking bayou."

I opened the door, closed it softly behind me, and walked to my car. Mug was snoozing. I got in very quietly. He needed his beauty rest. I wished I could sleep but my mind was a cauldron of stew spiced with Angela and O.J., trying to work out a plan before I took off.

I knew O.J. would be tearing himself apart about Angela, reliving all the guilt and failures from the bayou and glassblower women. He was already blaming himself for screwing this case up, too?

I didn't think so. We both knew Angela's story was a crock.

Or did we? Yet, what could we do? O.J. seemed to think Buddy was with her, by his own volition, which made him an accomplice until proven otherwise. He was probably pissed at Buddy. But he knew Buddy was weird about women. Even if a woman had done something wrong, he always gave them the benefit of the doubt.

Yeah, I should talk, right? Me and Angela. I was right there with Buddy. This case was a class A cluster.

At sunrise, the white panel van I'd come to know pulled in behind O.J.'s crappy little Honda on my left. It had the Colorado flag painted on the side with bold lettering under it: *Poudre Valley Crime Bureau*. PVCB. Catchy if you liked acronyms. O.J. had some issues with one of the PVCB guys, Blue, so that was another reason I stayed. Friends need support. Usually O.J. could handle Blue, no problem, but this case had too many personal complications for him. Blue had graduated from coroner's helper to CSI guy last year, a few months after the glassblower case, and every time I'd seen him since, I liked him less.

I heard the driver's side door open and close, and Blue walked around the front of the van to my window. His sky-blue CSI jumper was bright in the morning light, matching his wide grin. "Hello there, Var. How's the hardware?"

His voice was loud and the tone sour about my prosthetic. It bit me. I hated that he'd crawled under my skin, yet again. Mug flinched awake.

"Grand, Blue. Just wonderful. I'd appreciate it if you'd call me Dr. Lenus unless we are playing poker. And could you tone it down a bit? We've been here all night and one of us was sleeping."

Blue lost the smile, which was good by me, and bent over to peer at Mug. "Sorry I woke you. Wow! You're … really … big."

Mug nodded. "I get that. I'm Mug."

"Did you say Mug?"

"Yeah. It's a long story, but I'm not awake enough."

Blue looked back at me with his *Blue's Clues* dog face. This morning I was not into his cheerfulness.

"Where's the rest of your help?"

"O ... I mean Detective Cromwell said he just wanted me for now. Where is he?"

O.J. stood in the opened front door. "Over here. I'll just show you the layout and you can get your stuff."

Blue walked over to O.J., looked at his face then down at his shoes. "You don't have shoe covers."

O.J. looked at him like he'd said the sky was blue or his crappy little Honda still looked crappy.

"Right," Blue said. "I'll get some for you."

I eyed O.J. as Blue went to his van. "You gonna be all right here?"

He backed his head off his neck and gave me the *Are you kidding?* look.

"You sure? I mean, a lot has happened, and you and Blue are ... not the best of friends. You should probably call some more people in."

"I'm good. I want to make sure about Buddy first." His voice teetered on disgust. Was it in response to Blue or my perseverance?

"Okay. I'm headin out."

He squinted at me. "If Angela calls again, you'll let me know?"

"Of course." I started the car and backed away, avoiding his eyes.

I drove at a reasonable speed following the winding county road over foothills laced with sagebrush and pines, then east on Highway 34 out of the foothills, past Devil's Backbone, a jagged outcropping of reddish-tan sandstone and granite that looked more like a giant stegosaurus's back. We were soon in the outskirts of Loveland, and I dropped Mug at his townhome north-west of town, which seemed to me a come down for a previously wealthy guy.

Motoring home, I envisioned a big hamburger, making up to and making love to Lisa, and afterwards a wonderful nap.

My phone trilled. It was Angela. I glanced in the rear-view to see how far I was from Mug's. His house was not in view. I pulled over and answered the phone.

"Var, I need to review some things with you. Please, can you meet me now?" She sounded so … sweet. Jesus. Did I just think Angela was sweet?

She gave me directions and I drove north like a good little puppy dog. I love puppies, but sometimes they do dumb stuff. I-25 rolled through plains and buttes, a breathtaking vista that at one time was home to wild Cheyenne Indians. I sighed at the jagged power lines and robot-looking towers that held the lines, scarring the once-pristine land. The Rawhide coal turret billowed gray smoke into the cloudless Colorado blue sky. Progress. Yeah, destructive progress maybe, like me going to see Angela.

Forty-five minutes later, I parked the 4Runner and walked to the door of the truck stop off I-25 just south of Cheyenne, Wyoming. I hadn't had a lick of sleep for twenty-six hours but didn't need any coffee. Now would be a good time to call O.J. Yeah.

I opened the door and surveyed the restaurant. The prospect of seeing Angela again made me lightheaded. … Not sure I felt my feet as I walked to the door of the truck stop and pushed it open. So, I'm stupid. I have brain damage, after all.

She sat in a booth in the back, her thick raven hair transforming a simple shaft of sunlight into a sheen of iridescence. Her dark eyes sparked with vibrant energy as if fed by a nuclear reactor. Much cleaner than coal, but more dangerous. Yet so beautiful. Her skin was like poured gold, not a gram of bronze in it. Pure. The white blouse was so thin there was no doubt she was braless. She smiled at me, and I felt like a fly to the spider. My legs got weak. Probably all the blood going to the wrong head, the one without a brain.

CHAPTER 32

Angela

"Hello, Var."

"Angela." Moving quickly, hoping my weak legs wouldn't stumble and that she hadn't seen my tented pants, I scooted into the booth.

"I took the liberty." She pointed to the steaming cup of coffee. "Black and strong."

I nodded. Quite the conversationalist. Maybe if I sipped the coffee, I might settle down enough to actually get out a full sentence. Right. Coffee, the best relaxant known to man. I took a drink anyway to be polite. It was a good thing I was in great shape. A heartrate of over two-hundred a minute could lead to a heart attack in a lesser man. This was stupid. Why did she have this effect on me? I was over her a long time ago. *Keep thinking that, Einstein.*

Her gaze faltered and fell, and tears came. I was touched. My eyes even watered.

"The Judge is gone," she said.

The Judge? Are you kidding me? "I'm sorry, but I thought ..."

"I know. The Judge and I had our differences, but lately he'd been so good to me. And to see him dead was ..." She opened her purse and pulled out a tissue.

I watched her closely. Was she really that good at

acting?

She blew her nose. I took a deep breath and let it out slow. I thought of Buddy's smiling face. He was my friend and I had to control myself. My heartbeat decreased to an even more reasonable rate and I felt calmer, more rational, if not betrayed. I wanted to ask her about Buddy and what happened, but she would tell me, and the way she told it would be important. The detective in me was poking through.

I beckoned the waitress. I know, "server" is more PC, but PC and I weren't really holding hands today. She came over and Angela ordered the breakfast burrito with chorizo and two pancakes. How she kept her figure I would never know. The waitress must have agreed because as she jotted it down, she raised one eyebrow. I ordered a Denver omelet and sourdough toast with a side of bacon.

"Ice water, as well," Angela added.

"Oh yeah, water for me, too, before the meal, please."

The waitress had nice blue eyes and clear skin but had the smell of cigarettes wafting around her and large hips. She smiled at me and started to walk away.

"Wait," I said. "Are those Krispy Kreme doughnuts in the glass up there?"

"Yes sir. We get them every morning, fresh."

"Could you please bring me two crullers? Like, right away?" The sips of coffee were grumbling at my stomach already.

"Sure." She smiled again, knowing I liked what she liked. I gave her a smile, avoiding any suggestion in it, though I think she took one anyhow.

I looked at Angela and said, "You want a doughnut?"

She shook her head.

The waitress left, and Angela kept shaking her head at me. She wiped her eyes and I detected a slight smile.

"What?"

"I didn't know you liked them big."

"I was just being nice."

"She thought so."

"Give me a break."

A dark cloud crossed her face. "Like you gave Mr. Hollister?"

Okay. Here it is. "Look. Buddy Hollister is harmless, unlike the Judge."

"Buddy, is it? A friend of yours, I gather."

If I was going to get anything worth anything from her, I could not let her know that. "I've known him a while, that's all. He wouldn't hurt anyone." I could swear my nose grew.

"That's not what the Judge and I found out about him and his aunt."

"Yeah? What did you and the Judge dig up?"

She looked at me, her lips and eyes close to a smile, but more a face of utter confidence. "Enough."

She was right and she knew I knew it. Buddy's juvie case when he'd been accused but never convicted of killing a guy who'd been bopping her aunt. Since Buddy had been a minor, the details of the case had been sealed. But Angela had probably dug up a microfiche from one of the newspaper accounts. She would spread it to the press, and they would of course believe every word from a prior journalist and have a field day with Buddy's history. And when they found out he had been discharged from the Marine Corps for PTSD. Well, heroes were not heroes if they insanely killed people. Even if it had been war.

After all, war was sane and civilized killing. Everyone knows that.

"He was only a kid." I paused. "Besides, I'm not sure I'm buying you and the Judge being on good terms. What's with the tears?"

The waitress and her blue eyes brought the crullers. I smiled at her and she smiled back. She glanced at Angela and her smile disappeared. She walked away, very rapidly.

"The Judge," Angela said, "saved me from my father. Fucking football players."

Years ago, she'd told me her father had abused her and her mother on a regular basis. She never revealed the extent or the method. But filling in the gaps wasn't too hard. Though the bruises she came to school with spoke of physical abuse, it wasn't hard to believe a woman as beautiful as her had been sexually abused and her adult lust was the result. A sick twist of sexual abuse for some women that went against all rationality.

I picked up a cruller. "You want one?"

She looked at me. Her smile had disappeared, too. *Maybe I should go sit with the waitress.*

I needed to think. I bit into the doughnut and savored the taste. Took a sip of coffee, swished it around with the cruller, trying to think while I chewed. No use. Every conclusion was the same: I had to help Angela to find out the real story.

After I'd savored that bite—the coffee really made it better—I sighed. "Okay. What do you want me to do?"

She looked around and leaned forward. "The Judge," she said in a very quiet voice, "had been doing some illegal things, and we need to bury it."

I wasn't okay as Buddy's friend, and I was beginning to wonder if she really did still love me, but apparently I was definitely okay helping her cover up the Judge's illegal past. Then again, maybe she wasn't at fault and it had been the Judge who'd been pushing the illegal trafficking. Was that even what she was talking about?

The food came and the waitress poured us both more coffee. This time Angela smiled at her and she got a bit flustered and almost dropped the coffee pot.

I ate in silence. When was the last time I'd eaten? I should be hungry. But each bite tasted sour and I pushed the food around the plate. I was going to betray a friend. She was a dainty eater, but fast, her appetite not affected at all by her grief. She finished before me, drank her coffee and looked out the window. Not a care in the world.

I looked at her. "Illegal, like what?"

"Are you done?"

"Yeah." I wrapped up the cruller in a napkin and drank down the remaining coffee. Even though it tasted bitter, I would need it.

She got up. "Meet me outside." She walked to the door. I guess that meant I was paying. Sure: the doctor, the PI, vs. the rich sex trafficker. No contest. I had to pay.

CHAPTER 33

Ah, Love

Outside she told me to follow her in her Lexus. I didn't balk. Right now my choices were limited. And her perfect breasts under that sheer shirt didn't hurt her cause. I knew that, but sometimes the midbrain can bulldoze the cerebral cortex into submission. And there were memories in the temporal lobe that overrode logic. Sure, she might be luring me to an early grave, and she might be lying about both her husband and Buddy, but I also remembered nights of tenderness in medical school and her researching a drug for her brother's asthma. She was a complicated woman and I was a simple guy. If I could help her I would. The question is, how far would my reconstituted love take me? I also needed to find out what else she was up to and where these girls were? If my telepathy hadn't stopped, I would know already. But that was a sign I was getting better. Yeah.

We drove south and east, of all places, not where I thought we'd go. My heart continued to pound, and the dizziness returned. Jesus. I was such a sucker for her. Or maybe it was my anxiety at getting closer to her stash of illegals. I had thought they were in some private place in the foothills. But the further east we went, the more I realized how few people would ever come out here, unless you were some oil guy. I thought of O.J.'s words in Estes: a frackers' party. Fracking had taken over farming and ranching lands big time, though with the price of gas going down, most of the wells were sitting idle. It cost too much to dredge up oil shale from a two-mile sideways rig. The word was sixty dollars a barrel for crude was the tipping point for profit for frackers. And here we were at forty-eight dollars. Maybe the fracker bigwigs had bragged one too many times to OPEC that the US of A was now independent of them. The Saudis increased production, drove down oil prices, and now the big boy frackers were putting their capital in another venture. They weren't meeting with OPEC anymore. Couldn't afford to fly their Lear jets. Until the next oil upturn. What an industry.

Putting their capital into other ventures. Hmm. Could Angela be working for the bigwig frackers? Maybe they got a cut of the earnings? I'd read that some of those sex traffickers made ten grand a night. And as many men as those bigwigs employed in as many dusty, deserted areas, they could make a killing even at twenty percent, and there was no law for a hundred miles—okay, not no law, but essentially the same as when there was one county sheriff per fifty square miles. I imagined it was the Judge who got the twenty percent and the frackers the eighty. Angela fit in there somewhere, too. But where? Was she really the victim?

I felt my shoulder getting heavier, my neck aching, my eyelids scratching my sleepless eyes. The breakfast was counteracting Angela-shock and overriding my sleepless night.

Pretty soon we were on a dirt road. She must be hating this, getting her pretty black Lexus dusty and chancing dings from rocks. Not to mention possibly incriminating herself with a former lover. Her words on the phone kept echoing in my brain-damaged mind: *I still love you. I always have.*

Off in the distance, getting closer by the minute, was a drab olive double-wide. Were the girls in there? She probably wanted me to help her unload them. And whatever else she'd planned to cover up for the Judge. I took a few deep breaths; that bitter coffee finally kicked in and helped me concentrate.

Her car almost bottomed out on some of the small dips in the dirt road. I was thankful I had the 4Runner. It could take much worse roads. Yet those dips were small. I paid more attention. We came to a curve in the road, a sharp ninety degrees around a farmer's property line. She turned right and her left rear wheel bit down hard in the dirt, the axle tilted more than I thought was usual for a well-built Lexus with merely the weight of a driver. The Lexus slid almost to the edge.

There was no other explanation: She had something heavy in her trunk.

The dust behind her got thicker as she sped up after the curve. But it didn't block the view of the fancy L in the middle of her trunk. Oh, man. Was it possible she had another dead girl or two ... or maybe even three in there? Shit.

She stopped in front of the trailer and got out, beckoning me to come with her. Somehow the top four buttons of her blouse had come undone. Her purse strap hung over one side, pulling the blouse to the side. She had a devilish grin on her face. Double shit.

I took my Smith & Wesson out of the glove box and waited for her to go into the trailer before stepping out and cramming the gun into the small of my back. Safety on. I didn't need any other parts blown off. I wanted to run to the Lexus and punch the trunk opener beside the steering wheel. But there might be others inside the trailer, others with guns. Maybe I should have been closer to her when she walked in. Maybe I shouldn't have driven here to begin with. Maybe I should get back in the 4Runner and eat the cruller. Maybe that would lower my heartrate. Why was it beating so fast? It was way too hot here. Did Angela really cause all that?

The door opened and she was there, shirt unbuttoned and hanging open from neck to navel. "Are you coming?"

I stopped. "Who else is here?"

She spread her arms wide. "Just you and me. I've been waiting a long time for this."

Wasn't she just crying about her dead husband? I felt guilty about the hard metal in my lower back, but not the hard wood in Dorkmeister. There's something about impending sex with the woman of your dreams that pretty much kills rational thought. But it was about a lot more than just sex. She'd been the first and only until Lisa, and now I had a chance to redo a part of me that I'd lost going to war.

I walked toward her wondering if she would find my missing parts repulsive. My hard part got a little softer. I felt a little dizzy. What was I going to tell Lisa, the only other woman I had been with, the woman who kept me in line? She was probably making up my bed after sleeping there all night, wondering where I was.

Angela unzipped her shorts and they dropped to the floor. She stepped out of them. Her white shirt fluttered open, and I saw her black panties. I walked faster. I don't think I even had a limp, though I still felt dizzy. How could she have this effect after all these years? Why was I even thinking about hopping in the sack with a probable murderer? The mysteries of logic escaped me. I felt hot all over.

I walked into the trailer and before it hit me, I briefly saw the kitchen with a broom propped on the Formica table, the spartan furniture in the living room, mattresses stacked in one corner, and the doors closed at two back bedrooms. She closed the front door and it hit me. Maybe it was from too little sleep, guilt, or something else. Who knows? But it hit my arm like a flame thrower. I must have cried out because she frowned and crossed her arms over her chest. "What?"

My vision blurred and black gnats crowded the periphery. Now I knew why I'd been dizzy and why my heart had been racing and why I'd been thinking so stupidly—not just lack of sleep and not just Angela. This was going to be a bad one. And I'd left my phone in the car with my earbuds.

I turned around and started for the door, took one step and collapsed, the linoleum floor jolted my butt and shoulders. I rolled onto my back and she leaned over me, genuine concern on her beautiful face. "What's wrong?"

"I need my … phone." My lips moved but hardly any sound came out. I forced it out. "In the car."

She lifted her phone out of her shorts pocket, started to dial then stopped. "Should I drive you to a hospital?"

Here she was, being chased by O.J. and soon half the Poudre Valley police, and she was going to take me to the hospital. My love for her had not been misplaced. Maybe I wasn't as stupid as I thought.

"No." I gritted my teeth and took a deep breath. The next sentence was critical to get out and have her understand. "I'll be okay. I just need my iPhone and the earbuds. They're in the drink holder. Hurry."

Somehow, she understood. She tossed her phone onto the shabby gray couch and ran. I heard the door to the trailer bang open, and felt the breeze on my forehead, but my vision was all gray and black and sparkles. I should have gone home or at least to the bathroom at the truck stop and cleaned off the stump. I needed more antibiotics, too. Where were they? I couldn't think.

I felt the air move across my face and knew she was back. I blinked a few times to clear my vision. "Get me to a mirror. And I need a chair."

She helped me up and I leaned on her, limping to the bathroom mirror. The ringing in my ears was so bad, I could barely hear anything. I saw a tiny lighted tunnel inside dark fireflies. I had to make it to the mirror and plug in and get the pain gone before I could clean off the wound.

I propped myself against the sink while she dragged a kitchen chair over. I plopped down in the chair, fumbled the earbuds in, and tried to swipe to open the iPhone screen to iTunes, but I couldn't coordinate things. I heard myself whimpering.

She leaned over to help. Her blouse was buttoned. Damn. She swiped the screen. I moved to iTunes, picked James Taylor shuffle and looked into the mirror, clenching my left hand, my brain converting it to right hand, and the pain eased. Rivulets of cool sweat poured down my back and the gun felt like a sharp rock. I reached around and pulled it out and put it on the bathroom countertop.

"You don't trust me?" she said.

All I could muster was, "Stupid."

I started to take off the arm prosthetic and she helped. She was very tender in her ministrations. She helped me wash off the wound, sucked in her breath every time I groaned.

The washing, the pain, the watching her help me so carefully: it was all over in the shortest ten minutes of my life. The wound didn't look that bad, but it had probably keyed the phantom limb pain. Afterwards I explained about the infection and remembered where the antibiotics were—in my pocket. I pulled two pills out and she got a glass of water and I used it to swallow the pills.

She helped me take off my leg prosthetic then washed me off, head to toe. Slowly. Tenderly. Erotically. I forgot about the residual ache in my arm. Pretty soon she had her mouth on parts I loved and I had my parts in areas she loved. It was like old times, only she was unquenchable, an animal. But after a three-peat I fell back, exhausted.

Finally, she slept. I remember watching her breathe easily. I fell into a blank bliss.

I woke up, it seemed like a day later I was so refreshed, but I knew it could have only been hours. It had always been that way. A few hours and I was good to go in med school, internship, and then in Afghanistan it had paid off in spades. My exhaustion was gone and I knew the infection was minimal, but I wanted to cry. Not for love but for guilt. I thought this was what I'd wanted: Angela and me an item again; making love to her and her loving me despite my ugly wounds. But I could only think of Lisa and how much this would hurt her. And Buddy and O.J. and how I'd let them down.

I eased to sitting and looked for my prosthetics. We'd left them in the bathroom. It wasn't like they were outside, but I still had to crawl.

I pulled on my tee shirt and pants, slid off the bed and started a wobbly crawl on two good knees and one hand, bringing back memories of falling during a PT session. A humiliating way to move, and the thin carpeting not much padding for my bony knees.

"Where do you think you're going, mister?"

I craned my neck around; at first, I thought she was joking and wanting more. But she was sitting there naked and pointing my gun at me. Something about looking at the dark hole of the gun took away from her perfect breasts, and the waning love I had for her dribbled out of my heart.

CHAPTER 34

Love and Friends

Cromwell had to walk away from the Judge, the garage, and his spinning thoughts. He strode up the flagstone steps along the side of the house to the back patio. The view overlooked the plains and the rising sun. How long had it been since he'd watched a sunrise? There was really nothing for him to do, so he plopped down, his eyes glued to the east. Low clouds started indigo, then red, then orange like a fire that was dying had come back to life. He traced the horizon to the west and saw one final star blink out. How insignificant was one man? Could he make a difference? Even after so many failures?

Blue had kept up a barrage of conversation, well, more like chatter—conversation meant more than one contributed. He kept trying to twist a humorous knife about the prior glassblower case that he knew Cromwell had botched, but Cromwell just stood behind him with his mouth closed. Any answer would have egged him on. Except Blue just kept going.

Once he looked back at Cromwell. "You okay?"

"Tired." He didn't want to open up. Not to Blue. He didn't want to say this case reminded him of another more distant case in a bayou of Louisiana. His obsession with that case had lost him the best woman he'd ever had. The case had driven him to put the barrel of his gun in his mouth nightly for two weeks. God how he missed his lush green home. Yet he had to come here to these dry mountains to be near friends he'd relied on in combat. All he had were friends. No wife, no kids. Relatives he hated were strewn around the South.

No, he could never tell Blue about the hot, humid bayou where he'd found a man and his three children strung up like marionettes, rotting in a dilapidated frame shack, their feet in cool fresh water they desperately needed but couldn't get to, their necks tied to a post. The sly wife with large brown eyes and cherub cheeks had gotten off because Cromwell had been a sucker for her beautiful innocence. Her planted and contaminated evidence screwed him in the ass at the trial.

Worse, if Blue ever knew the truth about the glassblower case he kept needling Cromwell about, Cromwell would have to leave the state. It was another woman, this one found dead with a murdering psychopathic glassblower here in Poudre County. Cromwell had assumed she was like the sly bayou woman. But she hadn't been sly or a murderer. She'd been innocent, and Cromwell had gotten her killed.

And now there was Angela. Had she pulled the wool over his eyes like the bayou woman had? Or was she merely an innocent bystander for a murder Buddy had committed—a friend who'd once saved his life in dry mountains of a torn country with savage people where the only thing that had mattered was friends?

Cromwell stared at the rising orange orb for too long, then squeezed his eyes shut and rubbed his temples, enjoying the residual lighted globe on his closed lids. The sun would not give up on him. He smiled to himself and wished Blue would quit yammering and finish the job, so he could get some sleep. Just a few hours. If he was lucky. He was sure his boss would be calling him soon to find out about the Estes Park woman, and then Cromwell would tell him about this one. His boss had already accused him of bringing New Orleans crime rate with him. He opened his eyes and spotted a bald eagle, smiled at the wonder, and watched it fly to the horizon. He sighed and walked back down the flagstone steps into the side door of the garage. The West was just like any other place. Population and the times were finally catching up. More people meant more bad people. Bad people made bad shit happen.

Blue stood by the kitchen door, his puppy eyes following Cromwell in. "Okay. I'm done. I'm assuming I can take the body to the M.E."

"Yeah. Let me help you."

Blue gave him a suspicious side glance but rolled in the gurney. They bagged the body and Blue rolled it out to the van. Cromwell helped him collapse the gurney and roll it into the waiting space. Blue slammed the doors, the sound like the Judge's gavel at trial. He looked at Cromwell. Cromwell stared at him and blinked once.

"Yeah," Blue said. "I'll let you know when the post is." He actually seemed a bit concerned. Pretty unusual after all the shit they'd said in the past to each other.

Cromwell nodded. "Thanks."

"It's my job." Blue's voice was deadpan. He walked around and got into the van and drove off.

Once an ass, always an ass, Cromwell thought. He dragged himself back into the garage. One last look.

Fingerprint dust gathered like snowflakes on the doors and inside on the seats and steering wheel. He thought it through again. Buddy would have had to be in the passenger seat to kill the Judge. Why would he be there and not Angela? From what Buddy had told Cromwell in his office, the Judge didn't like him, thought he was some hick. Assuming Buddy's story was true, which Cromwell did and other people would not, Angela had threatened Buddy with a knife. Why would they let him ride up front with the Judge? On the other hand, Buddy definitely didn't like the Judge because he thought the Judge was going to kill Angela, or that's what he'd said a few days ago. Yet, Buddy hadn't killed anyone after the Corps, though back then he'd certainly proved he could do it. Absolutely. In spades.

Too many maybes and what ifs.

"Shit!" He'd forgotten to ask Blue to search around the house for footprints that lead away into the hills. He needed sleep, but there was no one else to do it.

Outside, he searched for footprints, starting very close to the house and making bigger and bigger circles. Loose divots like small volcanoes appeared here and there in the sandy soil, but no defined footprints. Hell, Buddy would have known enough to get rid of any prints that led to him.

His phone jingled and he pulled it out—*Unknown Caller*—probably the Captain calling from his personal cell. Sergeant Rupert had probably filled him in. The Captain never gave out his personal cell number to any of the worker bees, except Rupert. The Captain and Rupert smoked together outside by the flagpole and hunted for elk every fall. Some said Rupert and the Captain had a thing for each other in the hunting tent.

Right after this call he had to call the Captain.

He answered it. "Cromwell."

"Detective C, we're in trouble." It was Buddy.

Cromwell's jolted fully awake and scanned the perimeter. Trying to keep this case quiet, he'd not had his cell monitored by Kip the geek in the department. "Where are you, Buddy?"

"You'll figure it out. I gotta go, but I had to tell you, the Judge is trying to frame you."

"Me?"

"Stop by the meadow on your way home."

"The meadow?"

"Has the Judge hurt Angela yet?"

The Judge hurt Angela? Cromwell's thoughts churned, and he couldn't say anything for a few seconds. Finally, he said, "Look, Buddy. I need your help. Tell me where you are. And where are those other girls?"

"I gotta go. Call you later." He disconnected.

The meadow? Shit, there were hundreds of meadows. But there was only one like Buddy said, "on your way home." Then there was the other thing: If Buddy killed the Judge why did he ask about him hurting Angela? Was he with the other girls?

Cromwell had a feeling there was a lot of information there and if he wasn't so damn tired he could figure it. He had to get some sleep. On the way to his house and his bed he would think about it all and maybe something would shake out. Though, he already had a feeling about the meadow Buddy was referring to. A bad feeling. Maybe something would...

His phone rang again. *Unknown Caller.*

"Buddy?"

"Who's Buddy?" It was the Captain. "And why haven't

you reported in. We have a murder, I understand. Didn't you think that was something I should know?"

Maybe he wouldn't be going home after all. "Hello, Captain. Just about to call you." That forever, dyed-in-the-wool asshole, Blue, must have got to the Captain.

Cromwell filled the Captain in, avoiding naming Buddy as the owner of the Glock. He didn't know, really. And come to think of it, why would the gun be his? He wasn't stupid. They would have to wait for prints. Thankfully, the Captain told him to go home and get some rest, but to be in the office by 2 p.m. *What was with him being nice?*

Cromwell glanced at the scene again, decided it was taped off well enough for him to leave. Besides, Blue and he had taken lots of photos. If anyone disturbed it, he would know, or maybe not. Right now he didn't care about the crime scene or the Captain.

He locked up the house, then got into his crappy little Honda, cranked the key, once, twice. When it didn't start, he tipped back his head and rolled his neck. He cranked it again and it started. He told himself for the umpteenth time he should get a new car, or at least a new used car, and drove away.

On the way home, the cool morning breeze woke him up enough for him to experience the usual buyer's remorse. Hell, the car still ran good. Probably just needed a new starter. Why spend the money on a new car? Yeah. What money?

It took about thirty minutes to drive home, plenty of time to think. If Buddy wasn't in the front seat with the Judge, it had to be Angela. She was the alpha female. No way she would let one of her girls sit up front. And as a crafty bitch alpha, she probably knew the

Judge was planning on killing her and beat him to the punch. And wrapped it up with a neat little bow around Buddy's suspicious little neck. But to get the splatter on the windshield and powder burns on his forehead, she would have had to use her left hand and leaned way over. She wasn't left handed. Something didn't make sense.

He kept going back to the glassblower case. Innocent until proven guilty. Maybe Angela really had been a victim and Buddy had actually killed the Judge from the backseat. Cromwell blinked his eyes hard a couple of times and stretched his neck again. He needed sleep.

He pulled onto the road to his rented house and hooked around the curve and stopped at the meadow he knew Buddy meant. Numerous fresh piles of dirt pocked the meadow. His stomach crawled around like a voodoo curse of snakes. The Judge had set him up, Buddy said. Shit.

The air smelled of pine trees and grass and dirt. Still about a quarter mile away, he saw the sun gleaming off his house. His bed would feel great right about now. Too bad he'd be going into the meadow with its cloak of mist and lumps of freshly dug dirt. He knew he should call this in, but he also knew Buddy was right. It was going to be a mess.

The long grass was matted and trampled in a straight trail that led over several deadfall logs. One reason he loved it out here was the morning light and its natural beauty, the way it fluttered over the grass. But today the early sunshine took on a more ominous cast. It outlined an oblong mound of brown earth, clearly tamped by a shovel. There were at least five more of the same dirt mounds sporting some weeds and sprigs of grass.

Bodies buried right in his backyard.

He wanted to scream. Just when he was getting used to this place. It had only been a year, but he had a nice home, a few friends other than Buddy and Var, even had been on a date or two. Now his landlord would ditch him like his department had in New Orleans. The rotten bayou had followed him. He shook his head. His rental was going to be the least of his worries.

He got back in his car and drove the last quarter mile home. Found the glass pane Buddy had left outside his door. Saw Buddy had taken his pack, food and camping gear. Buddy had been here, not near the Judge's. *What the hell happened last night?*

Whatever had occurred, Buddy was on the lam and in survival mode. He sounded sane enough on the phone, but once a person entered into survival mode, his thinking changed. Buddy would become protective of his friends, and he would try to save Angela, despite her sins. He would think the Judge had caused it all. Maybe Angela had gotten Buddy so riled up about the Judge that he *had* killed the old fart. A riled-up Buddy was nothing to mess with. But he didn't sound that way on the phone. And from what he'd said, he still thought the Judge was alive.

Words. Lies. Truth. He couldn't think straight. Had to get some sleep.

He decided he would find Buddy before he called into the station about the graveyard out back. Graveyard. Yeah. Who the hell was buried there? Could they have been offing some oil guys who didn't pay up?

In the kitchen, he drank down a cold glass of water, then walked to his bedroom and fell onto his stomach on his bed, thought about the Suburban and the blood splatter on the windshield, the gun behind the garbage can, the three kids in the bayou, and ...

A high-pitched wail. He stirred. Saliva drooled out of the side of his mouth. He pushed up on one hand, blinked at the light. Where was he? Another scream like a dying rabbit caught outside his window by a coyote. His neck was stiff, his eyes caked with matter. It was hot and stuffy. He blinked and saw his bedroom. Oh yeah. Must have slept most of the morning. Great. Now he was even further behind on finding Buddy.

The scream his brain had imagined had become a ring—the phone. He found it and touched the green phone icon, "Cromwell."

CHAPTER 35

Sex, Drugs and Wiley Coyote

I do like Cromwell's voice. Even when he's just waking up it sounds authoritative. Just like a sergeant and a former MP. I was so glad he answered and didn't let my call go to voicemail. I said, "I thought you'd be at work, so I called there first, but they told me you were home. You okay?"

"Peachy." I could hear him drag his forearm over his mouth and beard-stubbled cheek. I envisioned him doing what he always did when I woke him up for a watch in Kabul. He'd open his mouth wide and stretch his face then blink hard twice. "Where are you?"

"Can't tell you that. Client confidentiality."

"Shit, you're with that bitch, aren't you?"

I responded with stone cold silence. Angela stared down at me through the sites of *my* gun, pointed at *my* stupid head. Pretty good motivation to stay on her script.

"Var?"

"You and Buddy have been very bad boys. I know all about the killing fields in your backyard. Now you've got Buddy working for you. You guys were always tight. I hated that in Fallujah with ISIS, and now I know why. I'm headed to the DA with this info. You were once my friend, so I thought I'd let you know."

I hung up. A person will say almost anything when the woman he loves has a loaded Glock pointed at his head. It doesn't matter if you don't really love her anymore (yeah, sure) and you have a stupid, screwed up, barely-with-the-program head, you can make up shit pretty quickly.

And though it sounded like a nasty thing to say to my friend, I'd never been in Fallujah with O.J. or Buddy. Or Angela. I just hoped she knew as little about the war in Iraq as ninety-nine percent of Americans did. ISIS wasn't even called ISIS until 2013. They weren't in Fallujah until 2014. Way past when O.J. and Buddy were there.

She lowered the gun. Marvelous view of those superb mammary glands. I wanted to look away, but testosterone had eons of control I could not override. Then there's Buddha. He would say try to enjoy every moment. Okay.

"I'm not sure," she began, "if I believe what you just said." She paused and shrugged her shoulders. "But it will keep him busy while we get out of here." She stepped out of the bed covers, padded around me, walking casually with the Glock in her hand as if she always strolled around nude with a fire-ready gun in her hand. She stopped to pick up my cell phone and then proceeded to the bathroom. She put the gun on the floor, tossed me my arm prosthetic, closed the door and turned on the shower.

I had to admit, she was a classy bitch. What she thought she knew was that I couldn't leave without my leg prosthetic. But I always kept a spare in my car. Granted, it was the climbing prosthetic, not made for walking fast. And I'd have to crawl to the car—or grab the broom I'd noticed propped on the kitchen table—and use it to crutch it out there. If I made it, I'd be driving away and gone in less than three minutes.

The door to the bathroom opened, steam billowing out, her Venus form silhouetted against the light in the steam, legs apart, one hand holding the gun again, the other with something else in it. She tossed out the something—handcuffs. "Cuff yourself to the bed."

"I'm offended."

"Do it or you will be offended and also lose another leg." She pointed the gun at me.

"Geez, aren't we touchy?" Of course she wouldn't do it. Of course. She watched me put on my arm prosthetic, then fumble a bit and get the cuffs clicked to my right wrist and the bed's head rail.

She closed the door and went back to her shower. I sat back wondering what the hell I'd done, though I knew O.J. would never fall for my DA remark or how I hated him being tight with Buddy. We three were like the three musketeers, without the French names. One for all and all for one.

And even though I got what I thought I wanted, making love with Angela, it was like the apple in the Garden of Eden: I felt dirty and stupid and fooled. If I ever wanted to feel like a real human again, I knew I had to take Angela down.

But how does one take Wily Coyote down? Make him think he's smarter than you and then throw him off a cliff with a piece of dynamite.

I looked at the bed rail, my arm, the cuffs, and then at the couch. Yeah, she had *my* cell phone, but I remembered her tossing *her* cell phone onto the couch when she came in. I patted my pants pocket and felt the key ring. Wily Coyote wasn't so wily.

I pulled out the key to the cuffs, removed them, and looked around for a quick fix to slow her down if she came out of the shower, catching me red-handed. I scooted on my butt to the lamp on the nightstand. Both the lamp and the nightstand were cheap things, not very heavy and easy to move quickly, which I did, and quietly placed them in front of the bathroom door, lamp on its side on top of a sideways lying nightstand. It would be a minor obstruction, but with them on their sides, they were low enough she might trip over them if she were in a hurry, and if she tried to move them, it might take even longer.

I scooted and crawled toward the couch like a three-legged dog trying to win a race. Damn. The cell phone was not on the couch. There was a pink lipstick, not Angela's color, and a single pair of purple bikini panties. I held up the panties. Not Angela's size. Where was the cell phone? Maybe it fell between the cushions. I lifted them up and the phone plopped onto the carpeted floor. Also under the cushions I came across another prize. A bottle of pills. I picked them up daintily with tips of fingers and read the label: RAZR. I needed to get prints on the bottle, and get the contents analyzed. Find a ziplock baggie. In a hurry.

First the phone. I put the bottle on top of the side table, grabbed the phone, and swiped a finger across the screen—*Password?* Hmm.

I shoved the phone in my other pocket and tri-podded over to the kitchen table, pushed up using the table, pulled out a couple of drawers and found a zipper baggie shoved one in my pocket. I hooked the bristles of the broom under my right armpit and took a hurried step, the bristles sticking like pins. The end of the broom slipped on the linoleum and, like a cartoon character on ice, I fell. No problem. I used my combat and football skills to roll quietly rather than plop noisily. The linoleum was too slick. I grabbed the broom and crawled to the carpeted living room. I reached and pinched the pill bottle with finger tips and put it in the baggie and stuffed it in my pants.

The humming flow of water in the bathroom stopped. Unless she put on makeup, which I doubted she would, she'd be out in under a minute. Maybe less.

Switching into a faster gear, I used the wall to brace and stand, and hooked the broom bristles under my armpit again, then hopped and lurched as fast as I could across the carpet. The broom handle bent a bit but held. I made it to door, stopped to open it with my good hand, and heard her humming in the bathroom. *Please, take all the time you want.*

I crutched like a jackrabbit on a pogo stick across the threshold and over the gravel to my car, the broom slipping and bending, but not failing. My therapist in Pensacola would have been proud.

I pulled on the handle of the 4Runner. Locked. Why had she locked it? I propped myself against the car and fiddled in my pocket for the keys. They were the keys to her Lexus. I jabbed at a button and the Lexus trunk popped open. Shit. I'd have to close it to get moving. Inside were boxes. Not a body. That was good. But, it must be loaded with something heavy the way the car had been moving in front of me on the way in. Two open boxes revealed bottles of pills. I crutched over on broom, reached in and picked up a bottle. RAZR.

A racket sounded behind me and Angela shouting

"Shit!" She must have stumbled on the bed stand and lamp. I had maybe twenty seconds.

I shut the trunk and took a long crutch plant to the driver's door of the Lexus. The broom slipped out from under me. The keys flew out of my hands. Out of the corner of my eye, I saw the fender of the Lexus rushing at my right eye.

I jerked my head and the fender missed by an inch. Just what I needed: another blow to the head. I scrambled around on my knees in search of the keys. I sighted them a foot under the car, then grabbed them and started to get up when I heard her voice.

"I'm glad I always lock my Lexus." Her voice was calm, and I looked up and saw her standing at the open door, my handy Glock in her right hand. She had a black bra and panties on. There was a wan grin on her face. Her left shin was bleeding. A nightstand in the wrong place will do that. And those bonks on the shin could be very painful. Maybe the pain would slow her down. Maybe I could unlock the door, get inside and start it and maybe get it in gear before she shot me through windows. ...Yeah, the already broken windows from shots she would have already taken. Even slowed down, even if she crawled to the truck, I was screwed. At that moment I cursed Samuel Colt for inventing the revolver, the Great Equalizer that began the American worship of handguns.

I sighed and stood as straight as I could. "Okay. Now what? You gonna kill me, too?"

The trill of my cell phone she held in her other hand made me flinch. She looked at it and smiled, touched a finger to the screen and answered it. "Hello, Mr. Hollister. Or should I call you Buddy like this phone says?" She moved the gun in short flexes of her wrist, motioning me to come back inside.

"Var? He can't come to the phone right now. He's not being very good." she said to the phone. "Yes, I know. The Judge made me do a lot of very bad things. I need you to help me get better. Will you do that?"

I crutched toward the door, the sticking of broom bristles in my armpit even worse, the broom end sliding around on the gravel with each plant, the shaft bending to almost breaking twice. My previously strong left leg felt noodly, and the arm on the crutch like I'd been curling at the gym all day. Angela stood back, the gun pointed at my good leg, as I wobbled past her. I made it to the couch and collapsed onto it. The front door slammed behind me.

"Oh, I'm so glad," she continued plying poor Buddy. "Where can I meet you?"

She uh-huh'ed as she padded around behind the couch. I didn't see what was coming next. The gun butt was fast, hard steel on my slow, soft brain—a shooting pain on the back of my head—fleeting, memorable, and violent. Morpheus kissed me as I made my way into the gentle darkness. I didn't care if I ever woke.

CHAPTER 36

A Complicated Woman

When you're unconscious you can still think, or at least on your way up through the dark fog, you can. Sleep is much better than being knocked unconscious, at least in my experience. Well, maybe not. Dreams and the unconscious world are like some weird fantasy land where monsters you never even suspected become real. And they somehow scare the shit out of you, or confuse the hell out of you, even if you're not five anymore.

IEDs notwithstanding, Angela coldcocking me with that gun hurt more than just the pain of the gun on my skull. I get it—she was pissed. But the pain hurt more because I didn't really think she would risk hurting me permanently. I thought she still had feelings for me. It hurt more because I still had feelings for her. Jesus. Was it love? Love. Why couldn't I control it? I knew the answer to that. I'd always believed love was something so ethereal, something a mere mortal could never control. I wasn't married to her, but I believed in "for better or worse." Yet, there comes a point, though, when a man has to grow some balls and move on. Then again, maybe she had knocked something back in place that I'd started to lose.

I gently shook my head to climb out of my confused

semiconscious funk. Each shake felt like a loose hammer smashed my skull from the inside. Light started to register, and I remembered the call from Buddy. Oh, man. Now I would have to put up with Buddy slobbering all over her beautiful bare feet. And if I got too many more head bonks, I'd become one of those pro-football, post-concussive, Parkinsonian droolers. As it is, I'm only a bad step or two away from a wheelchair for life. Angela had tended to my stump infection so tenderly. She must still have feelings, so why hit me so hard on the head? Though, she could have shot me.

Maybe it was that other part of me that kept hoping for good, the part that seemed to be getting things wrong about Angela. I wonder if Freud knew that the penis was the ears for the id? Ears, eyes, fingers, tongue, nose, and of course the brain. Yeah, Sigmund knew. Probably thought about it every time he bonked his wife's younger sister. Or maybe talking with all those patients about sex every day was like a confession to a Catholic—kept him as clean as Jesus. Was Jesus clean? A thought registered about Freud: He wasn't Catholic. He had to be Buddhist to see good in so many weird things.

I blinked and pursed my lips. I had to wake up. These thoughts were not only scary, but totally nuts. Freud was an atheist for most of his life, until he got into that foxhole of old age when he reverted to his Jewish heritage. Foxholes will do that to you. Or maybe it was the nature of scientists, after they found out how totally non-objective science was. Oh, man, I was not in a foxhole but a rabbit hole. I needed Alice.

I could feel the bouncing of a car ride. I opened one eye and could finally focus. Angela was driving my 4Runner. Sitting in the backseat, my right wrist chafed at being handcuffed to my left prosthetic hand, both pulled by the connecting chain through the door handle. It had the effect of twisting my body right, my head lolling left on the seat back. Awkward; I could feel a cramp starting in my side. If I pulled real hard and got my left stump out of the prosthetic, I could lean towards her and beat her with my stump. Except, with the stump infected, that would hurt me more than her. I might even get another joyful ride on the phantom-limb roller coaster of pain. I had a feeling she might laugh if that happened. No more tender loving care.

I licked my lips and took in a deep breath. The skull hammer was subsiding. "Why did you have to hit me on the head?"

She glanced back at me. "Would you rather I killed you?"

I grasped my prosthetic with my right hand and cranked my stump at an angle to the prosthetic, trying to break the suction. "No, but I don't want to be a blithering idiot, either. You do realize I already had traumatic brain injury from an IED and had difficulty recovering to where I am now." I pondered her beautiful face. "What happened last night? You seemed so tender with my stump. Was making love just a bedtime story? At one time you cared about people, and I thought you cared about me. Was I wrong?"

She stared down the road. Her face didn't change. She was probably wondering why I was asking this stupid question, since I was the one who tried to leave. I pulled on the stump connection, felt the suction loosen on the rubber.

"Okay, I guess that means yes and I was stupid to think you might still love me and you could care less if I become a brain prep, organ donner in some nursing home with glazed eyes watching birds out the window."

I paused, but no answer came. Not even in the form of a twitch. I pulled my left arm and held onto the prosthetic with my right hand. I thought the connection was loosening, but it didn't move. A little harder, and I could at least have my good hand mobile enough to smack her.

"Okay. So you've turned into a hard bitch who runs illegal whores for oil men and has no problem setting up my friend for your murder of your husband. You not only hurt those you once loved, but you kill them as well. Now you're going to kill me and make Buddy take the fall for that, too."

I stopped pulling on my prosthetic, hoping my words finally got to her and that she would react.

Nothing.

I rolled onto my side and felt the bottle gouge into my thigh. The pills. Why did she have them in the trunk? Had she used one before last night to help her get over my appearance and have wild, passionate sex?

No, I couldn't think like that. She loved me.

Yeah, I was an idiot. But let's just say I'm not and I believe the pills had been for the girls—to make them sexual maniacs. That made sense. But why so many pills? There had been boxes and boxes, enough for a thousand girls.

I decided to give the prosthetic one last tug.

Just as I grabbed my prosthetic with my right hand, she stomped on the brakes and whipped her head around, glaring at me. Her eyes were overfilled lakes. "Your friend, Buddy killed the Judge. I have to say

I'm glad he did. The Judge was going to kill me soon enough. He was all about money. He forced me to do his bidding with the girls. I loved that girl who killed herself in Estes yesterday. I love them all. The Judge gave me some of his money, so I could continue the research on the asthma drug. You *do* remember my brother, don't you?"

Tears streamed down her cheeks. Her gaze had changed to someone who had just witnessed deeds of pain and inhumanity that only doctors knew.

"But most of all..." she looked at me in the rearview mirror, her eyes the only thing I could see, eyes full of tears and truth.

She looked away. "Oh, never mind. It's all over."

I was sure she was going to say, "But most of all, I loved you." I could not swallow. I squeezed my teeth down so hard my jaw cramped. But I wasn't going to cry. She had to be playing me.

She swiped a hand across her cheeks and glanced at my hand. "What are you doing?"

I cleared my throat, though the lump stuck and my voice sounded funny. "My infection itches and is starting to hurt. Just wiggling things to prevent another major pain reaction." I smiled at her and shrugged my shoulders. Me and lying were never good poker partners.

She turned forward and the car sped forward.

Was she playing me? Did I believe her? My heart did. My brain, though really stupid, was beginning to come around and take the other side. I had my doubts about Buddy, but she'd already proven her other side with handcuffing me in the living room, pointing a loaded gun at me, coldcocking me, and now this. Why would she handcuff me if she really trusted me, or even had reasonable plans for me? Was she going to enrage Buddy enough to have him kill me, too? And what about the pills?

I looked out the window. We were traveling southeast, getting deeper into the boonies. We passed a few distant oil derricks and some natural gas tanks and a house or two. A field of wheat straw in the distance. Oil shale had been the end of dry-land farmers. Why work your ass off rolling the dice for rain (or no bugs, or no hail), when you could just say yes when the oil guy called and wanted to pay you to lease a few acres of your land for enough money to get your kid into college and pay off that pickup truck. And if you got royalties, too—*if* they struck something with their miles of sideways drilling—you'd be set for life. Or as long as the wells produced. Which had become a short-term proposition in many fracked oil wells.

That head bonk must have scrambled my thinking or put it into tangential mode. I needed to concentrate on getting loose and get away from this woman whose plans for me seemed eminently dangerous, and possibly deadly. Even if she just dumped me out here alive, I'd be hosed. Now all that tangential thinking made sense. I looked west. No city visible. If I stood on the roof I could probably see five miles to the horizon. I could walk okay on my prosthetic for a few miles, but not five, or the more likely ten I'd need to reach the nearest population. My leg nub would be bleeding hamburger. Then again, bleeding was better than dead, brown, and drawing flies.

The next thought came to me with crystal clarity: she wasn't going to dump me out alive.

All I had to do was get my arm stump off. Then I thought I would be able to pull the cuff off the upside, pull it through the door handle and get myself loose. I'd whack her on the head with my good hand and hopefully grab the wheel without the car crashing. Then I could crawl over the seat as the car slowed. I'd also need to find my key to the cuffs, cuff her in the very back compartment of the 4runner, and drive her to O.J.

The question of the morning was, where was the Glock? It wasn't on the center console or in the center drink holders where I would have put it. I couldn't see the front seat from my angle. If she had it there, I'd have some time. But if she had it in the side net pocket of the door where she could reach it with her left hand ... I might be in serious trouble.

Either way, I would have to be quick.

She slowed the car, glanced back at me, and turned towards me a bit, holding the wheel with one hand and pointing the Glock at me with the other. "Forget trying to get away. I'll let you go soon enough."

The car slowed even more, and she guided it to the wrong side of the road coming up to a mailbox at the end of a dirt road that connected to a house about a hundred yards away. It looked to be a simple white-framed ranch with poplar trees in various stages of death shading the western side. There were three squares of freshly leveled dirt containing two cylindrical tanks and low pipes coming out of the ground, each square located within about stone's throw from the house. One on the left, two on the right: frackers natural gas tanks.

She stopped in front of the mailbox, adjusted the rearview so she could see me better, and opened her window. She pulled down the mailbox door, pulled out a brown envelope, threw it on the seat beside her, closed the mailbox, her window and whipped a U. She sped up and we were cruising again, back the way we'd come.

I still had my chance at her, though at the speed she was now traveling, knocking her senseless would be risky.

In the rearview, her dark, beautiful eyes studied me. I was having a hard time reading them. Was it mistrust? Was it regret? Was it frustration at being in a situation she hated? It really didn't matter. I'd been wrong so far.

All I knew was I had to escape. But with her constant eyeing me, I would have to undo my stump, the cuff, everything by feel and without moving my head.

She turned and pointed the gun at me again. "Don't make me shoot you."

I thought about telling her I knew she wouldn't. But I was afraid I might say something else that might set her off. And when people get stressed, sometimes they pull the trigger without thinking.

In ten minutes, we were back at the double-wide, her Lexus still dusty and parked outside. She unbuckled her seat belt and looked back at me, put the key to the cuffs into the center drink holder, sighed heavily and got out. She placed the Glock and my phone on the 4Runner's hood, smiled at me through the windshield, then got into her Lexus and drove off.

A very complicated woman. The things she did. I could not give up on her.

CHAPTER 37

The Finger

I t took me about one minute to get out of the cuffs, get my arm prosthetic back on and find the leg in the front seat. The area on the stump was improved. The antibiotics were kicking in. I looked in the rearview mirror and felt the small lump on the back of my head. No blood on the hand. Nothing on my face. The haziness after Angela's head bonk was gone, and my old energy returned. A weight had been lifted. I didn't know if it was due to knowing she left me without killing me, indicating she really did have compassion for me, or if I'd finally decided I was done with her.

Another minute and I had my Glock in my pocket and O.J. on the phone.

"What?" He was in a mood. This might be difficult.

"Hey, I just got totally confused and wanted to help you."

"Help me what—get more confused?"

"No ... I mean ... Shit." I thought about it. I really wanted to tell him about Angela. Should I bring Buddy into this? "Wait. You're confused already?"

"Worse than that. I'm in deep shit. That bitch Angela screwed me to the wall."

"No, that's what I did to her last night," I wanted to say but didn't. It's a guy thing, you know, boasting about sexual prowess. Lisa popped into my banged-up head. I think Angela screwed me to the wall more than I did her. Sometimes I think it would have been better if Dorkmeister would have been damaged in that IED explosion. Yeah, right. As they said in Wayne's World, NOT!

"Yeah," I said. "I hear you." I paused. "You knew, right, that I would never give you over to the DA? I mean, I was never with you in Fallujah."

He didn't say anything for a long, thinking moment. "Neither was ISIS. Wait. Are you with her?"

"No. Why would you think that?" Jesus. I should have told him she just left so he could maybe track her faster. Those little omissions. I was so-o-o glad my dad wasn't Geppetto and my nose wasn't wooden. Although, technically it wasn't a lie.

He paused again, his hamster brain wheels moving so fast I could smell burning glial cells. "So" he paused just long enough to unnerve, "what *did* you call about? And yes, I knew you wouldn't be a tattletale. I am a detective, you know. I'll still have a beer with you."

I wanted to tell him I'd solved his cases, and all he had to do was find Angela, who, by the way, was here a few minutes ago. I wanted to tell him our friend Buddy did not kill anyone. I wanted to tell him Angela had plied her girls with RAZR and had tons of the drug. But really, what hard proof did I have? I'd never seen any girls. I had a bottle of pills labelled RAZR that could have been Viagra. Hadn't even opened the bottle. I had no real idea what was in them. He would probably believe me that Angela hit me on the head, held me at gunpoint and then left me. Probably. I did have a bruise on my head. All in all, I didn't have a damn thing. All I had were gut feelings that Angela had lied, that Buddy was too smart and too good a guy to leave his own Glock at the scene of a murder with his prints all over it, and that ... Angela had lied.

Yet, she had cried. Yes, I went to war, but I was a doctor. I have empathy. I'm a sucker for any crying man or woman. But Angela and tears ... That got me deep.

I had to find her again and find out the whole story. O.J. would not give her any slack.

I said, "I just wanted to tell you I'm available to help, if you need me. I got some sleep and...Did you get any sleep yet?" Deflect, parry, avoid. What a loser I am.

"You woke me up with that call about going to the DA. Remember?"

"Oh yeah. I knew you wouldn't believe that."

"What the hell is going on, Var?"

"Yeah. There's stuff. Umm, could we meet for lunch? I'm kinda hungry, and I'm sure you are."

"No. Not hungry."

"Yeah. Figures. What about a climb. Might help you think."

What the hell was I thinking? Angela and Buddy needed finding. But we really had no clues where they were. Angela was probably out of state; Buddy deep in the wilderness.

I remembered how in Afghanistan we all would have a quick pickup game of basketball or flag football between raids. I mean, we may have just been up all night, some guys had killed several Taliban assholes, or lost buddies, but you just figured this might be your last hour on earth, so why not take the time and enjoy it. None of us were NBA material, but playing blew off steam, and if you made a few shots you suddenly felt better about yourself. Maybe that was one of the good things about being in a war. You learned priorities. Beauty and fun trumped killing and the job. Every damn time. Though O.J. seemed to require more convincing nowadays.

Yeah, it was a long shot, but he'd told me several times that when he rock-climbed it helped him puzzle through cases. I felt pretty good, physically, but my mind needed to get away from all this shit for a while, and I needed a little adrenaline surge that climbing always gives. But I figured he would never agree. He was too focused.

He said, "Meet me at my house in half an hour. We'll hit the Finger."

I almost dropped the phone. But I had to be cool about it, like this was something I expected.

"Sounds like a plan. You got any food at your place?"

But he'd hung up. I'd stop for a mini pizza at a Loaf and Jug on the way.

I started driving.

We named it the Finger because it looked like how you felt after trying to climb to the top and failing all over again: Mama Earth had just given you the finger for thinking you could overcome her. Well, maybe we would conquer the sixty-foot spire of jagged red and brown rock with few holds today.

Half an hour was cutting it close, but the Loaf and Jug wasn't busy, the 4Runner needed no gas, and there was hot pizza just made. And on top of all that they had cold Fresca. I needed to mark this place on the map. I got three sodas: one for me now, one for me later, and one for O.J.

I never took the climbing stuff out of the back, crash

pad and all. I'd been climbing for about five years, O.J. for much longer. When I first started we hit the rocks twice a week together. Lately it had mostly been Lisa and I. Lisa ... Yeah. What a shit I'd been. I would have to talk to her about Angela. Yeah, as if she didn't already know. She *had* been in intel and surveillance. But that didn't mean she knew all about me and Angela.

I took the bagged pill bottle out of my pocket and stuck it into the glove box, behind the owner's manual and oily rags, then jumped in and drove as fast as I could safely while eating pizza and guzzling Fresca. He was waiting outside his house with his climbing stuff, ropes and rings and pitons in his hands and a sour look on his face.

I was glad I'd already hidden the pill bottle. I still wasn't sure what to do about that: analyze them with my private resources or give them to OJ. It opened up a whole other can of worms, including my case with Mug. I might need them for evidence to clear him, and if O.J. got them into his investigation, Mug's might have to wait.

O.J. opened the back and threw his stuff in, clanking and plopping onto the floor, then got in next to me.

I pointed to the pizza box in the backseat. "There's a couple of pieces left. Got you a Fresca, too."

He glanced back. "Thanks, I had some Cheerios and Greek yogurt. I'll take the Fresca, though."

"Damn. You getting healthy on me?"

He popped a Fresca and guzzled it, then said, "I really want Scotch, but I need a clear head to think this through. Plus, this is a good break time for the investigation."

"You wanna talk now?"

He took another swig and looked out the window.

I backed up and twisted the wheel and started back the way I'd come. A meadow came into view.

He put a hand on the wheel. "Stop."

I pushed on the brake pedal with my good left foot. He pointed to the meadow. "She buried bodies out there. Looks like about ten to me."

I squinted into the noonday sun. Pretty clear there were several freshly dug patches of brown earth interspersed between the waving prairie grass. And many more mounds with new grass dotted the meadow. Shit. I wanted to go back to his house and shower off hard and scrub Dorkmeister off, twice. I'd made love to her last night. But she said it was the Judge who made her do it. Sounded like a sick song, *The Judge Made Me Do It*. I hadn't been using my own drug—music—nearly enough lately. The pizza sauce started bubbling up into my throat. It felt like all the energy flowed out my mouth with each breath, taking some garlic and tomato sauce with it.

"Ten?" was all I could muster.

"At least."

"You sure you wanna do this? Shouldn't you be tracking down leads or something?"

He looked at me, his eyes hard. "I got a BOLO out on Angela. Buddy will be found whenever he wants to be. Angela's house is secured. And these dead bodies point right to me. I've been mulling over what to do, but it's getting jumbled up. I need some space for an hour to decide what the hell my next step is. Kick it in gear."

I looked at the "killing fields," as Angela words in my little speech came back. *Her* killing fields. It could have been the Judge, but it felt more and more like O.J. was right about her. My arms felt disconnected from my body. Nothing moved right. I needed some space, too. I picked my iPhone out of the cup holder, tapped on a play list, then looked at him. "Is music okay?"

He shrugged, then finished the Fresca and crushed the can. Guys do that. It feels good.

I tapped the black play arrow and Idina Menzel sang "Defying Gravity."

I felt the steering wheel, hard and cool in my right hand, gripped it hard and mashed the accelerator. We heaved forward, my tunnel vision only seeing the road. Soon, Idina's fantastic voice and the lyrics relaxed my grip and I started to notice the outside world: the deer in the trees, the smell of pine, the motor sounds of my 4Runner doing its thing against Nature that could never be fully tamed. Idina hit a few high notes, and I felt the old determination fill my chest, just as it had in Pensacola after falling one too many times on my new leg. Idina had been with me then, too.

Maybe it was Angela's knock on my head, or maybe my brain was finally changing. Whatever it was, I didn't know Buddy was watching us.

♪ ♫

Buddy heard the 4Runner gunning around the corner as it entered Detective C's road. He threw the last of his stuff into his pack and jogged back around the rocks and trees that hid him from whatever occasional traffic came through. Like Var's 4Runner, which turned west and jounced up the old two-track toward him now.

He squatted behind a rock and waited. The smell of the pinion trees reminded him of cat piss. But it wasn't, and it smelled much better than the stench of human excrement he'd experienced in some of the hovels he'd had to invade in Iraq and Afghanistan. The odor yanked hard at his memories: two particular abandoned hovels, abandoned except for a tortured woman who'd been left to die.

He gritted his teeth, wishing he had Faith and his video game to play while he bounced on his haunches in a slow rhythm, matching it with equally slow, deliberated breaths. That shit in the Marines was over. Now he had to help his friend—he looked again at the approaching 4Runner—friends, plural. Var and Detective C.

He stopped bouncing. Maybe he should stand up and walk to them. His thighs tightened in preparation, but then he relaxed back again. He took in a deep breath through his nose and let it out. First, he had to find out what they thought about him and Angela. Going to jail was not a future he could envision. Many of the mountains behind him had no roads or paths—an easy place to disappear. He'd survived the Hindu Kush with Taliban on his ass, IEDs on every road, and snipers from every crag and rooftop. The Colorado Rockies with Thompson County Police on his tail would be a piece of cake.

♪ ♫

I drove the road from O.J.'s out. It jagged right just as a rocky, unused two-track hung left. I turned left, toward the western sky, just like the song's lyrics, and we bounced over the trail for two miles until we came to a clearing below the Finger—a sixty-foot spire of jagged red and brown rock that had few holds, at least to me.

"Defying Gravity" finished and I stopped the SUV, turned the key and got out, looking at the tip-top of the Finger, a spire of red and tan against a blue western sky.

Maybe I would "fly" today. That's how it felt when you got to the top of a tough climb. Even if we made it to the top, though, there was only room up there for one guy to sit.

Right. But neither one of us had ever gotten to the top. Maybe today. Who would it be?

I would have taken my iPod with me so I could play the song again, but I hoped O.J. might loosen up on the climb and we could talk.

I tossed the rolled-up crash pad to O.J., in case we decided to boulder instead of climb, and grabbed the duffel bag full of climbing equipment, set it behind the 4Runner, unzipped it and got out the two climbing prosthetics. I changed into a spandex blend tee shirt and shorts, took off my leg and fit on the climbing leg, more like a mountain goat's leg and hoof with rubber on the bottom and pointed toe. Then came the climbing hand, a two-hook affair that could get into almost any small crack. O.J. was going to have to work today to best me.

He stripped off his shirt and pants and pulled on climbing shorts and a small fanny pack for chalk.

"No bouldering. I need to climb," he said.

We got the ropes out and he led the way, walking to the base of the Finger. He left the rolled-up crash pad; it wouldn't matter if one of us fell fifty feet onto a mattress-sized cushioned piece of rubber. If we got discouraged early on the Finger, and weren't too tired, we might use it bouldering on one of the lower rock faces.

The Finger started out pretty tough with very few hold areas, then had a craggy midriff, a smooth neck, and a last face with very particular, wide spaced cracks. We'd both been up there three times. As unprofessional climbers, it usually took a half hour to reach that spot just six feet from the top. Then it took another half hour of failed attempts before we scaled back down.

"This might take a little more than an hour. Are you sure?" I asked.

He started up without looking at me, testing pitons we'd previously placed a month ago, then clipping in and moving up. I guess that was a yes. His sinewy, muscled back and arms and legs moved like a cat's. OJ was a smooth climber, very few jerks or jumps. Unlike me. I liked the rush of crashing up and hoping for a good hold. We took our women the same way. He preferred safe—me dangerous.

He kept going up, taking a different tack than any prior. He looked like a spider going up a web. When he stopped to hammer in a new piton, he looked down.

"On belay?" I asked.

"Belay on," he said.

"Climbing."

"Climb on."

♪ ♫

Buddy watched Var pull the 4Runner to within thirty feet of him, just below the Finger, and get out. Var stuck on his mountain goat leg and sloth hand. Detective C started to climb as easily as he had in Afghanistan. He'd even done it back then with a loaded backpack.

♪ ♫

We climbed steadily for the next fifteen minutes. I found it easier with the prosthetic hand to hold on for-seeming-ever to a small hold, no danger of finger cramps or giving out. The hoof would also support me better than a real foot, resting on a crack that only a mountain goat would love. It was almost unfair to O.J.

Except. Yeah, except he looked all human and I looked like part scrap metal.

Who was it that said, "If you look good, you feel good?" He was wrong. I feel great climbing. Fuck the way I look.

I watched his face relax and his eyes study the next hold about two feet up and to the right.

"I wasn't with her when you called," I said. He seemed relaxed. I couldn't keep it from him any longer. "She'd just left. But I was with her most of last night. And—"

His glance down at me stopped my words, his face tightening, his gaze seeming to look through my head. He blinked and breathed in and out. His face relaxed and he looked back up, reached with his right hand, found a hold on the top of a slight mound, stepped up with his right leg, followed with a left-hand reach and left leg up. He clipped into a prior piton, tested it and said, "On belay."

He was pissed, but did I worry he might have faked that test on the piton? Not pulled hard enough on the rope, so if I fell, the piton would pull out and I would just keep falling? He and I had been through too much to let a woman get between us.

He was right, of course. We were here to forget that world.

"Climbing," I said. I pulled a little harder than usual, testing the rope before I stretched up with my hooks and shoved them into a crack, the metal grating sound unnatural in the quiet, but also felt good and secure as I pulled on it. The goat foot fit easily on the lip of rock the size of two bent knuckles on a normal hand. I pushed up with that leg, grabbed another purchase with my left hand, and found a more sizeable ledge for my left to support me. My chest expanded faster and deeper with each breath, and the cool Colorado air suffused me with confidence and hope and calm.

I glanced up at O.J. He was staring out at the plains, now high enough to see over the small lump of a hill we'd driven around. Staring and breathing easily and slowly in and out through his nose.

We were getting there: leaving the stress of the sympathetic nervous system, redirecting the adrenaline into the parasympathetic system, like a yogi and his bed of nails. But I was sure this was much more enjoyable than lying on nails.

We could see the meadow pocked with mounds of earth that should have cute prairie dogs poking about them. But there were none. I loved the view to the far side of the meadow: red buttes and crags at the top of the first foothill. These were apparently left after the dome of rock that had formed millennia ago had collapsed. The other side of the collapsed dome was part of the Finger. The meadow and valley near O.J.'s house had been the lower belly of the rock bubble way back before the dinosaurs. I guess it had been softer rock and more fertile and...Ah, what the hell did I know about geology? The sights seemed to enter my eyes and go directly to my chest and stomach like a cup of warm cocoa on a cold day.

A large raptor, almost as big as an eagle, floated above us, screamed once, and soared away over the eastern buttes: a red-tailed hawk.

We climbed on and made it to our usual place, about a man's height from the top. He studied it, looked out at the meadow again, took a deep breath, then, without even attempting to go higher, said, "This helped. Thanks. But, you're right. I need to get moving. Let's go down and talk."

Somehow, I didn't feel like the Finger had given it to me today. I went down first, and he followed.

CHAPTER 38

A Tangled Web

Buddy watched and listened as they climbed. Detective C, unencumbered by a pack, could have made his way to the top of the Finger in a few minutes, Buddy was sure. But he waited for Var, patient and unassuming.

Buddy's heart ballooned into an aching, engorged mass in his chest, his tongue choked the back of his throat, and his eyes watered watching Var go up the Finger, sticking his sloth-hooked metal hand into cracks and pulling himself up, an awkward mix of robot and human. He'd really made something of himself when he came back: a doctor, a PI, a biker, and a rock climber.

Buddy dropped his head forward, his chin tapping his chest. He squeezed his eyes shut, then wiped his eyes at the sides with his hand and looked back at his friends. Angela needed his help. He had to find out what they knew.

Their clipped words cut through the air: "On Belay? Belay. Climbing. Climb on." Var started to say something about Angela, but Detective C cut him short with a look. Buddy knew that look, though he hadn't seen it since Fallujah when he'd gutted the guy in the room with her. Her. He squeezed his eyes shut again and shook his head quickly trying to rid himself of the memory gnats that flitted inside and bit his brain.

Then they were near the top, almost there. Detective C could have made it up in three seconds, but he looked down at Var and said, "Let's go down and talk," and they did.

Buddy listened and knew exactly what to do.

♪ ♫

Once down, I felt a bit nervous about O.J. wanting to talk. I took off the harness and peg-legged to the back of the 4Runner, unfastened my leg and hook and replaced them with something more presentable and easier to walk forward into the public. The thumping in my temples slowed, the exertion over.

"So, you were saying about Angela," O.J. said, studying me.

I felt my face warm and the thumping of my heart speed up again. Ugly truth time.

I told him: Yes, all about the double-wide, the sex, the attempt to leave, her trapping and cuffing me, the weird thing with the drive to the mailbox, and finally her leaving. I glanced at the 4Runner and thought about telling him the about pills in the glove box, but left them out. I might need them for something else.

"You think the girls were there yesterday?"

"She'd cleaned up the place. But I did find lipstick she never uses and a pair of purple panties I think were too small for her. So, really, no evidence." Those pills in the glove box were becoming more and more annoying.

"Probably belonged to one of the girls Buddy and I saw at the Stanley. They were very young and quite thin." He paused. "Were there any signs of restraints, like bars on the windows or maybe remnants of Plasticuffs?"

I felt my face burn even hotter. I'd already failed to keep my lips from puckering and I looked away in shame. He thought Angela had been starving them, cuffing them to the beds. And me, Mr. Puppy Love, I had wallowed in her arms. Would I ever regain his trust? "I didn't really inspect the whole place. Not that much time, you know."

He gave his hundred-yard stare and walked to the passenger side, opened the door, got in and gently closed the door.

Okeedokee. Talk time is over. Time to go back to his place and change. I needed more music.

I flicked my finger over the play list, found the song, and played "Demons" by Imagine Dragons. The song started, he gave me a look, and I drove a little faster than I should have, my head touching the roof over a couple of rocky bumps. The song ended a little before we got there, but I turned off the music before another song started. It was quiet, but I wanted to keep that tune in my head and my mood elevated.

Once there, I switched off the SUV, said, "You know how much I loved her, right?"

He said nothing and went straight into the bathroom. For sure, he got first dibs on the shower. Little grubby dogs like me didn't deserve a shower. I grabbed a washrag and towel out of the linen closet, went to the front sink and washed my pits and dried and changed into my clothes from last night—Navy blue Chinos and blue pin-striped long-sleeved shirt—it had a few wrinkles but smelled okay.

His cell phone rang on the kitchen table. I took a step and picked it up, read the screen: *Unknown caller. 2:03*

PM. Probably his Captain. That's why I put on the presentable clothes. Had a feeling. I laid it down. No way was I talking to the Captain. Not sure O.J. would even want to. But I was sure he had a few things figured out. Anytime he got this stubborn and antisocial, he had something big he was going to do. At any rate, I was dressed in presentable clothes to go with him and help. That look was what he gave me in the hospital when he told me he was quitting the Corps. Eight years, Sergeant and MP school under him, he said, "After this, and what they did to Buddy, I'm done."

The door to the bathroom opened and he stepped out. "Was that my phone?"

"Yep. Unknown caller."

"Probably the Captain. I should have been in there by now." He had on gray suit pants and a white dress shirt, neck button fastened, each side of a black tie under the collar, ready to tie. Definitely getting ready for something big. He usually wore a Stones big-red-lips tee shirt.

I raised my eyebrows at him and squinted like I was waiting for his retribution hammer to fall. "What have you decided?"

"Nothing more than what we said outside. I have to find Angela. So do you. I'll send someone to poke around the trailer. Once the Bolo finds her, we'll interrogate her."

"That's it?" I was sure it wasn't.

He tied the knot in his tie, too slowly, sighed heavily and looked at me. "Look, I know you love Angela and Buddy. But I don't know how I can protect you and Buddy, this time." He paused. *This time.*

The war and military never left us, did it? He could

cover up things in the war. War allowed for certain … indiscretions. Like how I'd been driving the Hummer, the doc, not the driver, and I'd been joyriding when the IED almost killed me. Like when Buddy killed five Iraqi noncombatants because they'd been taunting a woman. No, war never left us. And even though we were friends and Buddy had saved his and my life at least once, he was right. This time was not war.

He continued, "Not to mention protect me. Angela seems to have tied a bow around those bodies and my head is at the knot. I gotta figure out what to do with that. I probably need to tell the Captain when I go in. I might not be coming back out as a cop."

"And once we find Angela? Well she's toast. There's this Blue Campaign from Homeland Security coming in and teaching us all about sex trafficking. It's an international crime—a big deal. We've been getting briefs on it almost daily. And guess who'll be breathing down our necks as soon as the Captain knows about this? Mucho Federales: not only Homeland and the FBI, but Immigrations and Customs Enforcement—and believe me, those guys are just like their acronym ICE—they have ice in their veins. They will put any offenders down in a heartbeat. And that's just the beginning. If she's been using any drugs on those girls …"

His pause made me fight to look away, to show any sign I knew about the RAZR in her trunk. Though I was sure just by the pause that he knew I was holding back something about drugs. I could feel that pill bottle in the glove box expanding, the evidence growing larger and larger. Soon my 4Runner would explode and there would be pills all over the driveway.

"You get it," he continued, "there's a whole shitload

of federal agencies that will be poking around with long knives, bright lights, and no mercy. None of these agencies look favorably on any accomplices like Buddy, even if he is a veteran with PTSD. And you—your knowing what she did and failing to say anything until she was gone ..." His voice faded off.

Yeah. I was hosed. Buddy was going to the Super Max. I might get visitors between anal inspections at some lesser institute for sex puppies of sex traffickers. But Angela? I hoped to God when she drove away from me earlier that she left the country. I hoped she was long gone, back to Brazil or wherever the Judge got those girls. I didn't want her to sex traffic anymore, but I absolutely didn't want her going to the Super Max. I still loved her. What a guy, huh?

I had to find out about all those pills in her trunk. Had it all been the Judge? And if everything else could be tied to the Judge, then she would be cleared. Right?

Another thought circled my mind like one of the turkey buzzards I'd seen so often in the foothills. I think it was a realization that my mind kept blocking.

"You want me to come with you?" I said.

"I need you to find her and Buddy." He pulled on his gray suit coat. I think I'd only seen him wear that once, to a funeral of a squad mate who blew his brains out after he got back and couldn't keep a job or his wife.

He eyed me. "We *are* on the same page here, right? No more lies. You find either one, you tell me."

I saw the hopefulness in his face; he still had faith in a friend, and I could not let him down. "Yes," I said, and I really did mean it. Right after I figured out how all the pieces fit. Once that goddamn buzzard stopped circling in my mind and lit.

He started walking towards the door, shoving his Glock into his armpit holster. "This is serious shit, man. Not just because of the Feds and the penalties. Those people who traffic immigrants for sex have no regard for human life." He looked at me. "Don't go out there like the Lone Ranger, like you did with that IED. I wanna see you at the top of the Finger one day, and with no other pieces missing."

I wanted to run over and hug him and give him a big slobbery kiss. But he was out the door before my words "I won't, dude," came out. Did he know me or what?

Does anyone really know another person? Probably the closest you come is when you're dodging bullets together in a rat-infested hovel, drinking boiled and iodine-treated water from a Taliban-fouled well, eating dog stew from a communal soup spoon, and dragging a guy whose leg has been blown off to safety.

O.J. was pretty close. Buddy? He was inside my head.

My phone alarmed. A text message from Lisa. *Riana died last night. Making arrangements. Be back soon. DON'T CALL!*

Oh, man. Riana gone. And me making it with Angela while Lisa was with her dying sister. Shit! I had to find Angela, tell her we were done. Except she'd already showed me that. In spade. My one-way ticket to Angela needed cancelling.

I thought about calling Lisa even though she told me not to, to tell her I loved her. But I put the phone away. *Give her space.*

I heard the squirrel in O.J.'s crappy little Honda pound out rpms and soon the reverberations of the bad muffler disappeared. I gathered my clothes, myself, and trekked outside to the 4Runner and jumped in the driver's seat, tossing my stuff into the passenger seat.

Buddy popped up from the backseat and I nearly shit my pants.

CHAPTER 39

What Are Friends For?

I turned around and looked at Buddy. He immediately looked away.

"What the hell are you doing here?" I said.

He kept looking at the floor.

"Wait." I turned and adjusted the rearview mirror, so I could see him. "I'll look through here."

His eyes came up and he shyly looked at my reflection. "I want to help you and Detective C, but he's too intense right now."

"You're in deep shit, Buddy. Why did you kill the Judge?"

His shy eyes got confused. A frown darkened his face even more than it already was under the baseball cap I'd never seen him wear before. Usually he wore the same grimy cap, but this one made him look, I don't know, more believable, more respectable—not like some skid row bum. Maybe it was because it had the New Orleans Saints logo on the front.

"I didn't kill the Judge."

"Right. You've been pissed at him ever since you delivered that mirror to his house. O.J. even said you thought he was going to kill Angela."

The 4Runner had been a little warm in the afternoon sun, until I said "Angela." Buddy's gaze became cold and angry, the eyes I'd seen when he shot a guy in Kabul who'd beat a woman then shot her in the head, point blank. I didn't want to be this close to him. I reached for the door handle to leave and—

"You slept with her." His flat statement froze me.

I looked away, pausing to gather my thoughts. Then I looked directly at his angry eyes through the mirror. "Yes, I did. I loved her ... Maybe I still do, and I thought we might get together or something. It's like those dopes you see on TV talk shows: Past love affairs of two soul mates lost, then years later drawn back together. She seemed to think the same thing. At least, she convinced me last night. I thought. But now?" His eyes seemed to soften a bit. "Now, I'm not so sure. She told me you killed the Judge, and you say you didn't. I think I'm more inclined to believe you. Maybe you should tell me exactly what happened with you and her from the time you two partnered up at the Stanley Hotel in Estes Park until now."

He gazed into the distance. "I know she did bad things, but she has something deeper, something good. I just wanted to help her."

"I do too, Buddy." Then I digested his whole sentence. "What bad things do you mean?"

His gaze returned to me, but the sides of one eye crinkled and his lower lip pouted just enough to show doubt. "You'll tell Detective C and hurt her."

"No ... well, I might tell him, but we won't hurt her. If she's been a victim of the Judge forcing her to do things with those girls, she won't come to any harm. We just have to clear her name."

He pursed his lips but didn't answer.

"Do you know where she is?" If he didn't, I was going

to need a good crystal ball.

"You promise you won't hurt her?"

"I love her, Buddy. I couldn't hurt her. Ever." After all was said and done, if she had killed the Judge, had lied to me, and had implicated Buddy, I was so glad Geppetto was not even a distant uncle.

I could see that black turkey buzzard in an ever-smaller spiral coming down to land on something I didn't want to see.

Buddy looked away and crooked his jaw and started tapping his eye teeth together. Thinking.

Was I lying to him about Angela and not hurting her? Sometimes we lie for good reason. I glanced at the glove box. I'd lied to O.J. about not knowing about the pills because I hoped it wasn't Angela, and I wanted to have a case for Mug. I needed to get the pills analyzed, maybe get some prints from the bottle. I'd noticed a weird lock on the bottle lid, a larger childproof lock than I'd remembered seeing on other bottles. Maybe they were unique enough to be traceable. To do that, I had to get both Mug and Lisa's help. Mug needed to know there was still hope when it came to his case—maybe even more than hope. And Lisa was always good at finding out things.

Lisa. Yeah. Shit. I needed to be with her, comfort her about her sister. It wasn't a good time, but I had to talk with her. Was it possible for me to tell her the truth? She didn't need it right now.

I looked back at Buddy. Truth was becoming an alien concept. But Angela had lied. I was sure O.J. had lied. Buddy? He was pretty straight but probably didn't give me the whole truth either. Doctors got hit in the head every day by patients who lied—not really on that diet, drank more like six beers not four, watching a football game and not once a week but three times a week, yadda, yadda, yadda. I was just like every human being. An ordinary, lying sonofabitch.

"Look, Buddy, when I said—"

"I might know where she is, or at least where she will be," he said, interrupting my thoughts. I looked at myself in the rearview. Got off easy, you fucking liar.

"Yeah?"

"You live close by the place."

"Good. I need to go home, anyhow." I started the 4Runner. "Why don't you come up in the front seat? Would that be okay? You can direct me better up here, and I won't feel like a chauffeur."

He nodded and got out. I grabbed my clothes and stuff, and tossed them in the back. He got in, slipped out a mirror from his pocket and held it in his lap, tilted so he could watch me.

I put my seat belt on, he fastened his, and I pulled out.

"So," I hoped a bit of misdirection might get more out of him, "Who killed the Judge?"

He palmed the mirror face onto his thigh and looked out the window. "Don't know."

"Who do you think did it?"

"You know."

Yep, I think I did. I was pretty certain it wasn't one of those girls. Angela would never let them have the gun. That left only Angela. Jesus Christ on a crutch, as my Aunt Donna used to say.

But from what I knew, the Judge probably had it coming. And yet, something kept nagging at me about all those pills in Angela's trunk. Why would she want to clear his name if she had killed him?

The mind-buzzard landed, and I could not help but see what it started picking at. By saying she wanted to clear his name, Angela had led me to believe the Judge had been the trafficker—so I would feel sorry for her.

I beat a palm on the steering wheel. Damn.

I hoped Buddy was right when he said she was close to my house.

I mashed the accelerator.

CHAPTER 40

Women

Angela drove south after leaving Var, through empty fields that had once been wheat and soybeans and sunflowers. During the fracker heyday, the fields got gobbled up by dirt roads and white pickup trucks and tanker trucks all moving back and forth between the high stanchions of fracking driller rigs. It was ugly. Yet, she realized what she had done was more than ugly. She hated herself for it.

But it had to be done, and she had to keep going. She had to lay low, out of Colorado for a few days. She and Salvation Lab were so close to getting the ideal asthma drug. Just a little more time and money. The Judge's death might bring that with the insurance, though it would take at least a month—if no one figured out who really killed him. A quicker source of funds was the football connection. In one week, max, they'd be on the way.

She drove fast on a back two-lane, through the green light at the Highway 34 intersection, her thoughts coming back to Var and how pitiful he'd been with his stumps. Pitiful and yet he still loved her.

She pulled over on the side of the road, jerked the door open, ran to the other side of the car and vomited in the drainage ditch. She beat her hand on the passenger door and kicked the dirt with her shoe and stood. *God damn him.* She *had* loved him once, and now all she could feel was pity. Or was it merely pity? Hadn't she felt love for him last night? Hadn't she felt the old surge after washing him off. It hadn't been all RAZR. Had it?

Yes, it had! She did not love him. He left her. Went off, did the manly thing and joined up, no better than those other damn football players, all thinking that if they were macho enough they could rule the world, save the world, save all the poor, pitiful, weak women. Well, their world was about to end, and a woman would do it.

She wiped her mouth with the back of her hand and got into the car, stomping on the accelerator and twisting the steering wheel. The car spun into a screeching U turn. At Highway 34, she turned left toward the mountains and Var. She was going to finish this. She held on to the steering wheel with one hand and made a call on her cell phone with the other.

♪ ♫

I gunned the 4Runner around the bend of the small foothill that hid the meadow from O.J.'s house, feeling like Buddy and I could fix everything. Then I saw it. The KWJN TV news van—blue globe and large orange lettering on its side—parked at the meadow. A local Colorado news station, not national, and pretty nice people, not the assholes that some of the national people that covered the High Park Fire. KWJN had helped me in the past with publicity on a few hit-and-run cases, posting vehicles we were looking for. That was great, but it made me a known figure now. Had Angela upped the ante and called KWJN about the bodies? Who else? Had she told them Buddy was the main suspect? If they stopped us and got photos of Buddy and me ...

There was only scant space on the road between the rear of the news van, a knee-high rock, and a juniper with a broken branch pointing at the van like a specter. I thought of the beautiful sunny day a month ago when I'd waxed the forest green 4Runner. Still looked like new, then.

"Put your head down," I told Buddy.

I slowed the 4Runner. If I stopped and asked them to move forward, would they?

A guy in denims and a Harley tee shirt hoisted a TV camera onto his shoulder. He sported a graying Fu Manchu moustache and ponytail and all I could think was, *This could get ugly*.

I pressed the accelerator gently and joggled over the rock on my side, the broken branch of the juniper screeching down the side of the 4Runner. That hurt, but not near as much as seeing my face on the news with Buddy would.

I heard voices and punched it, one last cracking scratch from the juniper. Yelling from behind me, a few waving hands in the rearview, but a curtain of dust between me and them, hopefully obscuring my license plate.

I kept a hand on Buddy's head until we were well out of sight.

"I sure hope we find Angela where you think she is today. That news crew will have the story on the evening news, and you, me, and O.J. will be the next big thing to happen to Poudre County."

Buddy looked out the window at the sage, rolling hills, and sparse pine trees. "Mirrors don't lie. The Judge didn't knife Angela, but he still killed her."

I heard it but what can you say to something so

weird? I shook my head and drove.

Soon my humble abode came into view. I needed food and a nap, but Lisa's black F-150 in the driveway told me I would get neither. She was standing at the front door, smiling. How could she be smiling? Her sister just died. And I couldn't tell her about last night and everything right now. She'd decompensate.

"Don't say anything to her," I said, glancing at him. "Let me … just let me tell her. I know: I'm all screwed up. But," I gave him a hard look in his mirror, "you don't perfectly understand women, either. Right?"

He nodded.

I got out and she was already on me, arms around my neck, warm lips kissing the soft and tender spot she knew I loved behind my earlobe. "I was so worried about you."

"It's been a crazy twenty-four hours. But, what about your sister?"

She backed off and wrinkled her nose. "You smell like sweat and …?"

"Yeah. I need to clean up. I did some climbing with O.J." Damn. Women can smell things even a dog can't.

I started for the front door and saw a mountain bike leaning beside the garage. It wasn't mine or Lisa's.

"Is Mug here?"

"Yeah. He said he was nervous at his place so he rode over here to see if he could help me find anything else about the RAZR. He's really nice."

She frowned. "Actually, about Riana, I feel relief. I think I slept better the last four hours than I have in weeks. Now, maybe you and I can …" She paused "Except, that is *not* just sweat I smell."

Twelve miles. Not bad for a beefy guy like Mug on a

mountain bike.

"Yeah, probably pizza and maybe some blood from the crime scene and the lunch I had." Uh-huh. The smell she was catching had nothing to do with Angela's sex on me. Maybe it was a Freudian slip to not wash off Dorkmeister after we climbed. I never liked Freud.

I leaned toward Lisa and whispered, "Might be Buddy, too. He doesn't take showers too often."

She looked at Buddy who had just stepped out of the 4Runner. She squinted at me, not really buying it. Could this be her limit? God, not now.

"Anyway, I'm so sorry about your sister. We need to talk, but things are moving fast in this case. I'm glad Mug is here. I've got something I need you to investigate with him. If it has the right prints on it and we can find out where it was filled, we might be able to solve this RAZR case." I walked past her, trying not to be too obvious in hurrying out of her nose's range and ignoring her frown and hands on hips.

"Mug," I shouted. "I've got good news."

He lumbered out of the hallway, his gargantuan mass filling the door frame of the kitchen. He wore tan shorts and a bright yellow tee shirt with *Colombia* in small lettering on the left side of his massive chest, and his flip-flops slapped as he walked over the tiled kitchen floor. Must have changed out of his biking clothes. I looked at his flip-flops. How could people wear those things between their toes?

"Hey, Var. Thought I'd come over and help Lisa. She's done so much for me, you know." He glanced at her, smiled sheepishly then looked at the floor.

What had been going on between these two? I gritted my teeth and took a deep breath. Jesus. She'd just lost her sister; I was the guilty one and here I was trying to make Mug just as stupid as I'd been.

I pulled out the clear ziplock baggy with the pill bottle inside and strode into the kitchen and laid it on the table. I chose my words carefully, fuzzy about how much I'd told Mug about my love for Angela. "I think these are RAZR pills. After I dropped you off, I found this in one of the Judge's cars. We need to get an analysis of the pills and get prints on the bottle and pills if possible. Also, try to see if this bottle was manufactured anywhere special."

Lisa walked past me on the right and picked up one baggy by a corner. "Looks like simple pill bottle to me." She faced me. "What happened the rest of last night?" Her voice had a definite tone about it, and not a good one.

I kept walking, around the left side of the table and Mug, keeping her at a distance. I entered the hallway and said over my shoulder, "There's a weird childproof lock on the lid. I gotta get a shower and take a nap so I can think. Tell you about the rest when I wake up. Promise." I was halfway down the hallway to my bedroom and turned around. "Thanks. Both of you. I don't know where I'd be without you. You have no idea how important you are to me." I made sure I looked right into Lisa's buckskin eyes. I wanted to get lost in them. I wanted to tell her everything.

"I'd give you a hug, but I stink, and I gotta take a shower. If I'm not up in two hours, please wake me."

Buddy had come in and was looking at me through the mirror and shaking his head. I turned, walked in the bedroom and closed the door.

The tingling burn in my arm had started again. I

needed the shower and antibiotics and the rest, not just to wash off Angela and give me time to think of a way to come clean to Lisa, but to figure out if this infection had progressed and how to stop it. It would be faster if Lisa helped, but that was not an option right now.

CHAPTER 41

O.J.'s Review

On his way to the office, O.J. thought about the crime scene again. Had Buddy killed the Judge at the house or in the meadow? If in the meadow, there should be signs of the Judge's blood there.

He called Blue to tell him to check the meadow for blood. Blue's phone began to ring.

Then O.J. changed his mind. No one in the department needs to know about the cemetery in the meadow.

He was about to hang up but then had another thought and let it ring.

It rang once more, and the tiny speaker clicked. "Hello, Detective Cromwell."

"Hi, Blue. I've been reviewing the crime scene again and wondered if you could give me a preliminary report concerning whether the Judge may have died somewhere else and was driven into the garage?"

"It would be purely speculation. Nothing definitive, yet."

"So that means you might have something?"

"I have evidence, but nothing to lead me to believe either way, exactly."

"Exactly? Quit fucking with me, Blue."

"I wouldn't do that. Let me explain. Ambient temperature in the garage changed overnight, from some unknown temperature to the time I got there when I measured the rectal temperature, which was eighty-eight by the way. If the ambient temperature started at ninety-nine, then dropped to eighty when I got there, the calculation of time of death would be very difficult. If the body was in the Suburban at say seventy-two for an hour before, driven while dead to the garage where it was ninety-nine and then sat until I got there, then the calculation would be even more difficult."

"Difficult, but not for you, right?"

"I'm flattered, Detective Cromwell. But you fail to see the biggest problem with the body temperature in discovering time of death in this case." He paused, a pregnant pause way past its due date.

"Are you going to tell me?"

"It's that I have no idea what temperature the body started at in the garage, or if driven there, in the vehicle it traveled in. So what I'm saying is body temperature is out."

"So you don't have any idea what the time of death was?"

"Not really. The other two indicators, lividity and livor mortis, revealed that the body, if driven, was not driven more than about fifteen minutes. Un—"

O.J. barged in, now angry. "Why didn't you say that to begin with?"

"If you will let me finish, Detective. As I started to say, *unless* there were activities the person was involved in that sped up his metabolism before death. If that were the case, then he could have been driven there perhaps an hour or two from the place of death."

O.J. pushed *End,* killing the connection. *Fucking Blue,* he thought. Never could give a simple answer, even when playing poker. No wonder he won so much. Everyone beamed frustrated with his slow play and that caused them to make mistakes.

He unrolled his window and took some deep breaths, turned right onto Hancock Road towards town, and re-started his train of thought.

If he would have thought this out, he never would have called Blue. It was clear that Buddy had not been to the garage. If Buddy had killed the Judge at the meadow, and Angela hit him with the shovel there, she would have had to drive the Suburban back to the house, trying to see around the Judge's brains on the windshield. Possible, but very unlikely Why would she do that? Maybe she'd had the illegals in the Suburban and didn't want to chance being found with them.

It all pointed to someone killing the Judge while he sat in the Suburban in the garage. If she was sitting in the driver's seat and did it, why were his brains on the windshield and not the passenger door and window? Maybe one of the girls in the backseat had offed him. Unlikely. No way they would have a gun. Maybe Buddy *had* been there in the backseat and killed him and took off like Angela said and hitched a ride to the meadow. He had sure been to O.J.'s house. But why had he waited until the Judge turned around to the backseat and shot him in the forehead, instead of just giving it to him in the back of the head?

He pounded his palm on the steering wheel. "Shit!" This wasn't making any sense.

What did make sense was Var calling him and telling him he knew about the meadow and the dead bodies.

He'd been with Angela, and she'd told him about it. She knew it because she'd just been there.

What it boiled down to was O.J. had to find Buddy and talk to him.

He took another deep breath of the fresh air pummeling him through the window. Var would help him. He could count on Var.

O.J. began thinking of what he would tell the Captain and how he would get out of the department as fast as he could to get back out there and help Var, when he turned down Main Street and saw the KWJN TV news van and Pamela Sanderson and her tight black skirt and low-cut, white, spaghetti-strapped tank top. She always flaunted her pretty little ta-tas and tight ass. Got people to watch the news. But she'd never liked him, even in a Stones tee shirt. He didn't understand that, because most women loved his avoidance of typical police dress and haircuts. Except the Captain. And she was no Captain.

He started to turn the car, thinking about a U turn, but she already had the camera man pointing the big lens at him. Probably had recognized his crappy little Honda.

Screw that. He turned left fast, giving the camera man the passenger side of his car, and sped into an alley that led to the back of the police department. He hoped he'd turned fast enough so they didn't see his license plates. Less chance the network would ID his car. There were lots of crappy little Hondas around.

But why was she here? And why was she so interested in him? She hated him. Unless … She must have known about the bodies in the meadow and wanted to see him squirm under her lens like a bug under a magnifying lens focusing the sun and burning him to death. Boy was he glad he'd passed last week on buying her a drink at the Cowboy Bar. She was a looker, part Mexican and part Irish, with those dark brooding eyes and smooth olive skin, but she had to be a ball buster. What was he thinking—she already *had* busted his on other cases and was after him again. Could that be a way of flirting? He got hard under his pants.

He parked the Honda, jumped out, adjusted himself, and ran down the stairs to the basement entrance to the records office, fidgeting with his key ring to find the one he needed. Around the corner, Pamela's frantic screaming at the camera man echoed in the alley, as did their running footsteps. She was getting close. His groin tingled. It was like foreplay for torture. He got a sense of why some people like S&M. But he could *not* let her catch him. Not now. He'd have to work on this later.

He hadn't been in this back entrance to the department for over a year. He fiddled with his key ring, located the key and hoped it would still work.

CHAPTER 42

O.J. and the Captain

He stuck the key in and it fit but wouldn't turn. Pamela's voice was nearing. He jiggled the key. "Come on!" He pushed and jiggled and it finally twisted. The door opened, but only halfway. Damn. He pushed harder and the door opened slowly, like there was someone pushing back. Finally he was in and he closed the door behind him. He thought about plastering his face against the window next to the door with his tongue out at Pamela. Better not. If she had been flirting, that would kill it. Besides, he didn't want his contorted face on the news.

There was a pile of files on the floor behind the door, apparently had been leaning against the door, partially blocking it. His entrance had pushed them over from their semi-neat pile, now more like fifty-two card pickup, papers leaking out of them all over the floor.

He twisted the key and the deadbolt made a satisfying clunk. He bent over and quickly straightened the files in a semblance of a neat stack against the door then turned and walked through the records office. Pounding began on the door behind him. He kept walking. A balding pudgy guy sat at one of the cubicles with a Styrofoam cup and open files on the work desk. He looked up at the banging and tracked O.J. It was Cranston, one of the other detectives.

"Do *not* open that door!" O.J. said.

Cranston smiled. "Didn't even know that door did open."

"Well, just leave it locked and shut. That KWJN TV news woman is after my ass."

Cranston smirked as he went back to his files. "There are worse things."

Yes, there were.

O.J. bounded up the stairs into the large open room with four modular office cubicles fit together. O.J.'s was on the right. It was an economical use of space and money. On the south side was a glass door to the Captain's office, which had a southern window. Rank has its privileges. The southern window had been nice for a year after the Captain moved in. Then Gorilla Covers, the company that made covers for smartphones, built their three-story building twenty feet away. If he stood close to the window and looked to the side, the Captain could still see a glimpse of the park beyond, a few cottonwoods and grass. At least he had some natural light and didn't have to listen to three other conversations on the phone and stare at gray walls all day.

The Captain was sitting at his desk, munching on chips and sipping a Coke. The permanent lines of the scowl on his face deepened when he spotted O.J. walking toward his door. That natural light did nothing to improve his personality. Could be he noosed his tie too tight. It was striped today, blue and gray, but still tight enough on his crisp white dress shirt encircling his toad-like neck that his face had its usual purple hue and his neck veins stood out. The guy was a stroke waiting to happen.

He brushed chip crumbs off his beer belly and stood when O.J. entered. "You're late."

"Had a few things I needed to clear up about these cases."

The Captain's face relaxed, as if O.J. might actually have something that would please him. "Close the door and sit down and tell me about them. But make it fast. The TV people are wanting you for supper."

O.J. shut the door and sat in front of the Captain's large mahogany desk. "Yeah. I saw that. Almost had a run-in with Pamela Sanderson."

"If she talks to you, send her my way." Did O.J. detect a sly smile on the Captain's face? Jesus. He was married. Yeah, as if that mattered.

And then he got it: The Captain was relaxed and smiling because he *was* pleased, not with O.J., but with himself.

O.J. nodded at him. "Let me start with the Stanley Hotel case. That looks like a suicide, no signs of murder, so not really our concern."

"Yeah? So, where's the body?"

O.J. glanced out the southern window, wanting one branch of fluttering leaves to look at. The trees always made him and his problems smaller. He remembered a phrase from a Sioux Indian he'd read once: *Only the trees and rocks live forever.* "I'll get to that."

The Captain leaned back in his chair and raised his eyebrows, as if waiting for more, yet looking even more relaxed and very confident, as if he already knew what was coming.

O.J. wanted to steer away from the meadow of bodies. He needed time to prove Angela had framed him. Yet he knew if he did, and they were discovered—which it looked like the TV news had already done—then it would look like he was hiding things. It would look like he'd put them there. It would look like he was guilty.

"The body is probably in a meadow close to my house."

The Captain's bloated upper eyelids almost covered his eyes, like a lizard watching a grasshopper crawling up a stalk of grass, right towards his hungry mouth. "Do tell."

O.J. did not like his smug tone.

"Look, Captain, I know how it looks, but I had nothing to do with that meadow. I have reason to believe that the woman who buried that suicide, Angela, has been running a sex-trafficking operation out of her house and buried several dead girls in that meadow."

"This woman—Angela—would she happen to be Angela Craghead, the Judge's wife? The same judge who was found in his garage shot in the forehead?"

"Yes. I found him there early this morning."

"You found the Judge." He stood and grabbed his index finger with the other hand. "You have several bodies buried in your backyard—that's two." He grabbed the long finger and started ticking off numbers like he was playing three little piggies went to market. "You never liked the Judge or Angela. You have a war buddy who's wacko, probably joined the service to escape another murder charge, and he drove away with Angela. Your friend's gun with his prints on it was at the scene with the Judge. You, as I seem to remember, have a grudge against women, after your New Orleans stint." He held up five fingers on one hand and one on the other. "There's a lot of *you* that keeps coming up in both of these cases." He put his hands on his hips and stared down at O.J. "Did I miss something?"

O.J. had his molars ground together so hard he was sure he'd need another crown for a cracked tooth. He'd stared straight ahead and breathed slowly during the Captain's accusations.

"Yeah," O.J. said.

The Captain shook his head and looked at the ceiling. "You mean there's more?" Sounded more like a comedian's punch line than a real question.

O.J. stood. Being two inches taller, he looked down at the Captain. It felt good. "Probably not that your pea-sized brain would ever understand. Should I call Blue in here to make sure you didn't miss something? I'm sure that asshole gave you all that erroneous information."

He stepped forward into the Captain's face and the Captain stumbled back and plopped his ample ass on his huge desk, a desk that hinted at overcompensation almost as obviously as his red 350 Magnum truck in the parking lot did.

"Here's the deal, Captain. If you'd ever actually gone into the courtroom with the Judge, you'd know how big a hypocrite and ass he was, how many innocent people he put away, and how much he hates good cops. And if you'd been out on the streets doing actual police work, you'd know that he and his wife, Angela, have been running a sex-trafficking operation from their basement for what could be years after he retired and that he used his contacts in the upper echelons of power in this state to contact traffickers in Brazil. You'd know that he and his beautiful wife, Angela, have been killing off these illegals after they'd used them up and burying them in the meadow a quarter mile from my home. But, if you trusted me as an investigator, you'd know that Angela is trying to frame me and my good friend, Mr. Hollister. But you wouldn't know these things because you sit on your fat ass in front of your sixty-inch flat screen every night, eating pepperoni pizza and popping one beer after another watching mindless television shows, not even caring that the cops who care, like me, are out there actually doing their jobs. You wouldn't know because you've never been in a rat-infested dirt hole wondering if you'll live to see the next day, knowing friends like Buddy Hollister are the only thing that keep you alive."

He stared down at the Captain, whose countenance had changed from confident to worried. Pale and anxious.

"Are you getting this, Captain?"

The Captain nodded once, then his toad eyes rolled up inside his toad lids and he flopped over onto his fat, toad side onto the oversized desk, pencils and pictures flying off and crashing onto the ground.

"Ah, shit," O.J. said. He opened the door and screamed. "Call an ambulance! Get the AED. The Captain's having a heart attack."

He pulled the Captain off the desk and started pumping his chest, CPR style. No mouth-to-mouth. He'd heard the pumping was the most important part. Someone else would have to blow into the toad's mouth.

God, how he'd wanted to say to the Captain before he crapped out, A lot of *you* kept coming up in my words, if you hadn't noticed. But he was pretty sure someone (or possibly many people) outside the Captain's office had heard the yelling through the walls and seen how he'd almost pushed the Captain onto his desk. Even if he saved the Captain's life, O.J. Cromwell was done as a detective in this county. He pumped harder and faster.

Cranston had walked from the cubicle room and watched now, just outside the office. "Cranston, can you help me with this? I forget if I press five times and one breath or fifteen and two? I seem to remember not even needing breaths."

Cranston had always been the teacher of their biennial CPR courses. He bustled into the room, pushed O.J. aside, and knelt beside the Captain. "Let me take over." He was such an expert.

Cranston took over pumping, and O.J. gladly stood aside, gradually back stepping and sidling through the gawking cops and staff until he was behind everyone. He watched from the rear and saw Rupert, the Captain's smoking partner, standing off to the side, wringing his hands. He glanced at Cromwell with a look that was pure blame. Cranston looked up from his pumping and caught Cromwell's eye—a big question mark in his gaze.

O.J. turned and walked downstairs to the record room. He looked through the window beside the back door—no reporters—kicked the files leaning against the door out of the way and went out the way he'd come. He turned to lock the door, then thought about the reporters everywhere, the Captain, Rupert, and Cranston eyeing him. They deserved each other.

He left the door unlocked. He walked to his crappy little Honda, got in, backed up, turned the steering wheel, and drove out of the alley, taking a right into the street, smiling at the view of the TV van in the rear-view.

He focused on the road and sped up. He had to find Var—he was the key to getting Buddy and Angela, and clearing up this mess.

CHAPTER 43

Pablo

Angela felt her hands getting sweaty and she licked her lips too many times as she put the Glock 26 back into her purse and started driving. She drove west faster than she should have, west on Highway 34. There were traffic lights at Centerra Promenade shops on the right, the overpass of the busy I-25, then another mall, and after that mostly a blur of strip malls. She wanted to stop and get a Coke or something for her dry mouth. What she really wanted was to turn around. This was way too dangerous. But she had to try. The gun would give her the edge.

Her vision seemed to narrow as she thought of what she must do. Landmarks barely registered, only enough to know if she should turn: farms growing squash and pumpkins, a high school, many square salmon-colored brick business buildings, and roads that lead to neighborhoods. She felt her jaw clenching and her pulse start to race as she kept pushing her speed, knowing if she got caught it would be the end, but also knowing the faster she ended this, the faster she could move on. She kept going west on 34 through streetlights, into town, by Loveland Lake, then out into the periphery of town, getting close. She turned right at the foothills, on the last president street, Wilson Street. The terrain changed to wheat fields and plowed earth and rolling hills with higher foothills on the left, and the town of Fort Collins coming up north. She passed a few suburban neighborhoods, took a left on Harmony to Horsetooth Reservoir.

Her hands were getting so slick they slipped on the wheel. He was a very dangerous man. But she had RAZR. She took a few deep breaths and let them out slowly. It had to be done, if she was ever going to get out of here.

At the top of the hill she pulled over and stopped, the long waters of Horsetooth Dam on the right. Ahead to the left was construction on the road that curved to the left above the lake and toward a small town. Once again, she thought about turning around and driving back to the interstate and speeding south. But it was time. She held her right hand up. It shook like a palsy. RAZR had screwed her up, her body, and more of her mind than she wanted to admit. Another twenty minutes, and it would be done.

She popped the glove box, took out the bottle of RAZR, opened it, took out four pills and stuffed them between her breasts, under the bra strap. She took another one out and swallowed it. She closed the bottle and put it back and took another deep breath before putting the car into gear. She turned right onto the causeway and drove north. The road was hilly and winding.

Fifteen minutes later, she slowed, saw the 4Runner in Var's driveway and sped up again. A few more miles of winding road passed under her wheels before she turned west into the foothills again onto a dirt road. In another two hundred yards, she hung a right on a two-track where red rocks spiked into the air like tongues.

Around one of those rocks, she came to a dead end and another trailer. This one used to be white, but a brown fringe of dirt had formed from years of rain splash. A black Mini Cooper sat outside: Pablo's.

She took a deep breath and let it out and looked all around the trailer and her car. No one guarding him. That might make this a bit easier.

She pulled the Glock 26 from her purse, stuck it in the sweaty small of her back, pulled her shirt over it and got out and walked like a woman with no cares toward the front door. Ten feet from the front step the door opened, and Pablo stepped out, a half-full glass of cognac in each tattooed hand. A silver skull ringed his right middle finger, a smile creased his acne-scarred face, and black eyes peered at her, as cold as death.

"My Angel. I knew you would come. We have more girls to move, eh?" He held out a glass to her. "Let us toast to your getting away from the pigs."

She went up the steps and took the glass in her left hand, the steady hand, but which also allowed her to twist, putting her left side toward him and quite naturally her right hand unseen behind her back. She smiled as she brought her lips to the glass and reached her right hand to grab the gun.

A vice of a hand clamped on her right wrist before she could get the gun and her arm was pulled up behind her back and another hand steadied her left shoulder.

She screamed, "No!"

Pablo slapped the glass out of her hand and it crashed onto the trailer door, glass flying everywhere. He leaned into her. "Yes. Oh, yes, you little bitch. You think you can drive your fancy car in here and kill me when you owe me money? And," he put the back of his right hand on her cheek, "you owe me a lot of money."

He turned and took a few steps back into the trailer. "Come in to my humble abode."

The silent man who held Angela forced her forward. She smelled his sour sweat and the sickening sweet cognac on his breath. Pablo disappeared into darkness inside the trailer. She stumbled through the door and saw the high-backed metal-framed kitchen chair sitting in the middle of the kitchen floor. All the other furniture had been cleared out. There was a ten-foot by ten-foot black plastic sheet spread out very smoothly under the chair.

She remembered vomiting on the road south not an hour ago. She should have kept driving south.

The beatings began after he tied her to the chair. That wasn't too bad. The RAZR pill helped give her strength, though not nearly enough. She'd had worse beatings from her father. It was the cutting with the razor blade that got to her. Her blood ran down her chest, down her arms. After she had told him about Var and that he probably knew everything about the girls, Pablo left her alone. She sat and sucked breaths through swollen lips and heard the *plop-plop* of her own blood on the plastic sheet under her.

Pablo was looking at a laptop on the kitchen table. He found Var's house on Google Maps, laughed, and came back to her, cut her ties and dragged her back to her Lexus. "You and I are going to find this Var and since he is your problem, you will make sure he doesn't tell anyone what he knows."

She could only see hazy shapes and her legs wouldn't support her, so the helper opened the passenger front door and threw her in and slammed the door behind.

Her head smacked the gearshift and she groaned, but it was like a slap in the face. She righted herself and sat and started thinking. The gash on her cheek oozed and dripped onto her white shirt. His silver ring was large and multifaceted and had done its work. Her thighs slipped and slid on the leather seat. She couldn't help a scant smile. It was going to be a bitch cleaning the blood off.

She watched Pablo tuck her Glock in his pants and nod to his helper, who went back to the trailer. Pablo walked in front to the driver's side, and when he wasn't looking, she slipped her finger and thumb inside her bra, brought out the four pills, slipped them into her mouth and swallowed. She was dead anyway. Might as well fry the rest of her brain and go out with a bang.

Pablo alone got in and drove back toward Var's.

CHAPTER 44

Caught

I took two of the antibiotics, gingerly washed off the wound in the shower, and hit the rack. I instantly slept but kept dreaming about Mug and Angela and Lisa in a weird sex triangle. I woke and sat up, wiping my palm over my face. "Jesus."

The clock said I'd been out for an hour. I felt worse than if I'd not slept. I must be getting old. I'm sure Freud would fill a large tome with the significance of my sexual dream, but I just wanted to forget it. Still, I kept wondering why I wasn't in the dream. I thought about lying down, but there was no way I was going back to sleep. Maybe if I snuck out and got a bike ride in, I could clear my head. Or did I just want to avoid thinking or dreaming for a while. I needed to do it alone, no distractions. I dressed in my gear, grabbed the GPS odometer, got my bike prosthetics on, and was out the back door to the garage in less than five minutes. It was a warm day, but not over eighty, perfect for a ride in the fresh breeze off Horsetooth Reservoir. I needed to get a few endorphins going and to listen to tunes. I pushed the earbuds in and picked a favorite track on my iPhone, heavy metal mixed with the occasional Barenaked Ladies, stuck the phone in my back shirt pocket and picked my favorite road bike, the Trek. I pumped the tires to 110mm Hg, fit the GPS unit onto the handle-bar mount, put a leg over, and coasted down the drive-way. If I went straight out someone would see me, so I curved to the left and was on the road south, I hoped, before anyone inside was the wiser. I had an hour—time enough for twenty of the one eighties. In those pain and torture sessions in Pensacola, I'd gotten by on only three of the one eighties, just a minute under my allot-ted break of ten minutes.

I shoved my shoes into the clips and started ped-dling. Soon I was in a good rhythm, each rotation matching the beat of the song. Very few cars were on the road; the mild heat felt good, and soon nothing mattered but wind, breathing, and Joe Walsh's guitar riffs. It was like being a moving cog of nature. The glare of the sun off the reservoir, the long-distance views of hills and valleys and roads and campers by the water, and soon the endorphins kicked in and I felt that I could conquer everything and everyone.

Going up one hill, I had to pedal hard and shift down until I was barely moving forward despite my legs pumping furiously, pushing it up the hill. My lungs felt they would burst but I made it to the top and floated over the crest like the Monarch butterfly I'd seen, shift-ing up, catching my breath, taking a drink through my Camelback tube.

I heard a car gunning its engine a good distance be-hind me and hoped I would make the turn before it got close. I hated assholes who sped too fast on this road, but it happened all the time. I gripped the handle-bars and started down the next hill, over the dam and around the corner to the right, coming up to that same area I'd met Mug: jagged rocks and water below on the right and construction ahead on the left.

A jackhammer prevented me from hearing the car behind me, but there is a sixth sense that bikers get, or maybe it's paranoia I carried with me after my accidents that told me a car was coming up. In my hurry, I'd forgotten the postage-stamp rearview mirror I usually clamped onto the stem of my dark glasses, so I had to risk a quick glance behind me to the left. It was Angela's Lexus, only a Mexican-looking guy was driving it. He must have seen me as I'd pulled out of my driveway and followed, picking this narrowed road at the construction site to pin me close. Angela was in the passenger seat and her face was a mess, bruised and cut. Her eyes looked glazed and I knew instantly that the guy driving had beaten her. I didn't like what she'd done to me, but you don't beat up women. You just don't. You might kill them if they are carrying some IED trigger in a war. But that's war. And even then, it's a quick bullet to the head. You don't beat them up. Unless you are some bully of a terrorist who gets his power trip jollies that way.

This guy wasn't a terrorist; I was pretty sure. Everything clicked into place in a half revolution of my pedals. Amazing how a brain can do that. This guy was Angela's boss. He must have been running the organization that brought in the Brazilian girls Angela had been using. Now I knew. It hadn't been her. It was the asshole driving. And he probably was not Mexican, but Brazilian.

I also recognized my danger. That guy had used her to find me. He likely wanted to know what I knew about the organization. He was mopping up before he pulled the chocks and put his private Lear jet into supersonic.

Angela and I were dead meat, right after he obtained the information in my head.

Another half revolution of the pedals and I figured it all connected to RAZR, the drug used to spice up the girls' sex life. And kill them. But this guy and his organization didn't care about killing girls. They were the detritus of power and money.

I was about to become the same.

CHAPTER 45

Here We Go

O.J. sighed in relief at the brief view out the rearview. No TV news personnel followed. They were all plastered on either side of the ambulance that was backed up to the front door of the station. Death vultures. Had to get a piece of death, swallow it, and defecate it onto the news. Everyone loved to hear about someone important dying. He shook his head. The human race never ceased to disappoint.

But he didn't know the Captain was dead. It was just wishful thinking.

Once out of sight of the news van, he'd gunned it. The crappy little Honda still had a little get up and go, so he stuck the magnetic flashing light on the roof and gave her most of what he dared. Too much and he knew the poor old car might throw a rod and then he'd be stuck.

As he'd been getting into the Captain's face, some thoughts had crystalized. Var probably knew where Angela and Buddy were. But O.J. didn't want to call him and scare them away. He would drive to Var's place and confront him there. It was only a few minutes away.

♪ ♫

Mug found a hit on his internet search about the type of pill bottles. He put a fist in the air and went in to tell Var, but he wasn't on the bed. The covers were barely rumpled. The bathroom door was closed, so Mug walked over to it and knocked.

No answer.

"Var, you in there?"

No answer.

He opened the door. Empty bathroom.

He ran back to the living room and said, "Var's gone."

Buddy stood up and frowned. Lisa started pacing. She went to the front window. "His car's still here." She ran to the garage and ran back. "His best bike is missing."

"Maybe he just went for a ride to clear his head."

"No, it's not just that," Buddy said. "I didn't want to say anything when I came in, but I saw it when he passed the living room mirror. Someone's going to shoot him."

They all piled into her F-150, Mug in the front passenger seat and Buddy behind Lisa in the crew seat, and took off south, the way Lisa said Var always went to clear his head. If they didn't see him in ten minutes they'd reverse course. It wouldn't take long.

♪ ♫

I thought about speeding up to get closer to the miniscule town of a restaurant and vacation homes about a half mile ahead. Surely the guy driving Angela's car wouldn't kill me in front of witnesses.

But just before the construction, he passed me and pulled over to block my path. I had no choice but to slow down. Another car was coming from the other direction, so I couldn't pass. He stopped the car right in front of me, forcing me to brake hard and quickly twist and unclip my foot and prosthetic out of the pedals. I took the earbuds out and was off the bike, but the guy was quicker than me. He'd already put the car in park and was walking toward me, pistol in his left hand by his leg, clearly visible to me but hidden from any traffic that might come along. And I doubted the two construction guys down the road on the left would think anything odd about this encounter, if they noticed it at all. One was jack hammering while the other was driving the miniature front-end loader.

Angela's boss wasn't a big man. I didn't see anyone else, but Angela. I could possibly take him, if not for the gun. He had a dark, two-day beard covering an acne-scarred weak jaw. His eyes were his strong suit, though. It was like they held the River Styx and all the dark power of the underworld inside. This man was not to be messed with. I was probably toast.

"Hello, Var. I brought your girlfriend. Me and her had a…" he glanced over at her getting out of the passenger side, "a conversation about you." His accent was minimal, despite his poor command of grammar.

He smiled—a gesture that made me nauseous—and flicked the gun at her then me, motioning for her to go to me. "And she wants to talk to you about a few things."

She was walking on the passenger side toward me, the glazed look on her bruised and lumpy face one of intense concentration. Her previously sexy sheer white shirt was spotted with blood and torn over one shoulder.

"Var, I need to know a few things." She glanced sideways at the man. "*We* need to know some things, and then we'll be on our way." She kept walking, her gait becoming more sure-footed each step of the way. Her eyes were now clear, the previous glaze gone. Her cheeks were red. It looked like she was trying to appear sexy. But she failed miserably, her face looking like Joe Frazer after Ali.

"What the hell did you do to her, you piece of shit?" I asked the man.

He leveled an indifferent yet penetrating gaze in my direction. One that said he'd make me pay for dissing him. I heard the safety click off on his gun.

"It was me, Var," Angela said. "I tripped and fell."

How many times had I heard that one in my office or the ER? Why do women who've been abused lie about it? The answer in her case was likely fear of retribution. It would be much worse next time if she told. Bullies of the world knew that, and every day got away with worse abuse. One woman was physically abused every fifteen seconds, and many went back for more, sometimes to die. Well maybe I could stop this from continuing.

She was now a few steps from me, and I could see the cuts on her arms and more blood under her shirt. Her head shook in a slight tremor, as did her hands. Sweat soaked under her arms and around the waist of her pants.

She wrenched my bike from my hands and raised it over her head with as little effort as lifting potato chips. It was light, but not that light. "Tell Pablo about your investigation or I will throw this bike over the side" Then she murmured to me, "Or he will kill me."

Her breasts thrust into my face. I smelled her sour sweat, not the aphrodisiac of last night, but the smell clicked a memory of concern last night making love. I had hoped it was her desire. Now I realized the question that had lingered then at the periphery of my mind, how could she make love to me and my stumps? manifested again. Her strength despite her recent beating, her sweating, her red face, the sexual body language—all of it was from the drug she'd taken, the same drug she had been giving her girls: RAZR. She had probably taken it last night, too. Her seeming long lost desire for me had been a drug-induced fake.

I didn't care if she threw my bike, smashed it over my head, or ran me through with a knife. A moment earlier I had wanted to save her from this fiend who'd cut and beat her. Now I hoped she'd throw me over the side onto the jagged, cold rocks. It seemed I was no different than an abused and hurt Angela.

"Tell him!" Her scream was ragged, and she tossed the bike over the side onto the rocks. I watched my bike arc into the air and crumple and bounce down the man-made scree and land with the bent back wheel in the water, the handlebars twisted and pointed up towards me, outstretched arms pleading to come back. It had been my partner for three years, helping me get into shape and forget about a miserable two years after losing a hand and a leg.

Yet I would be happy to be that crumpled and worthless bike.

I looked into her eyes, the dark orbs of a drug frenzy. "I'm sorry I left, Angela. I love you. This is all my fault."

For an instant I saw a glimmer of regret in her eyes. Or maybe it was pity. Pity for this half human whom she could never love.

She picked me up like a rag doll, held me over her head, one hand on my waist, the other on my back. I should have been surprised, but I'd already seen the effects of RAZR: her sweating, the sexy looks, the toss-ing my bike like a potato chip.

I looked into the clear blue sky then closed my eyes and relaxed into her grip. I was ready to die. A gurg-ling sound come from her, a kind of sputtering of her lips and ragged breathing that almost sounded like cry-ing. I heard a car door open and steps and grunting. The ringing in my ears drowned out conscious thought. I concentrated on that. I remembered the feeling after the IED detonated, a detachment, a floating in a space between life and death, and I tried to reproduce it.

Maybe someone yelled, maybe more than one per-son. Maybe a car engine or two revved. I couldn't be sure; nor did I care. My body floated, and my mind was calm.

♪ ♫

Even though Buddy was sitting in the backseat of Lisa's truck, and she was driving fast, he saw Detective C right away. His crappy Honda started to turn after com-ing up the steep hill, then changed directions and kept going west. Buddy's stomach dropped like it had been punched. He saw Angela, beautiful and vulnerable An-gela, holding Var in a military-press position, with his horizontal body over her head. Crazy. No way she was that strong.

Lisa drove them over the dam causeway to the place Angela held Var when Buddy saw Detective C change directions. Soon his car pulled up beside Angela's Lexus, which was muddy, not at all the way Angela liked it.

Mug's jaw went slack. "Shit, that girl must be real strong to pick up Var. I mean he's no bruiser, but he's substantial."

"That's Angela," Lisa said as she got out of the car. She sounded angry to Buddy, like she was ready to hurt Angela.

"You can't do anything to her," Buddy said.

She slammed the door and started walking. "Watch me."

"Is that the Angela Var likes?" Mug said.

Buddy nodded, feeling each nod get deeper and deeper. His stomach roiled. He wanted to get his mirror out to watch Mug and Lisa, but he kept his eye on Detective C, who'd already pushed the Mexican-looking guy onto his belly and cuffed him behind the back—and now Detective C had his gun trained on Var. Or was it Angela?

Through Lisa's open door, Buddy heard Detective C shout, "Stop, Angela! Put him down. Please. Come on. I've got this Mexican cuffed. He can't hurt you. Please!"

♪ ♫

I felt my floating body descend, as if she were flexing her legs and arms to push me up and out to my death. Not so bad, really. At least I wouldn't have to worry about being a demented idiot from too much brain trauma.

Though ... I suppose it was possible that I might not die from landing on the rocks. My body would suffer, and my head ...

Shit!

I opened my eyes and felt my pulse spike. That's when I began to struggle. I'd lived my life both before and after my accidents as an active, productive man. I could not imagine watching the world move on around me while I was trapped in a cage of concussion-induced dementia.

There might have been another shout. She stopped her heave at my struggle, likely losing her balance.

A hoarse, choked whisper came from her. "You can't love me."

Then I felt my body start to ascend.

A gunshot broke my thoughts, and I fell on top of her limp body. It was soft and warm. She did not move. I twisted my head to look at her and found her open eyes staring at the blue sky. I could not hear her breathing or feel her heartbeat. I wanted the rocks, the hard and cold reality I deserved. She was dead, and Pablo had killed her. I was alive, not demented. But I had not saved her. Had I not struggled, perhaps she could have dodged the bullet. Had I not struggled I would be on the rocks, perhaps to die, perhaps to never think clearly again. But I might have seen her smile one last time.

CHAPTER 46

Oh, the Pain

Buddy wanted to jump out and run and help Var as he wriggled in Angela's amazingly strong grip. She was going to toss Var over the side. But she stopped for an instant, said something that Buddy couldn't hear, then squatted again and started pushing Var up.

"She must have taken RAZR," Mug said. "No way she could do that without it. I mean, her arms are bean poles."

That's when Detective C shot her.

Buddy looked at the back of the driver's seat. He couldn't move. He knew Detective C wouldn't miss. And he would shoot to kill. O.J. loved Var as much as Buddy did. But another woman was killed. Buddy wanted revenge for her. But O.J. was his friend.

"Jesus," Mug said, soft and sad.

Buddy glanced up: Var was squirming around on top of Angela's collapsed and unmoving body. Buddy opened the door, got out, and started walking toward them, then turned around and walked down the road to the east, away from everything.

"Where you going, man?" Mug said.

Buddy started running.

He knew if he would have had a gun, he could have

shot Angela's leg and Detective C's as well. Boom, boom. That fast and no one would be dead. He would have saved them all. Now Angela was dead.

He ran in the middle of the lane down the hill that turned south, a steep grade, not minding the cars coming up the road swerving to miss him. One guy honked.

He was halfway down the hill, tears spilling down his cheeks, his legs numb, when he heard the rattle of Detective C's old Honda behind him. The car pulled up beside him and kept pace.

"I'm sorry, Buddy." Detective C spoke out his open window. "I didn't want to do it. But it was Var, and she was stoned on that super drug RAZR. It was the only way."

Buddy slowed to a walk, then stopped and turned toward the car. He hadn't looked another person in the face for years. But he looked right into Detective C's eyes.

O.J. Cromwell hadn't seen Buddy straight on like this in years. He gazed into sad and caring eyes.

Buddy liked the way it felt to look someone in the eyes, especially Detective C, and especially at this time. "I know," he said. "It just hurts." He felt the traces of warm tears on his cheeks. He couldn't help it. They just flowed.

"Come on, Buddy. Get in."

An ambulance sped up the hill, veered around them, and continued towards Angela. Buddy watched it round the corner, then he walked around the back of Detective C's car and got into the passenger side.

Detective C drove back to the scene. There was another SUV there by Angela's—a black and white from Poudre County with the blue and white light-bar flashing. The ambulance had parked and its red and white lights added to the police lights that rivaled Christmas lights. Only the green was missing. But there was green; an olive green blanket covered Angela's body, now mere unmoving lumps. There were flares stuck in the road and a few cars backed up. Detective C maneuvered his car around the obstructions and drove up to the black-and-white and stopped.

"Don't leave, okay?" Detective C told Buddy, as he got out.

Buddy looked out the window and nodded.

Buddy saw cars backed up. Lisa was talking to some guy in a suit who held the Mexican guy by the cuffed hands behind his back. The Mexican guy's face was relaxed like he had nothing to fear.

He saw Var half-leaning, half-sitting on the guardrail, his gaze on the reservoir. Buddy hated that Angela was dead, but he hated it more that Var was hurting again. Buddy could go back to delivering stuff and playing video games, but Var—he had to go back to being a doctor and helping Mug and other people. Buddy always thought Var was much better than him and deserved more.

Buddy opened his door and started walking toward Var. He caught Detective C's concerned look and pointed at Var. Detective C nodded and kept walking toward Lisa and the suit and Mexican guy.

♪ ♫

I felt someone walk up behind me and put a hand on my shoulder.

"Sorry, dude," Buddy said.

I turned my head toward Buddy. His eyes were dry, but tear tracks stained his cheeks. He smiled with his mouth, but his gaze dropped, and he sighed and turned back to look at the water.

Buddy's head drooped, but his warm hand stayed on my shoulder. Another woman had died, but we were still here. We were still brothers.

CHAPTER 47

The Rest of the Story

Why had O.J. killed her? He was a great shot and didn't have to kill her. It kept running through my head like a bad dream every couple of hours. I wanted to smoke some weed, but after what RAZR had done to Angela, I'd decided to forget the weed. Four days of avoiding the weed, I'd used my other drug, music, a lot and had just made up my mind to get out for a bike ride. I was lying on the couch, plugged in to my iPhone, listening to "Piano Man" by Billy Joel, trying to get out of my funk. Lisa got up and answered the doorbell. She'd had a simple ceremony for her sister then poured her cremated remains into the Big Thompson River, a place she loved to go as a child. That had taken all of two hours. Then she was back. She just wouldn't leave. Didn't she understand?

I had unplugged and heard O.J. talking—his words sounded cheerful initially, then got a little angry and louder. Lisa's words were calm and low. She sent him away like I'd told her to—*If he comes in, I might hate him forever*. But then I heard her say, "Wait."

I closed my eyes and my insides felt empty. It had been the same with or without the music. Empty ... Nothing. And that was fine with me.

I heard her steps and felt her sit at the end of the

couch. I opened my eyes and looked at her.

"The post is in—."

I interrupted her. "She died of a gunshot wound. Duh. Just get rid of him." I closed my eyes and stuck the earbuds back in.

The weird part about it was that Lisa never even lost a beat with me. I'm sure she knew that I loved Angela. She knew I was grieving over her. But she stuck around and cooked for me, tucked me in, slept by me, held my crying head in her arms. Never once said, "You stupid motherfucker," like I would have to any stupendous idiot like me. I don't even think she thought it. Though, I didn't know for sure. My mind's ability to float around and read other's thoughts had completely abandoned me. I didn't deserve her. She'd been so loving and gentle.

Until now.

I felt the couch jostle at her abrupt movement. The earbuds were snatched out of my ears. I opened my eyes wide, prepared to berate her. She knew better than to interrupt my music.

"Sit up and listen to me."

Okaaay. What the hell was going on? I swung my legs around and sat up.

She sat on the coffee table directly in front of me and glared at me. "This is important, so listen up."

"What?"

"O.J. is your friend and you need to talk to him."

I looked down at the couch and started plucking off pieces of lint. "Not right now. Maybe later."

"No. Right now. He has something important that you need to hear."

"How do you know?"

"He told me."

"Well, just tell me."

"No. You need to hear it from him."

I took a deep breath and sighed.

She put a hand under my chin and raised my face to hers and looked into my eyes. Hers were wet. "He's your friend and happens to love you almost as much as I do, and you need to talk to him."

I clamped my jaw a few times. "I have to put my leg on." I hadn't put any of my prosthetics on the last four days. Why would I need to when I just lay around and did nothing? The arm stump was almost healed. No more redness, no more tenderness, just a scab over the scar.

"You don't." I heard his deep voice and his steps on the floor coming from the front door.

I pulled my chin out of her hand and looked away from her and O.J. I heard her stand and pad away, and then the flexing creak of the wood, the crack of his knees as he sat on the coffee table.

"Okay," he said. "You don't have to look at me. But listen."

I cupped my right hand over my stump, a natural reflex to hide it. I did not look at him.

"First, we got the trafficking ring. Pablo and his cronies will be going to the pen for a long time. It appears as if Angela and the Judge were broke, or nearly so. The Judge used his legal cases on trafficking to get in touch with Pablo. You were right, Angela was using her profits to fund an asthma drug. In fact, the drug was to start clinical trials in another two weeks, if she got more money. I believe she probably saw no other way, and was probably manipulated, at the very least psychologically, by that asshole the Judge."

He pauses. "You gettin all this?"

I nodded.

"So, I can see why you might have thought Angela was being coerced by the Judge. But then it gets a little hokey. Angela's prime target for RAZR was NFL players. If enough NFL players died from suicide, the league would go under ... The DEA is all over that now They found most of the players taking RAZR. It will take a few seasons for the NFL to rebound, so her plan worked a little, but in the end failed. I am assuming she did it for some kind of twisted revenge against her father. I remember you telling me, so I dug up some old records and found she and her mother and her brother were victims for many years. I get it. But she still did a lot of bad shit. Buddy told me about going to the meadow. She tried to put those murders on me. A pretty lame attempt, but it got me doing things I should have never done."

He sighed. "Anyway, Mug has a lot of help now in his injury suite. "But they will need whatever evidence you dug up. And Mug still wants your help. Court starts next week."

I didn't move, but my chest felt a little flutter of joy.

"Second, there were no prints on the Glock found under the seat in the Suburban, except one: The Judge's thumb print on the trigger."

I shrugged. So Angela had wiped the gun. No surprise.

"You're not hearing this. The coroner thinks the Judge pulled the trigger himself, not Angela, not Buddy. At any rate, the Captain lied to you, there were none of Buddy's prints. And it fits better than anything else. Not sure why the Judge was facing the rear of the Suburban, maybe he had partaken of the RAZR one too many times, like Angela, and just wanted a last look at the booty in the backseat ..." His voice trailed off. "We'll never know."

I raised my head and looked out the window. The buzzard that had been flying around in my head and finally landed and was picking at something that became more and more visible.

O.J. took a deep breath and let it out slowly. "Doc said Angela had massive amounts of some drug in her system. Probably RAZR, judging by the empty bottle we found under her car seat. A drug testing lab in Omaha has just developed a new test for RAZR, so they sent out some of her blood and brain tissue. Should have a definitive answer soon."

He paused again. I looked at him. He looked away.

"Doc also said," he ran his tongue under his front lip before going on. "Her brain was mush. Where it should have had firm areas, it had started to liquefy. Not postmortem changes. He thinks the drug literally fried her brain."

I looked at him and frowned.

His gaze was unsteady. His lips quivered, then started, "I don't think—"

"Thanks," I interrupted him. "But you didn't know that when you shot her."

He sighed. "Yeah." He stood and left, his heavy feet knocking on the wooden floor.

CHAPTER 48

One Eighty

After he left, I put on my prosthetics, plugged back in, and started out the door to ride my next-best bike.

Before I left, Lisa said, "You okay?"

"Yeah. Just need to think."

She held the door after I walked out and said, "Come back. I love you."

Otis Redding played "The Dock of the Bay," and I rode. It took that one eighty and two more before the rhythm and notes started working on me.

It took me back to therapy after the second accident. It took me back to thinking about Angela and how I had left her: my first one eighty turn. But she was gone and had been gone for some time. I had been stuck, like a nick in a vinyl disc that kept skipping back to a part you'd already heard, a part that was over. It was good to listen to again once or twice, but after a few redoes it just sounded old and worn out and sometimes ridiculous. But the guy who kept listening was really the ridiculously stupid asshole.

"You can't love me." Angela's last words and now I knew why. It fit, but it still hurt. Yet, I shouldn't have been so hard on O.J. All the bullshit about abused women and drug addicts I thought I could ignore in

Angela. I got sucked in, just like her. Yet, there was no way around it, my love for her was based on that old but true belief: for better or for worse. Yeah, we weren't married, but who said you had to be married to believe that. And the way she'd said those last words, and kept holding me up, knowing she would be shot? I had to believe she loved me so much she didn't want me to suffer any more with her. And knowing my stubborn for better or worse beliefs, she had to end it by dying.

RAZR's addiction had destroyed her brain and destroyed what I knew in my heart she would never have done had she been of sound mind. Just a few years ago, we'd been head over heels, she'd loved me, wanted a child, and I'd left so I could become a hero. The Judge sucked her in, preying on her rebound of losing me, capitalized on her prior abuse, then manipulated her into whatever he wanted. She'd been like many women in a bad relationship and thought a child would help. And that's when RAZR started, initially touted as a fertility drug. How the mind can fool you into doing the opposite of what you want. She thought the drug would help her conceive initially. But later on maybe she thought it would help her forget and get back at a father and men who'd abused her since she'd become a beautiful woman. Her beauty had acted like a mirror in a way, reflecting on her the knowledge that it's what brought on the sexual abuses. She'd hoped that selling RAZR would get enough money to develop a new drug, one to help asthmatics. It wouldn't bring back her brother, but it might save others. It was an honorable and justified goal. Honorable in that it would help all asthmatics forever, and justified to get back at all those macho, sexist men, all in one. Maybe it was a subconscious way of getting back at me for my macho hero worship that took me to war, and from her.

RAZR had twisted her reality. Another one eighty. It had done the same to the Judge, as it turned out, the meal that wonderful mind-buzzard had been picking at, revealed the flip side of the dead Judge. Now I knew why she was so adamant about Buddy getting charged with killing the Judge, or even the hints that she had done it. If the Judge committed suicide, there would be no insurance payout. If the insurance company even thought she had murdered the Judge, she wouldn't get the payout. She had needed more money to fund the asthma drug, finally getting what she'd started on her road to what she thought was salvation. But she got perdition. She hadn't seen how dangerous that road was until it was too late. She got addicted. The drug destroyed her brain. It all fell apart. Her one eighty.

I thought back to when she was holding me like a toy in the air above her head. The drug had done that. But it had not destroyed the last bit of humanity in her. Her last freedom of doing the right thing. She had purposefully ignored O.J.'s warnings. She probably hoped that pissing off O.J. as much as she had, that he would kill her, and she wanted it. She could not go on doing what she'd been doing. And, she could not have me going on loving any part of her.

Yeah, I still loved her. But that part was over. I also loved O.J. and Buddy and Lisa. They were still here, and I had to go on. Mug needed me. Others needed me. I had a lot of apologizing to do.

Those out-of-body, out-of-mind occurrences, where I could see others doing things, had stopped. My thoughts were clearing. I didn't feel so tangential.

Closer to normal.

I cranked on the pedals, rolled over the hills and down to the water but didn't stop at the overlook where Angela had died. After ten more miles and many musical one eighties, the warm buzz of endorphins had me peddling through memories as lovely as heaven's clouds. I flipped around and headed back and fell into Lisa's warm arms and started over. Now that Angela and Riana were gone, maybe we could concentrate on each other. And help Mug deliver his one eighty: ensure Salvation Labs received no deliverance from their sins.

Yeah, and I actually said, "I love you, too, Lisa." More than once. Way more. And boy was I glad she'd stayed. She was the truly "better" part. Maybe, with this final one eighty, there was hope for me.

The End

IF YOU ENJOYED THIS BOOK,

Please WRITE A REVIEW. Thanks.

About the Author

Milt Mays was winner of the Paul Gillette Writers Award in 2011. He grew up in Colorado, graduated from the Naval Academy and, after traveling the world as a Navy doctor, returned to the Front Range. He became a fly-fishing guide while working for the VA in primary care. He has four other novels, some set in Colorado, all involving the military. Please visit his website: www.miltmays.com.

For a FREE ebook go to www.miltmays.com
The Next Day
the first in the *Dan's War* Series
THE BEST KEPT SECRET AFTER 9/11.
Did Iraq have secret Weapons of
Mass Destruction?
Was there a biological attack on the US
that almost killed millions?

Alex Smith just wants to do his job—modify viruses in a secret US lab in Brazil—then go fishing. But something causes changes in Alex. Could he have been accidentally exposed?

After 9/11, Jabril El Fahd wants to finish the job—kill ALL the infidels with a modified virus. But when he is exposed, horrible, evil changes occur to him, and he loves it.

Can the new Alex stop the new Jabril from killing millions?

The Next Day, by Milt Mays
Chapter 1 *September 10, 2001*

Alex Smith awoke in a cold sweat. His heart hammered.
Holy Crap. That dream had been way out there, even for him. He lived for the edge. Job, hobbies, even his habits put him teetering on a knife blade, sharpened daily.
Yeah. So what? He was young. He could take it.
A jarring thump announced the 737 landing, bring-

ing him totally back to reality and ending the first five-hour leg of his journey from New York.

A humid haze cloaked Caracas, Venezuela. The buildings were dulled and grainy, the sun merely a meager white orb with a brightness as bland as the moon, only without the friendly face. The entire panorama was a surreal vision that made him wonder if he were still dreaming.

It was 12:30 p.m., Caracas Weird Time—a half hour earlier than New York. Who would choose to be a half hour off New York? They should call it Caracas Idiot Time. Though on a per capita basis, New York had more idiots, and most of those had PhDs from Columbia University. Who needed a PhD? Only someone with a desire for three dumb initials after their name and to do their research on biogenetics in some university-sponsored, white-coat lab. He was already doing more cutting-edge biogenetics in the lab in the Amazon than most PhDs would do in their entire lives. Probably change the world soon.

The exit door opened and he walked down the stairs. The air hit him like a sweaty net. Fetid aromas and distant ramshackle lean-tos reminded him of where he was. Another plus of traveling down here: experiencing the ambience of the fair city right away, instead of walking across a nice air-conditioned connecting ramp.

Even though he'd been here several times and knew what to expect, he wanted to leave, go home, have a beer, forget the whole thing. Now. If anyone found out what he was carrying, the USA and Venezuela and the one hundred and sixty-seven countries that ratified the Biologic Weapons Convention over thirty years ago would have him jailed. But they had to catch him first. It was one thing to ratify an important treaty, another to enforce it. He was pretty sure no one would find what was inside the 1.5-cm-thick false bottom of his metal coffee cup. Keeping the cup full—preferably with double-strength espresso—helped. If they wanted to inspect it, he could pour out the coffee, and they'd still find nothing. It required a few tricks to unlock and remove the bottom. Even so, he'd love to fit in with the locals better. All he needed was to lop off six inches at the knees, dye his curly blond hair darker, take off fifty pounds, and get rid of the Hawaiian shirt, blue jeans, and the green eyes that ladies found so memorable.

Customs was usually easy. A little pocket money to the familiar customs officer, a stamp on his passport, and he was out of there. But soldiers sometimes haunted the terminal with machine guns and suspicious looks. Reminded him of Mexican Federales. Only these guys were worse. Last time, one actually walked up to him and asked to see his passport. Dark eyes had coldly inspected every wrinkle of his clothing, so close that personal space was more than just violated. The smell of sour sweat and garlic had gagged him.

This time customs was as easy as ever. Hand over the bribe money, grab the bags, and start down the hallway to the taxis.

Except, at the end of the hallway, two soldiers waited—silent, staring vultures. *Holy Crap.*

Every movement slowed. The end of the hallway seemed a mile away.

Stay calm. Move casually.

Their eyes scrutinized every nervous lick of his lips, followed each drop of sweat down his forehead.

Any second they would raise their guns and—*blam!*
—right between the eyes.

He walked past them, slow and easy. Just another
turista on vacation, in no hurry. Time straggled by on
crippled legs.

They didn't move.

At the exit, he hid his hand next to his chest, slowly
stuck up his middle finger, and whispered, "Fuck you,
assholes. Made it again!"

Next was a short cab ride to a smaller airport. The
young driver was unshaven yet dressed in new Levis
and an immaculate white tee shirt. He spoke excellent
English, trying several times to start a conversation.
But Alex let the words die. The dream from the flight
barged in.

—

*He is a child in a two-bedroom house in Wyoming. His
father, Joseph, a small man with gray eyes, mousy hair, and
a thin, acne-scarred face—but whose rare smile could melt
ice—is hurrying in the door from the garage in his under-
wear. To please his wife he's taken off his work clothes in the
freezing garage and put them in a plastic bag before stepping
inside. Oily fumes would not come into her house!*

*His clamped jaw keeps his teeth from chattering. A
warm shower and warm clothes should come first, but
he stops and ruffles Alex's hair with callused, oil-stained
hands of an oil field roughneck.*

"Hey, buddy." Joyful voice. Sad eyes.

"Hi, Dad."

*A grating female voice streams out of the kitchen. Her
words hang in the air like frozen fog. "You know tonight is
Bible club. Couldn't you be on time just once?"*

His father runs up the stairs.

She whips around the corner, white hair up in a bun. Amber, laserlike eyes pierce Alex. A semi-smile shows gleaming shark teeth. Painted-on, arched black eyebrows and Bing cherry lipstick are sinister above a bright orange and green clown outfit.

She grabs his arm, and her words come out as a hiss. "You're going with me tonight to learn about God. I am not leaving you two here to talk fishing."

She drags Alex outside and slams the door.

His father's voice is muffled but audible. "Love you, Alex."

—

Alex closed his eyes and shook his head in a spastic shudder, trying to end the images.

Was Mom that bad?

The clown in Stephen King's *It* had given him nightmares and a wet bed for months as a child. If the clown-suited Mom of the dream had said, "Beep, beep, Alex! Beep, beep..." Goose bumps crawled up his back and he touched his groin to make sure his pants were dry. Stephen King must have had a really weird childhood. Or maybe he hated kids.

Alex's head bumped the roof of the cab, jarring him to look outside. The dusty back road ended at a shack with a dirt landing field cut out of the jungle. A lone Cessna amphibian plane waited, motor purring.

He gave the driver a tip, bigger than usual. "Sorry, dude. Shoulda talked more." Most of the locals were interesting, and usually Alex enjoyed talking with them.

The driver perked up. "No problem, Mr. Smith. Perhaps on the return trip you can tell me all about the Amazon."

The door shut and the cab wheels spit dust. Alex frowned at the cab's rear window as it disappeared around the bend. He didn't remember telling the driver where he was going, or his name.

It would have been nice to catch up on more sleep, but the flight to the Amazon Lab west of Manaus, Brazil, was a turbulent carnival ride. Once, his shoulder crashed against the wall so hard that he had to stifle a scream. Did the pilot even care about his lone passenger? Alex held on tighter. The jungle below was green. Leafy and green. Forever.

At 6:00 p.m. Brazil time, one hour later than in New York—at least the Brazilians liked whole numbers —the plane slid into the water of the Amazon river, and coasted to a stop at the pier—if you could call it that. They were surrounded by—what else—more leafy green jungle. Only this place was even more surreal than Caracas, a humid, hot Twilight Zone. He grabbed his pack and stepped out onto a narrow pier, a sharp-edged puzzle of mismatched wood. One misstep and... busted nuts.

Next was a murderous uphill path to the lab. There were side walls of thick green jungle (of course) and a quarter mile of cobblestones laid by a madman: ankle-busters.

He was young. He could take it. Yeah.

The end of the path marked the divide between local workmanship, shoddy as it was, and the twentieth century—boring but modern. On the other side of the gate, a smooth cement driveway led to a one-story, gray cinder-block building. Metal doors, barred windows. He panted and sweated and stopped at the gate.

He studied rolls of concertina wire fringing the top of the twelve-foot tall chain link gate and fence that surrounded the building. *Tell me again. Why do you do this?*

A barely audible hum of high voltage coursed through the fence and gate. *So comforting.*

In front of the gate stood a four-foot metal post topped with a square keypad. "Angled for easy viewing," they'd said on his first trip. He wiped sweaty palms on his shirt and typed in the code. Below the keypad, a metal shield whirred open. He placed his thumb on the glowing red pane of glass. A beep sounded. He jerked his thumb back to avoid the carnivorous metal shield zipping down and closed. The thing was getting faster. Must have developed a taste for him after the last nip.

The security camera inside stopped its preprogrammed roving and swung back to point directly at Alex. The gate opened with a loud click. He walked through, waiting for the gate to close and the electric hum to resume. What exactly would he do if the gate didn't close?

Turn around and leave. No doubt about it.

A similar procedure opened the metal door to the cinder block building. The door clanged shut behind him and there it was again—the same prickle at the nape of his neck he always got at this point. *Will I ever get out again?*

The high-speed elevator descended so fast he felt weightless for ten of the fifteen seconds. He jumped up at the end, as usual, though he was too tired enjoy the usual rush. He yawned. No sleep any time soon. He trudged to the sleeping quarters—some "bedroom"—dropped off his pack, took off his shirt, and sighed, placing a cool, wet washrag over his chest and face. The sweat came off and he felt a tad more awake, though when he got up again, his eyes in the mirror looked like some kind of zombie's.

Coffee.

Before sleep, in the break room, there was the customary two-hour "briefing" on the new viral codes so he could get started first thing in the morning. Why was he so tired? He'd slept much less so many other times and felt way better. It wasn't even 7:00 p.m. in New York. Maybe he needed a beer. Might help with the aches in his muscles.

Almost felt like he was coming down with something.

He drained the still-warm cup of espresso left in his carry-on cup, padded to the break room, and nodded through most of the videotaped briefing. After a quick snack, he went back to his Spartan bedroom. Without turning off the light or undressing, he lay down on the small metal-framed cot that jutted from the wall, feeling like a lonely book on a solitary bookshelf.

A brief thought of his dream from earlier slipped through his mind, and he murmured, "Miss you, Dad," then slept.

It was dark when something woke him. Was the bed vibrating? Probably another tremor. He'd been told the tremors here were not nearly as bad as the ones in Peru, and not as dangerous. He took off his clothes and went back to sleep, peripherally registering that his tee shirt was more than a little damp and that his muscles ached all over.

Shrieks, whistles, and nails scratched on a chalk-board. Alex bolted upright. What the hell? Oh yeah, the new Memory Stick Walkman alarm. Better than Colombian espresso.

He shut it off, feeling drained, his tee shirt still damp from yesterday. 7:30 a.m., September 11, 2001. New work hours was probably the reason he felt so tired. Reset the internal clock. Get used to it. The last several weeks he'd been doing research in New York, finding the right DNA proteases for the viruses between about 9:00 a.m. and 4:00 p.m. That left the whole evening for hops and barley research. Way too many Irish bars. He hadn't seen the early side of 8:00 a.m. in…yeah, six weeks at least. 7:30 was *way* early—6:30 New York time. Jesus.

He took a shower and took stock of who he worked for: La Riva Labs did *some* things right—good food, movies and music. Of course, they had to. Worse than a nuclear submarine: no contact with the outside world for a month.

What had they said? *You must concentrate on your research.*

They did supply outstanding equipment. And they hired great people. No amount of great food could ever make up for working with assholes.

He finished the shower, still achy but better, and dressed in the "Uniform of the Day," as M.C. would say: blue scrubs and Nikes. M.C., Master Chief, was their retired Navy Class IV bio-procedure manager. A short walk and Alex was in the small—make that tiny—break room, hoping for a quick bite to eat before getting started. The break room fit M.C. to a tee. But the sterile, white-walled room pinched Alex's Wyoming psyche. It was a mere closet made into a break room. He sat on the cold, metal picnic table bolted to the floor.

For easy cleaning—my ass! Just plain cheap, and uncomfortable. Have a nice break, only be quick about it!

He recalled the Amazon Lab had once been a Navy base—Tropical and Preventive Medicine. It was one of the first bases closed in the late '80s, and La Riva scarfed it up. Funny thing, though, the government fully funded La Riva. It was the Washington shell game: take one pot of money and move it to another.

Pays your salary. Don't knock it.

Jesse pressed into the seat next to him. "Hey, Alex. How's it hangin'?" The blue scrubs she wore barely contained all of her six-foot-two and well over two hundred pounds. Jessibelle Yanaha Macallan was beautiful, sexy, and one of the smartest microbiologists Alex knew. He liked her even more because she'd been a rebellious youth at the University of Arizona, once being jailed as a grad student for protesting sanctions against Iraq. She was responsible for decoding parts of the Ebola DNA and was helping him transplant viral codes from smallpox-like monkey viruses to the middle of Ebola DNA.

She always liked to sit close, too close. Okay, maybe he liked it a little.

"Hi, Jesse. I'm good. Except I think my mind is still an hour behind." Truth was, even his eyes ached. But he had to get going. Work meant money. "Give me a few minutes, though, and I'll be multitasking as usual. Right now, how about some of that good old Colombian?"

"Sure, baby." Her smooth voice was nonchalant. "But you know I don't bring any of that stuff with me to the job."

"Right...just pass the coffee."

Macallan was a weird last name for an Apache. She'd explained it as a Scottish trapper hired by James Kirker to tame the northern New Mexico Jicarilla Apaches. Raised on the rez, she hated government oppression. She'd told him Yanaha came more from distant Navajo relatives, and translated to *One who confronts her enemies*. Fit her perfectly. Y this. Y that. Fuck this. Fuck that. Oh, yeah. Alex also loved it that "Y" fit right in with the D.C. acronym game. The best part: it was only one initial.

"So how's Lora?" she asked. That was a new one. Not like Jesse to care about the competition.

"Good."

"Just good? Come on! This is her big day, right?"

"Yeah, she was a little nervous. But like I told her, all she has to do is strut her stuff and she'll get a Nobel."

Alex wished he'd stayed to see Lora do her thing. She was an amazing woman. Amazing. Hmm...why did he not think of her as "my dream come true"? Was it because he really loved someone else? Was Lora only a rebound after Rachel? If Rachel hadn't been a coworker...

Lora was good, though. Yeah. Good. Then there was Jesse. What the hell was wrong with him? Lora was it. He wondered what she was doing right now.

—

In New York City, Lora Livingston stepped out of the shower, slightly less nervous than when she'd awoken an hour ago, and more determined. Black hair and blue eyes of a Scottish father topped a tall, athletic body of a Viking marauder mother. The morning four-mile run had almost rid her of the butterflies.

She'd been working in the North Tower of the Trade Center for five years now, and today's presentation was the culmination. Her brother's senseless death due to a medication error had infuriated her, spurring her to develop software that should eliminate all medication errors—a certain Nobel Prize, according to her boss.

But first they needed funding. Today was the day.

She donned the pale blue blouse, the new gray business suit, and added black heels and onyx ear studs. She held up her grandmother's pearl necklace. It always gave her luck. Placing it around her neck drained a bit more tension. It was like playing tennis—after the first few serves she loosened up. Maybe Andre Agassi was right: image *was* everything.

She scowled and addressed the mirror: "Screw that! There's a lot more than image under this suit, and I'm going to show them."

A deafening sound permeated the room. She jumped, then remembered Alex's alarm.

They'd met last year at an Internet café and it was love at first sight—Alexander Smith, curly blond hair she could run her fingers through and mischievous green eyes that twinkled like new aspen leaves fluttering in a spring breeze.

She strode into the bedroom, shut off the eighty-decibel alarm, and wished he was here. She could still see him yesterday, waking up, rubbing his eyes like a little boy, apologizing for oversleeping again with his usual, "Holy Crap!" His one minor flaw was his inability to wake up without "noises from hell." She could live with that—and his lack of time sense. But how all those OCD scientists in South America tolerated him was beyond her.

Maybe they liked his ability to do three things at once. But it annoyed her. Like yesterday. Before she'd left for work, he was talking to her, dressing, finishing his packing, and eating. All at the same time.

Now she wished she hadn't scolded him: "Are you really listening to me? Why do you always try to do three things at once? It is a proven fact that if you do more than one thing at a time, then all the tasks get short-changed. So you're really better off doing one thing at a time."

He didn't flinch. "I get too bored doing one thing at a time. Anyhow, I had a professor who said the world is changing so fast that the next major mutation will favor survival for those with the quickest ability to adapt to change. Maybe I'm the first with the mutant gene!"

He'd looked so pleased with himself. If only she'd hugged him instead of rushing off to work. Maybe she would call him right now, to make up for it.

Except there was no phone number for him in Brazil.

When she had complained about his working there, he'd said, "You can't get those monkeys up here, so South America is perfect. And when we find out how to make monkey viruses suppress human melanomas, I might join you for that Nobel Prize."

She still hated it that she couldn't contact him for the next month. Rachel Lane, his ex, probably could. And there was also the possibility Rachel might visit the Amazon Lab. Alex had assured Lora it was over with Rachel. But how many times had Lora heard that from other guys?

Maybe she would surprise Alex in a month. He'd be

in Patagonia on a fishing trip. If this deal succeeded, she'd have the money, and certainly deserved some time off.

The taxi honked.

She grabbed her laptop and shouldered her new black Prada purse, a birthday present from Mom. Locking the door, she remembered yesterday as she was leaving—Alex grabbing her and starting to undress her.

She yelled at the door, "Dammit! I should have let him."

But she'd have been a half hour late. At least. And *that* would not have been a good example to her crew. Yeah, but it might have taken his mind off Rachel.

She climbed into the cab. In four weeks, she would undress him on a Patagonian river. Well, maybe back at the cabin. It was cold down there.

She opened her laptop and said to the cabby, "Twin Towers."

---

[1] *Luckenbach, Texas (Back to the Basics of Love)* sung by Waylon Jennings 1977, written by Chips Moman and Bobby Emmons.

[2] Excerpts from the Prologue of Dexter Filkins's book, *The Forever War, 2008. Hells Bells written and performed by AC/DC,* © 1981, J. Albert & Son PTY.Ltd. Copyright owner.

www.ingramcontent.com/pod-product-compliance
Lightning Source LLC
Chambersburg PA
CBHW051329250626
47155CB00007B/2510